All the S

"
—*Entertainment Weekly*

"Beach book extraordinaire! *All the Summer Girls* delivered me back to my college summers and the sweet spot between indulging youthful desires and becoming an adult. Donohue's three protagonists are irresistibly sympathetic as they try to unbury their true selves from the ruinous secrets of their shared past."

—Elin Hilderbrand, *New York Times* bestselling author of *Beautiful Day*

"*All the Summer Girls* celebrates the healing power of friendship for three very different young women with a shared past and different roles in the same guilty secret. Meg Donohue paints a compassionate portrait of what it means to be adrift—in love, and in one's own sense of self— with engaging heroines both flawed and utterly real."

—Nichole Bernier, author of *The Unfinished Work of Elizabeth D.*

"Donohue gives the chick-lit buddy trope an appealing twist and a lot of depth, turning a familiar yarn of regret, trust, and loyalty into an elegant ode to late bloomers."
—*Publishers Weekly*

"Donohue captures the beauty and frustration of reconnecting with old friends—they know you so well, and they don't know you at all. Perfect for a staycation for readers who like the beachy drama of Elin Hilderbrand and Susan Wiggs."
—*Booklist*

"*All the Summer Girls* is a beautifully wrought story about the tender yet resilient bonds of friendship and the damage of kept secrets. Meg Donohue writes with keen insight, prodding readers to re-examine their own past choices, while gracefully examining themes of family, friendship, and forgiveness."

—Karen White, *New York Times* bestselling author of *The Time Between*

"A fast-paced novel about the enduring friendship of three young women who spent their summers in Avalon on the Jersey shore before dispersing across the country . . . A good beach read."
—*Kirkus Reviews*

"Meg Donohue's *All the Summer Girls* is an intimate, heartfelt, beautiful exploration of friendship, family, and the ties that bind and the secrets that destroy us. Read it first, pass it to your girlfriend later. She'll be grateful."
—Allison Winn Scotch, *New York Times* bestselling author of *The Song Remains the Same*

"*All the Summer Girls* is an honest and engaging look at the complicated and powerful bonds of female friendship. Donohue takes us on a weekend reunion full of secrets, resentment, and regret—in other words, once you start this book, you won't be able to put it down!"
—Jennifer Close, *New York Times* bestselling author of *Girls in White Dresses*

By Meg Donohue

MEG DONOHUE

All the Summer Girls

wm
WILLIAM MORROW
An Imprint of HarperCollins*Publishers*

ALL THE SUMMER GIRLS. Copyright © 2013 by Meg Donohue. All rights reserved. Printed in the United States of America. No part of this book may be used or reproduced in any manner whatsoever without written permission except in the case of brief quotations embodied in critical articles and reviews. For information, address HarperCollins Publishers, 195 Broadway, New York, NY 10007.

First William Morrow mass market printing: August 2020
First William Morrow paperback printing: June 2013

Print Edition ISBN: 978-0-06-297575-1
Digital Edition ISBN: 978-0-06-220382-3

Cover design by Emin Mancheril
Cover photograph © Wavebreak Media Ltd/Corbis
Author photograph by Sarah Deragon

William Morrow and HarperCollins are registered trademarks of HarperCollins Publishers in the United States of America and other countries.

20 21 22 23 24   SBL   10 9 8 7 6 5 4 3 2 1

With love for my summer girls—
Anna, Carla, Erin, Jeannine, Leah, and Nancy

What you love will always be with you.
—Alison McGhee, *Making a Friend*

1

Kate

In Philadelphia, Katherine Harrington stands in front of the bathroom mirror, waiting to see if her life is about to change. It has been a while since she stopped and really looked at herself—not to smooth the frazzled antennae of fine brown hair along her part or to brush away the taste of her morning coffee or to apply the mascara she swipes on each and every day before work, but to just stand completely still and look. The parenthetical creases on either side of her mouth have deepened, and she worries they make everything she says seem inconsequential, unnecessary. (*Not ideal for a litigator*), she mouths to herself. (*Must buy wrinkle cream.*) She is studying her own wry smile when the sound of the door buzzer cuts into the apartment.

"It's me," Peter says through the intercom.

Kate feels a rattling sensation in her chest. Her fiancé has had a key to her apartment for years, so why the door buzzer? And he's showing up unannounced, something he has never done in the four years they've been together—his politeness, his sense of formality even after all the time they've spent together, is something Kate still can't decide if she likes or dislikes about him. *Dislike*, she decides now. It's a wall between them. She suddenly fears they're too similar, but with only three months to go until their wedding, these are problems that will have to be sorted out once they're married.

"Hey," he says when she opens the door. It's the beginning of June, and already Philadelphia is experiencing a heat wave. A cloud of humid air seeps into the air-conditioned apartment from the stairwell.

"What are you doing here?" she asks, hugging him. Peter is only a few inches taller than she, and they fit together well when they hug. Still, she pulls away quickly to shut the door against the heat. "What about your basketball game?"

Peter plays hoops with his law school buddies every Sunday morning. Actually, *his* law school buddies are really *their* law school buddies, but they've never asked Kate to join the game. Which, frankly, is fine with her. Sunday mornings are meant for early jogs by the Schuylkill River with

Grace Kelly (Gracie, for short), her sausage-shaped yellow Labrador retriever, followed by the *New York Times*, a tinfoil-wrapped egg sandwich from the Italian market on the corner (an eggie, for short), an obscene amount of coffee sipped from her favorite Tiffany blue mug, and a cheery, if brief, phone call to her parents, who live fifteen blocks away in Society Hill. Separate Sunday mornings are just fine for Kate, who finds that being alone is not bad at all, entirely pleasant, really, when you know your fiancé is out there somewhere in the city, a phone call or cab ride away. Still, she can't think of her Sunday routine without thinking of the phrase "creature of habit," which in turn makes her picture the Loch Ness Monster squeezed into yoga capris, sipping coffee with Gracie stretched out at his big-knuckled, muck-encrusted webbed feet. Why "creature"? she wonders. Why not "person of habit"? Even "animal" would be better.

"I'm skipping this week," Peter says, nodding toward her walnut-colored couch. "Let's sit."

Kate's living room looks like a scene from a Pottery Barn catalog. Which, more or less, it is. She'd spent years admiring how tidy the homes in that catalog looked, as if the adults who lived in those rooms were off leading healthy, productive lives and would be back at any moment to spin the weathered-looking globe on the side console, or to pull a prized first edition from an espresso-stained bookcase. Kate had intended only to buy the Hamilton sectional on page twenty-three when she went online, but she ended up ordering one of everything else on the page too—the pair of bulbous glass Josephine lamps, the Milton steamer trunk coffee table, the large mossy green balls that were piled artfully in the reclaimed teak Luisa tray. *Why not?* she thought, clicking the mouse again and again and again. *I can afford it.* The room has always felt warm and layered and peaceful to her, but looking around now as she settles into the couch, she wonders if buying a room for the life you want rather than the life you lead is a bit like tempting fate.

She sits next to Peter, knees turned inward, nearly, but not quite, touching him. "Are you sick?" she asks. "Where's your key? Do you want coffee? What's going on?"

Peter frowns. He's never liked her tendency to dovetail one question into another, preferring to wade rather than cannonball into conversation. Kate knows this, they've discussed it for hours on end, but there are some fundamental things you can't change about a person, and this, she feels, is one of them. Peter, for example, is never going to throw her a birthday party, or stand up for her to his perpetually undermining sister, Lacey, and that is just the way it is. Some things you accept and then move on.

"I'm fine," Peter says. He looks at her, his eyes blinking behind rimless glasses, and when he glances away, Kate realizes that he is nervous. Her heart begins the annoying rattling thing again. She loves how his lips part a little when his face is at rest, revealing a hint of orderly white teeth, how his dark eyebrows are set too low, overhanging his deep-set eyes, how his brow is always slightly furrowed, hinting at his analytical nature, the workings of his ever-churning brain. She reaches out to him, trying to break whatever spell has fallen over them. When she touches his cheek, she realizes he has not shaved. This is not good. His skin has the same pallid sheen it had after he used tap water to brush his teeth on the second night of their vacation in Belize the previous year. A fresh torrent of questions threatens to burst from her, but Peter speaks first.

"I take that back, Kate. I'm not fine. I'm sure you know that. You know things haven't been great."

Kate drops her hand to her lap and stares at him. She thinks of them last week, making love—yes, this is what she calls it—in his apartment, watching the Phillies game on DVR afterward. There was the fight they'd had weeks ago during (and after) their Pre-Cana meeting with Father Jerry, but she thought they'd moved past that. She was going to work on her issues, and he was going to work on his. "Um, no, Peter. I have no idea what you're talking about."

Peter flushes, the red creeping up his neck like a vine. "Don't do that."

"Do what?"

"Kate," he says. "I've been thinking a lot, trying to put my finger on what is going on with us. I know you're unhappy too."

Something is twisting inside of her. "Are you breaking up with me? Or, wait, are you trying to convince me that *I* want to break up with *you*? Peter, we're getting married in three months!" She waits for him to laugh, to tease her for jumping to such a dramatic conclusion, but his eyes are pegged to the floor.

"I know," he says. His shoulders slump forward. He has always had incredibly bad posture—it was the first thing Kate noticed about him when he sat next to her during their final semester at Penn Law. "I can't believe this is happening either. I wish things could be different."

"Okay, so we'll make them different. We'll work on things. That's what people do." Kate can tell Peter wants to speak so she barrels on. "We've both been working so hard. We need to take more time for our relationship." *Yikes*, she thinks. *Am I quoting from* Cosmo? "We'll have more date nights. Split a bottle of wine. There's a BYO on Chestnut Street that Lisa says is amazing. Let's look at our calendars; we'll schedule some dates right now. I've been wanting to see that new Woody Allen movie—it's one that we'll actually agree on and . . ." Kate trails off, her face burning. *What am I talking about?* "Come on, Peter," she pleads. "Let's look at our calendars."

"I don't want to look at my calendar!" He sounds so exasperated that Kate leans away from him, shocked. After a long pause, he says, "I'm trying to be honest." He's switched now to the plodding, thoughtful tone he uses with clients. "We're really good friends and, actually, that's fine with me, but I know you—"

"That's what marriage is!" she interrupts. "Really good friends who want to sleep together." Again with the *Cosmo.*

Peter sets his hands on his thighs.

"Oh," Kate says. "Oh, I see. You're not attracted to me anymore. We're really good friends who *don't* want to sleep together."

"Don't be ridiculous, Kate. You're completely out of my league. You know that's never been our problem."

Even in the middle of this fight, Peter's words strike a chord. Kate tucks them away, filing them in her *Self-Esteem Boost* mental folder for later use. *He thinks I'm out of his league!* This will come in handy, she knows.

"Well, I'm grasping at straws here, Peter," she says. "Tell me how I'm supposed to process the news that three months before our wedding, you're breaking up with me."

Peter huffs, and suddenly Kate is seething. *He's* not allowed to be irritated with *her*!

"I'm trying to explain," he says in a tight voice. "If you'll give me a minute."

"Please. The floor is yours."

"The only thing I'm unhappy with in our relationship is the fact that *you're* unhappy. You won't admit it, but I can tell. That's what all of this crazy control-freak stuff is about—why you have to plan every second of every day. Maybe if you talked to somebody about what happened. Maybe if you found a way to let go a little." He hesitates, and her mind charges forward, chomping at the bit as she struggles to let him finish. "I can't replace him, Kate, and I don't want to. We both deserve something more than—"

"Don't!" she says sharply. He's using the things she's told him in the darkest, quietest parts of night against her. "Colin has nothing to do with this."

"I'm trying to explain how I feel. Maybe we should talk about this later, after the dust settles."

Kate stares at him. She understands now that this is a done deal. He is done. She won't tell him anything more now, out of spite. "Just say it, Peter. Put me out of my misery."

"What?"

"You're not in love with me anymore. Or maybe you never were. Just say it."

Peter is silent, thinking. In this moment, everything changes. He is not hers anymore, and she is not his. Even the air in the room feels different, cold and dry against her suddenly goose-bumped arms. She's tempted to jump up from the couch and throw open the door and let the thick, soupy air flood in from the hallway. Maybe the heat would breathe them back to life. Maybe it would form a cocoon around them and keep them here, together, forever.

"I can't say that, Kate," Peter says finally. "I'm sorry."

But in that pause before he spoke, she heard everything. She stands up, twists the ring from her finger. Peter looks away, a coward in the end.

"We can take some time," he says. "There's still a lot to talk about. You don't have to do that now."

"I do," Kate says and presses the large, nearly perfect solitaire into his palm.

His spare tennis sneakers are under the hall table. Spotting them, Kate strides across the room and pulls a green biodegradable bag from the drawer where she keeps Gracie's leash. She stuffs the sneakers into it. Peter takes the bag from her and pauses awkwardly. He now has a fifteen-thousand-dollar ring in one hand and what looks like a bag of shit in the other.

"Let's talk in a couple of days," he says, using his lawyer voice again. When she doesn't answer, he says something softly, maybe her name, and kisses her cheek. "Good-bye."

And then he is gone.

The tears—which had not pricked her eyes even once during the entire conversation with Peter—brim and spill as soon as the door clicks shut. *How did this happen?* Kate drops onto the couch and hangs her head in her hands, feeling the cushions shift as Gracie lumbers up and nestles beside her.

"Oh, Gracie."

Gracie shoots her a quintessentially Gracie look—brown eyes bright, sprocketed brows lifted expectantly, tail thumping slowly against the couch. A look that is equal parts "Honey, I told you" and "When's breakfast?" and "I will love you forever."

As her despair begins to morph from acute pain to the fog of self-pity, the first person Kate wants to talk to is Colin. But her twin brother has been dead nearly eight years. She wonders if this fact will ever truly sink in or if she is going to live the rest of her life with the knee-jerk reaction to call her dead brother whenever things go awry. Thinking of Colin, even for an instant, which is all she ever allows herself, brings a wave of unwelcome memories from the day he died—burnt skin, too-hot sand beneath her feet, the silky feel of the ocean enveloping her as she waded in to escape her brother's flat, unyielding gaze. She stands from the couch so abruptly that Gracie's head snaps up, cocked and ready for anything.

"Let's call someone," Kate says.

Gracie thumps her tail in wholehearted agreement.

Kate fishes her cell phone from her purse, trying not to dwell on her newly bare finger. She should call Vanessa or Dani, her best friends from forever, now living in New York City and San Francisco, respectively. Kate is the only one of their little gang who stayed in Philly, not wanting her parents to feel completely abandoned. She stares at her phone, stymied. Who to call first? It's a dilemma she faces at every major life change, one of the downsides of having two best friends. Vanessa—who is married to the son of a famous news anchor and has a toddler daughter—tends to make Kate feel out of breath, as if she is perpetually a step or two behind, struggling to keep up; this feeling, she realizes, will be worse now. And then there's Dani, who leads an unconventional, nomadic life and hardly ever picks up her phone; if by some miracle she did, she would suggest Kate draw a bath and pour herself a stiff drink. This is Dani's remedy for everything from hangovers to heartache.

Kate sets the phone on the table, her head throbbing. The loneliness swoops back in so easily—its familiar weight on her shoulders makes her wonder if it was ever really gone. She could walk over to her parents' house. Or head down to the café, just to be around people. If she weren't so wiped out, she might consider slipping on her sneakers and compelling their law school friends to let her join their basketball game for the first time ever. *Her* law school friends, she corrects herself. Not *their* friends. Her friends. Her mood is skittering ever closer to panic.

"Waiting isn't going to change anything," she says to Gracie. She pats her thigh and Gracie hops off the couch and clicks down the hall tight on her heels. Kate reenters the bathroom and, heart loosening into full-blown rattle again, looks down at the pregnancy test she'd left on the sink's edge when the buzzer interrupted her.

Positive.

So it turns out she's not nearly as alone as she feels.

2

Vanessa

In New York City, Vanessa Dale Warren is dragging out the process of putting her two-year-old daughter to bed. Usually it's Lucy who does the dragging, asking for one more book, one more sip of milk, one more hug, until Vanessa has to shut the door on her sobbing daughter and hope she doesn't catapult herself out of her crib. Today, though, Lucy is sound asleep and Vanessa is the one stalling, anticipating what she will do once the blanket of sleeping-toddler quiet settles on their West Village condo.

She sings another round of "Twinkle, Twinkle, Little Star." Lucy's eyes flick back and forth under her shut eyelids, her perfect rosy bow lips moving along with the words even in sleep. Just looking at her daughter makes Vanessa's heart swell until it feels as if it might burst. When Vanessa was pregnant, she'd envisioned herself singing Ella Fitzgerald or Sam Cooke songs to her baby. Something with meaning and soul. But when she held her tiny daughter in her arms for the first time, she couldn't think of the words to a single one of those songs. She's been singing "Twinkle, Twinkle, Little Star" and "Row, Row, Row Your Boat" like every other mother in America—her own included—ever since.

When the weight of Lucy in her arms is finally too much, Vanessa sets her down in her crib and slips out the door. Drew is exactly where she left him: leaning against the kitchen counter, checking e-mail on his phone.

"Trouble?" he asks, handing her a glass of pinot noir.

She takes a long drink before answering. "No. Just too cute to put down."

He gives her shoulder a gentle squeeze and she melts into the pressure of his fingers before she can stop herself. Lucy is becoming more little girl than baby; Vanessa's muscles have begun aching in new ways.

"You're a good mom," her husband says.

"Thanks." She slides out from under his hand and begins to rinse Lucy's dinner dishes. What to do with a half-eaten bowl of buttered penne with peas? Toss, she decides, and scrapes the final bites down the drain. Some decisions are that easy.

"I wish I didn't have to go to this dinner," Drew says. She can feel his eyes on her as she loads the dishwasher. She's wearing her Mom Uniform: pencil-leg jeans and a black tank top, a brightly patterned Missoni headscarf her only remaining attempt at personal style. She used to wear black because it made her feel chic; now she wears it because it's slimming and hides stains. "We never finished our conversation last night," Drew says, wrapping his arms around her waist from behind and kissing her neck.

Vanessa had barely slid her feet under the covers the night before when Drew had asked if she was ready to have another baby. It wasn't the first time they'd discussed the subject, but it was the first time he'd brought it up since he'd confessed, months earlier, what had happened with Lenora Haysbach. She had the sense that he expected they'd start trying right then. He had that look in his eye. She evaded the question by mentioning her best friend Kate's upcoming bachelorette party—it would be her first girls' trip in *years*. Nobody in her right mind goes to Vegas pregnant, she told him, and a certain amount of alcohol was required when facing the volatile, thorny mess that was her current relationship with Dani. Then she said she needed a glass of water and swung her legs back out of bed.

It was the only time she had ever appreciated

that her desk was in the kitchen. Up until then, the sight of her desk—built into the kitchen counter-top, a constant reminder that her work was now officially of the domestic nature—had always made her feel a slight tick of annoyance. Before her good sense could steer her down a more construc-tive path, she sat in front of her computer, logged in to Facebook, and, finally, allowed herself to look up Jeremy Caldwell. And there he was: so easy to find. The hint of an early summer tan. Light brown hair; dark, narrow eyes; and a clean-shaven jawline that would make a J. Crew model question his job security. She couldn't access any information about him—Was he married? Did he still live in Philadelphia?—without requesting to be his "Friend," and she wasn't ready to take that step.

She had sat at her desk for several long mo-ments, looking at Jeremy's photo and listening for Drew's footsteps in the hall. Had the situation been reversed and Drew were considering reach-ing out to an ex-girlfriend, she would kill him. Even before what happened with Lenora, she would have at least threatened to kill him.

She studied Jeremy's profile picture. He looked so unchanged that she wondered if the photo-graph had been taken the summer eight years earlier when they'd dated. Was it possible she herself had taken it? Was he sending her some sort of sign? She peered closer. His lips were pressed together, just managing to suppress the smile that shined, redirected, from his eyes. He'd always done that—smiled with his eyes, like a child. Like Lucy. At this gut-wrenching turn of thoughts, Vanessa quickly logged out of her Facebook account and shut the laptop. By the time she'd slipped back into bed, Drew was asleep.

"You're sure I can't convince you to come tonight?" Drew asks now. His wineglass has left a red ring on the counter. These little messes are invisible to him; he simply does not see them. "Maybe Gina can babysit."

"She's in the Hamptons," Vanessa says, though she's not actually sure whether or not their downstairs neighbor has already left for her beach house. Drew's work dinners are inadvertently humiliating. None of the people he works with have the slightest idea what to talk about with someone who spends her days raising a child. Anyway, Drew had already, by telling her it was "just the guys," indirectly assured her that she did not have to worry, Lenora would not be at the dinner.

"We'll finish the conversation eventually," Vanessa says, using the measured tone that has become her default. She wipes away the ring of wine he left on the counter.

"Okay," he says. She can tell he's already

moved on. He's incredibly skilled at not obsessing over things. She suspects this is a guy thing—she doesn't know a single woman who could so easily place something she wants on the back burner.

Vanessa first met her husband at an opening at Nocelli, the contemporary gallery in Chelsea where she worked in the years after she graduated from New York University. Drew Warren was tall with a strong nose and thick brown hair that curled against his forehead—a walking David in a bespoke white shirt, open at the collar. Vanessa felt the eyes of the other women in the room swivel in their direction as they talked. Drew described himself as an aspiring art collector and the executive producer of *Estelle*, the new talk show of a feisty octogenarian comedian who had starred in a much-adored eighties sitcom. Vanessa admitted she had not seen the talk show but lied and said she wanted to. Drew admitted he didn't know much about art but said he was fascinated by it and eager to learn more. Vanessa had obliged by telling him about the paintings, a series of vibrant, slyly funny domestic scenes by a figurist named Francine Martin. Vanessa could see that the paintings did not appeal to Drew, but he had tilted his head and listened with what appeared to be genuine interest as she spoke, at one point putting his hand on the small of her back to move her out of the way of a passing waiter.

When she Googled his name in her apartment later that night, she was astounded—and a little thrilled—to learn he was the son of Thomas Warren, the famous evening news anchor.

Their first date was spent wandering the new galleries popping up on the Lower East Side; afterward, they ate grilled corn wrapped in tinfoil outside Café Habana and laughed when they caught each other surreptitiously pulling corn shreds from their teeth. Drew took her to parties filled with famous, creative people. When she mentioned she had always wanted to visit London, he whisked her away for a long weekend spent trolling the Tate and the Saatchi Gallery and Portobello Road. When she met his beautiful, articulate mother for the first time, she was so nervous that she momentarily forgot how to hold a spoon. On their drive back from Connecticut, Drew had thrown his arm out protectively in front of Vanessa at the very moment he stopped short to avoid hitting an aggressive driver who had cut into their lane. Later, as the city came into view, he admitted that he feared that his father, known for his insightful commentary on the events of the day, was not proud of him; as the producer of a talk show, Drew could not help but feel his contributions to the world paled in comparison.

In response, Vanessa found herself telling Drew

that her fascination with the business side of the art world, the fact that she loved the excitement of a big sale as much as the art itself, made her community-organizing, ozone layer–obsessed parents uneasy. She had so little in common with them, a fact that seemed to get more pronounced with each passing year. She didn't even share their skin color—hers wasn't creamy pink like her mother's or dark brown like her father's but somewhere in the middle. Her skin made her experience of the world different from either of theirs; her job made them worry about her moral compass. Vanessa hadn't expected to open up so much to Drew, but she realized that when she looked at him, she saw a kindred spirit.

At twenty-six, Vanessa was the first of both her high school and college friends to get married. At twenty-seven, she was the first to have a baby. Her decision to quit working when she had Lucy made Drew uneasy—not because they couldn't afford it, but because he knew how much Vanessa wanted to run her own gallery someday. So, really, he'd foreseen all of this. This discontent. But when the doctor had placed Lucy on her chest, Vanessa had felt a series of fireworks explode inside her, and her very first thought was *Oh, fuck*. Because she knew what this crazy new kind of love meant. If it wasn't a financial necessity, how could she possibly return to work and leave Lucy in someone else's care? How could any work accomplishment ever compete with how she felt when her daughter gazed, mesmerized, into her eyes and smiled? No, Vanessa wanted to be the one who cared for Lucy on a daily basis. But she also wanted—and this feeling has grown stronger lately—to hold on to the dreams she had before Lucy was born.

She can't win.

Once Drew has left for dinner, the noise of the city seems more muffled than usual and the condo throbs with quiet. Vanessa pushes open the window above the sink and inhales the unusually hot June air. Five stories down, an ambulance passes, its urgent siren filling the kitchen for a moment before fading. She makes herself a bowl of cereal—a favorite dinner from her single-girl-in-the-city days. Leaning against the counter, she closes her eyes and feels the city breathe against her bare neck. Echoing heels against pavement. Laughter. Fragments of conversation. "She only calls when she needs something," one woman says. "If he doesn't pay by the thirtieth, I'm kicking him out," says another. For long minutes there is silence, and then a set of passing cars sounds so much like the inexorable roar of the ocean that

Vanessa feels herself being pulled back through time. Her eyes flip open, and she yanks the window shut.

After attending a Quaker school for thirteen years, Vanessa is used to being alone with her thoughts. Friends schools, as they're called, are a dime a dozen in Philadelphia and are populated by kids of every religious background, with practicing Quakers being in the small minority. Vanessa Dale was the only one in her Philadelphia Friends School class who went to Friends Meeting on Sundays with her family in addition to the school's Wednesday morning Meeting; her parents are agnostics who like the idea of being members of a peaceful urban community. So Vanessa had twice as much time with her own thoughts as her classmates did. Or with God, as her teachers would have said; Quakers believe that we carry God within ourselves, making an intermediary like an ordained minister unnecessary. Want a tête-à-tête with God? Just hunker down with your own thoughts for an hour and let the light within shine.

"I spoke with God already," Vanessa's best friend Dani said one morning as they filed into the auditorium for Friends Meeting during their senior year of high school. Even back then, Dani wore all black, already trying to prove that under her conventional cuteness—her shaggy, pin-straight blond hair, her perky nose, her big, brown eyes—lived an edgy artiste-in-training. "When my alarm went off. She was pissed. Turns out she's not a morning person."

"Maybe she just couldn't deal with your dragon breath," Vanessa replied. Kate, the third point of their best-friend triangle, looked back from her spot in line and laughed.

"Wait," Dani said. Her loud voice carried over the line of seniors shuffling as slowly as humanly possible into the auditorium. "I think God *is* my dragon breath. Right?"

Dani and Kate looked at Vanessa expectantly, as though her double dose of weekly Friends Meeting made her an expert on All Things Quaker. All it really made her, she thought, was an expert at gnawing her fingernails into perfect crescents. She shrugged. "Hell if I know."

"I don't think so," Kate said, tucking her hair behind her pale ears. "I think that's Native American—you know, a higher spirit in everything. Quakers just think he's in people. Or maybe not. Maybe all living things? Like, animals too? I don't think God is in your bad breath though. Or even your good breath. I think once you breathe out, God is probably . . ."

Vanessa tuned out. Kate got herself particularly wound up on Wednesday mornings, per-

haps worrying about the blow an hour of silent
Friends Meeting would deliver to her daily word
quota. Vanessa let her gaze wander over her
classmates, finally landing on Kate's twin brother,
Colin. He stood in a cluster of his lacrosse team-
mates, staring into the middle distance as his
friends jostled one another. He might, Vanessa
realized, have been high. Lately he moved within
a pot-scented haze that reminded Vanessa of the
cloud of dust that surrounded Pig-Pen in Charlie
Brown's Christmas special. Hardly a month went
by that she didn't run into Mrs. Harrington in the
school's halls, coming from or going to another
teacher conference about The Problem of Colin.

Kate and her brother shared the same Irish
coloring—brown hair verging on auburn, pale
skin with a dusting of tiny freckles across the
bridges of their noses that darkened and spread
in summer—but otherwise you'd never have
guessed they were twins. Kate was fastidious and
thin, an overachiever; her cheerful chatter was
motored by sharp intelligence. Colin—who had
an athletic build, deep blue eyes, and unruly hair
that seemed perpetually overdue for a cut—only
appeared focused when he held a lacrosse stick
in his hand.

Colin blinked and caught Vanessa's gaze. A
smile flickered across his face, as though there
were some joke between them. She looked down

and felt a flush warm her cheeks. Since he was a good athlete and had clear skin and a sweet smile, it did not matter that Colin was introverted, moving quietly within the pack of puffed-up, wisecracking jocks at the school: most of the girls at PFS had crushes on him. But he was Vanessa's best friend's brother, and therefore off-limits to her. When she looked up again, she found Dani looking at her.

What? she mouthed. She steeled herself for one of Dani's searing pronouncements, which could cut to the quick if you didn't prepare yourself. But Dani just shrugged.

"All right, girls. You know the drill," Mr. Camden said as they neared the entrance to the auditorium. "Time to make like bananas—"

"And split!" Kate finished. Mr. Camden, who coached the debate team and wore his shirtsleeves rolled up to his elbows, was Kate's favorite teacher.

"We know, we know," Dani said, her words overlapping with Kate's.

The girls hadn't been allowed to sit next to each other in Friends Meeting since the incident that fall when Dani—spelling out her jokes letter by letter on her thigh—had made Kate laugh so hard that she choked on her own spit and sprinted from the auditorium in a burst of coughing and squeaking sneakers and slamming doors, causing a ripple of laughter to swell and break over the entire student body. Even using all the arsenal at their disposal—hisses and flashing eyes and pointed fingers—the teachers hadn't been able to entirely snuff out the laughter for the remaining twenty minutes of Meeting; in the very moment it would seem to at last peter out, a tremor would strike a far corner of the room and suddenly the entire auditorium would again become a churning sea of hands clamping over mouths, crinkling eyes, and shaking shoulders.

Now, they filed into separate rows in the auditorium. Vanessa sat near the door and had a view of her classmates' backs. Kate was four rows straight ahead, and Vanessa could see the line of Dani's blond hair falling over the back of a bench two rows up and to the right. She searched the room until she spotted Colin at the far end of her own bench, his eyes already closed. She considered sending a poke down the row of classmates toward him to keep him from nodding off to sleep but decided against it.

Though she never told them, checking the room for the whereabouts of Dani, Kate, and Colin was something Vanessa always did. She would have felt silly admitting the ritual. Looking for Dani and Kate made sense—the three of them had been best friends since the first day of kindergarten at PFS when they all showed up wearing the same purple-striped Gap shirt and had spent two cherished weeks together every July at Dani's father's beach house in Avalon, a tiny town on a seven-mile-long barrier island off the coast of southern New Jersey—but why Colin? Vanessa told herself it was because he was always around, always barging into Kate's room to see if he could copy one of their homework assignments or to reclaim the laptop he shared with his sister or—in earlier years—to peg one of them with a water balloon.

One recent afternoon he had wandered into Kate's room, sat down heavily beside Vanessa on the bed, and stroked her hair three times before Dani's scoffing laugh made his hand drop to his lap.

"Stop pawing her," Dani ordered. Dani and Kate exchanged a meaningful glance, and a lump formed in Vanessa's throat. These little shifts in dynamic were common, but knowing how quickly things could change didn't make it any easier when you were the odd girl out.

"Woof," Colin said, jutting his chin up to flick the hair from his eyes. When he looked over at Vanessa, she saw that his eyes were glazed over. After a few minutes, he stood and walked back toward the door.

"He's drunk," Dani announced after he left the room.

"Maybe," Kate said. "Who knows?" There was a note of warning in her tone that Vanessa felt she, in particular, was meant to hear. What would it be like to have a twin brother? Vanessa had two younger sisters who, at twelve and ten, seemed like babies to her.

"Should we see if he can spare any?" Dani asked.

"Dani!" Vanessa and Kate said together. They looked at each other and laughed and just like that the lump in Vanessa's throat evaporated.

"We have to finish this calculus set," Kate said.

Dani groaned. "Who cares? We're seniors. We got into college already." She had a point. Thanks to her writing portfolio and 800 SAT verbal score, Dani was headed to Brown that fall. Kate was going to Penn, and Vanessa to NYU. Vanessa couldn't wait to get to New York, where she suspected her real life would begin.

"But it's only four o'clock," Kate said, looking even paler than usual. "And we have school tomorrow." She'd recently admitted to them that the thought of college sometimes made her throw up. Even then, Kate was not a fan of change. Penn was a whole three miles from the town house in Society Hill where Kate had grown up, Vanessa and Dani had laughed to each other on the phone later that night. She acted as if she were moving to the moon.

Dani stared at Kate, shaking her head as she clapped her binder shut. "Live a little," she said. "I guarantee you'll thank me for this later."

Vanessa is on her third glass of wine, regretting it even as she drinks it. She misses the days when she could have more than one cocktail without immediately foreseeing the headache she would have to contend with while serving her exuberant daughter breakfast at six thirty the next morning. Drew could stumble onto the bus and sleep through the workday with his eyes open, but Vanessa would be on her feet from morning to night, making peanut butter sandwiches and negotiating the stroller through subway turnstiles and cursing the person who invented tambourines during a relentless hour of music class. Of course, she and Lucy could just stay home. She could put on *Sesame Street* and let her daughter zone out for an hour or two while she sneaked a nap on the couch. But if that's the kind of mother she is going to be, then what was the point of giving up her career?

She sets her wineglass down beside her computer and logs in to Facebook. She joined the site only recently, much later than most of her peers. She is now "Friends" with many of her old PFS classmates and finds herself continually amazed by the things they share—especially the men. All of those jocks who had been so cocky and obtuse—Dani had dubbed them the Rock Eaters—now post about runs they are doing to raise money for breast cancer research and bid one another exclamation-point–ridden birthday wishes. Some even post pictures of their babies. They are fathers! The whole thing makes her inexplicably sad.

Now, she does what she's known all along she would do that night: she pulls up Jeremy Caldwell's profile picture again. *Jeremy*. They'd met in Avalon eight years earlier when she and Kate and Dani had rented a bungalow on the island for the entire summer before their senior year of college; a couple of weeks into that summer, they'd wound up at a party at the house Jeremy was renting. Vanessa still remembers how his white T-shirt had made his tan skin look almost bronzed. She'd felt his eyes on her throughout the party, and her face had flushed with anticipation. Later that night, Jeremy walked her out to the house's small, stone-filled yard; the slight breeze was a relief after the densely packed party. When he told her that he was a graduate of the Rhode Island School of Design and that he worked at a graphic design firm in Philadelphia, she felt their six-year age difference crackling between them like a loose, charged current. As they talked, he pulled a wire hanger from a trash can and manipulated it into the shape of a long-stemmed rose. Vanessa thought she'd been in love before, but when she held that rose, the metal still warm from Jeremy's hands, she felt sure she'd never felt like *this*. This was something new, entirely.

As she looks at Jeremy's photograph and thinks of that metal rose, her mind turns, as it always does, to Colin. In her memory, she was still a kid on the morning two police officers knocked on the bungalow's door. After the officers told them that Colin's lifeless body had been found in the bay, she was an adult. Maybe if she'd grown up sooner, none of it would have happened. Colin would be alive and she and Jeremy would be— what? She never had the chance to find out.

Vanessa lets the laptop cursor hover over the "Add Friend" button. She tells herself that she's just saying hello. It doesn't have to be more complicated than that. She clicks the button, finishes her wine, and waits.

3

Dani

In San Francisco, Danielle Lowenstein is hung-over at work. Again.

Her manager looks at her as he straightens the rows of books on the New in Paperback table. She picks up the phone and presses it to her ear.

"Booksmith on Haight," she says, even though no one is calling. She pauses, types gibberish into the search database and then says, "We don't have that in stock right now, but I can order you a copy." She looks over at Roger and mouths *Patricia Cornwell*. Roger grimaces and then turns back to the book display. Unlike Dani, who is an equal-opportunity reader, Roger both literally and figuratively holds mass-market fiction between two fingers with the same mix of disgust and shame on his face that Dani imagines he wears when he carries a cup of piss out of the bathroom at his doctor's office.

When Roger leads a woman toward the self-help section in the back of the store, Dani lowers her forehead to the counter. She is trying so hard to ignore the taste of bile in the back of her throat that she doesn't remember to hang up the phone until it begins to bleat in her ear.

The night before, when she should have been writing her novel, she'd been lured out of her room by the cloying smell of pot that drifted under her door from the living room. Her roommates are a motley crew—Bruce is a predictably awkward programmer at an online gaming company; Rachel is a twenty-two-year-old SAT tutor and a guitarist in all-female folk-rock band; and Rachel's girlfriend, Macy, is a sociology graduate student and Latin dance instructor with a penchant for wearing sparkly tube tops under extralong old-man cardigans. The four of them share a two-bedroom apartment in the Haight, an enjoyment of pot, an intrepid attitude toward Craigslist roommate ads, and not much else. Bruce sleeps on the couch in the living room. Macy and Rachel share the apartment's larger bedroom (except when they're in one of their frequent fights, in which case Rachel sleeps propped up and open-mouthed in a sleeping bag in the rusting claw-foot bathtub). And Dani pays eight hundred dollars each month for the privilege of a private bedroom just large enough for a twin bed and a small desk.

"Finally!" Rachel said when Dani opened her door and stepped into the living room.

"What do you mean, 'finally'?" Dani asked. "I just went into my room five minutes ago."

"Did you write about me?" Macy asked.

People always want to know if she is writing about them. As if she doesn't have enough of her own shit to write about and needs to steal some of theirs.

"I started to," Dani said, taking the joint from Bruce. "I wrote, 'Macy's such a . . .'" They all looked at her expectantly. She took a long drag, feeling a cloud billow up behind her eyes and down her throat, into her chest, making her lighter and heavier all at once. "That's as far as I got."

"Macy's such a knockout," Rachel said.

"Macy's such a smart cookie," Macy said, her accent rolling the "R" in "smart."

"Macy's such a . . ." Bruce began and then trailed off, reddening, while the women all looked at him. "Such a . . ." he tried again, and trailed off again.

"Not so easy, is it?" Dani said. She sat down on the floor with her back against the couch and took a swig of the beer that Rachel handed to her.

And the whole time she sat there on the floor, she felt guilty that she wasn't writing. She'd been on her feet all day at the bookstore, hand-selling strangers' books to other strangers, thinking about how she'd rather be home working on her own novel. But now that she was home, with a long day's work under her belt, she wanted to have a few drinks with her equally underwhelmed-by-life roommates before facing the stern, unhealthy hum of her five-year-old laptop. The guilt didn't fade until beer number four, and by then it seemed like a fine idea to head down to the bar on the first floor of their building. So, yes, if moving in with pothead roommates from Craigslist was her first mistake, then moving into a building with its own bar was her second. One might consider sleeping with said bar's bartender her third mistake, but this act did result in numerous free drinks, which meant less of her paycheck was spent on alcohol, which meant she could work a few less hours and still pay her rent, which meant she had a little more time to write. So. Silver lining.

At two in the morning, Dani declined Brett the bartender's offer to walk her up to her apartment. He was cute, but her guilt had started gnawing at her again by then so she told him she was going home to write. Brett gave an ambivalent shrug and walked away, but then he came back and started scrubbing the bar so aggressively that Dani and her roommates took the hint and lifted and drained their beers before he snapped them over with his dish towel.

"You know we can't stop going to that bar, right? I mean, it's *downstairs*," Rachel slurred as their little posse trooped back up to the apartment. Then, petulantly, as though Dani had responded, "You should have thought of that before shitting where you sleep."

Macy shot her an apologetic glance as she unlocked the door. Dani shrugged. The difference between real friends and people who are just acquaintances is that real friends will always choose loyalty over convenience. *Or maybe,* Dani thought, her mouth suddenly dry, *that's the difference between old friends and new friends.* Bruce lurched into the bathroom where they could all hear him puking, as he always forced himself to do when he drank too much on a weeknight.

Dani poured a glass of tap water and sat down heavily at her desk. She read the last couple of pages she'd written. She'd felt elated after writing those pages, but now, rereading them, her heart sank. Her phone buzzed beside her computer and she picked it up. It was a text message from her friend Kate.

> *Happy birthday, Danigirl! I miss you! Call me back already!*

Well, there you had it. It was the seventh of June, and she was officially twenty-nine years old. Dani envisioned Kate, who had become an early riser in law school, texting her as she leaned against the kitchen counter in her apartment in Philadelphia, waiting for the coffee to drip at five thirty in the morning. She knew that in a few hours, well before she heard a peep from her father, she'd have a text from Vanessa, who, despite everything that had happened between them, always reached out on her birthday. Dani's dad, with whom she'd lived after her parents divorced when she was four, is always either scrubbed in at Children's Hospital or with his latest girlfriend, and wouldn't remember her birthday unless Dani herself reminded him. Still, she adores the man, a feeling that was sealed during her us-against-the-world childhood with him. Even when he forgets her, she never doubts that she is the most important person in his life; she clings to this belief more than she likes to admit to herself. Her mother had moved to Denver and remarried soon after the divorce and had appeased her new husband by essentially cutting Dani out of her life; Dani has two half brothers she has never met. Her mother calls on the morning of January first every year, as if speaking to her daughter is an annual obligation she wants to get out of the way as quickly as possible. She does not call on her birthday. Dani wonders if she even remembers when it is.

In the midst of these thoughts, the heat turned

on, rumbling and whooshing out of the floor vent below her desk, adding insult to injury. She would never get used to the heat turning on in June. Dani ached for summer, feeling for it and being struck by the loss of it over and over. Summer is Avalon, New Jersey: thick, humid air cut with the salty funk of low tide and flip-flops smacking against hardened soles and hair drifting around you like seaweed as the ocean lifts you up toward a cloudless sky and the feeling that you will never be anything but young.

Instead, San Francisco's June fog gave Dani a bone chill, and she couldn't remember the last time she had heard her best friends' voices, and it was now abundantly clear that there is no way she will have published a novel by the time she is thirty.

In the back room of the bookstore, Dani's head is still pounding. She pours coffee into a mug and stretches out on the couch, Amanda Eyre Ward's *How to Be Lost* in her hand. She'd picked up a couple of Valium at a party earlier in the week; they're in her bag now and she knows taking one would make her feel better but she thinks that if she just rests, she won't need it. Twenty pages later, she places the book on her chest and closes her eyes. When she opens them, her manager is standing above her.

"You're sleeping," Roger says, running a hand over his face. "You're supposed to be unpacking the new shipment."

Dani sits up and knocks the mug of coffee over with her foot. She gasps as the dark puddle travels speedily toward a box of new hardcovers. Roger grabs a fistful of paper towels from beside the coffeepot and throws them down on the floor. Dani drops to her knees and mops up the coffee. The scent of pot still clings to the blond hair that falls around her shoulders.

"I'm sorry," she says when the books are safe. "I was reading. Amanda Eyre Ward. It's really good."

Roger's hands are now folded across his chest. He is small with bright eyes and thick mutton-chop sideburns that Dani guesses are meant to make him look older or bulkier or maybe simply cooler. It's the first time she's had a manager who is younger than her, and this feels more like a monumental life shift than she cares to think about.

"You were late today," he says.

"I know. I'm sorry."

"I'm not finished," he says. But then he doesn't continue.

Dani stands and tosses the soaked paper towels into the compost bin. The dull thud of their landing is loud in the room. She waits, looking at him.

"You're good with the customers," Roger says

finally. "But, Dani, how long have you worked here now?"

"Three months."

"And you've been late fifteen times. Sixteen, counting today. What did I say after the last time?"

Since graduating from Brown, Dani has moved steadily west, leaving a stream of bosses in her wake. She's gone as far from home as the country will allow, and this will be the twelfth job she's been fired from in seven years. Her mind is doing familiar calculations—her rent is paid through the end of the month, but she won't have enough in her bank account to cover July. She's long since worn out her welcome on friends' couches; if she doesn't find another job immediately, her only option will be to go home. For a brief moment she considers telling Roger this, but she can't bring herself to grovel—she's not there yet. But she is, she finds, disturbingly close.

"It's okay," she says. She clears her throat and speaks loudly and calmly like someone whose spirit is far from broken. "I get it." She walks over to the hook on the wall where her bag hangs.

Roger looks relieved. He has no idea how easy it is by now for her to hide her humiliation— she lied about her job history on her application. "We'll send your last paycheck to the address on file," he says. "Unless you want to swing by for it?"

"Mail it." She retrieves the book from the couch

and dog-ears the page she'd been reading when she fell asleep. "Deduct this," she says, holding it up for a moment before dropping it into her bag.

He shrugs, scratching at one of his mutton-chops. "Forget about it," he says. Dani has already passed Roger and opened the door from the back room to the store when he adds, magnanimously, "Happy birthday."

On the sidewalk, she blinks up at the bright, foggy sky. She digs both pills out of her bag and swallows them. *What does it matter now?* she asks herself. She doesn't really want to know the answer.

She pulls out her sunglasses and begins to walk. Her first thought is to call Kate, but Kate's life is too predictable to understand anything Dani is going through—it's been this way for years now. Kate—who is a little prim—has trouble hiding the fact that she judges Dani's lifestyle. In high school and college Kate rarely drank, which made the nights she actually did cut loose all the more entertaining for her friends. It's a neat trick if you can pull it off, if the idea of going out and not drinking doesn't seem like the worst, least fun idea you've ever contemplated.

She certainly isn't going to call Vanessa, who she hasn't seen since her wedding to that television guy three years earlier. The wedding was held on the groom's parents' riverfront Connecticut lawn with a tented reception full of massive arrangements of white flowers that must have cost a fortune. Drew was flashy in that way that Vanessa, like a moth, had always been attracted to, but he gave a surprisingly heartfelt toast to Vanessa that made Dani like him despite the fact that he wore loafers with no socks. She gave them a fifty-fifty chance, which, for Dani, was optimistic. Vanessa's parents seemed happy about the union if a little shell-shocked, and Dani wondered if they were high. An hour into the reception, when she was sufficiently drunk, she decided to ask them, but as she crossed the dance floor, Kate appeared out of nowhere and took hold of her elbow, rerouting her to the bathroom. So Dani had made it through the wedding without causing a scene; she'd even hugged Vanessa at the end of the night. The regret she felt as she hugged her old friend was a dark, trapped, moving thing, water flowing unseen below ice.

If Kate's brother, Colin, were alive, he would have made Dani feel better, just by being himself, just by being alive. She isn't feeling well, and whenever she isn't feeling well, even when it's just a hangover, she thinks of Colin. During their junior year at Philadelphia Friends School, Dani had awakened one day with a slight sore throat that grew over the course of the morning to a whole-body ache; by second period she was curled up on a cot in The Mull—the students' name for the dimly lit, green-carpeted basement domain of Mrs. Muller, the school nurse who was rumored to have worked at PFS since its founding in 1691—with a fever of 101 and glands that felt like tennis balls. Muller kept trying to reach Dani's father but was told he was in surgery each time she called. Dani lay on the cot, shivering, working to keep herself from crying as she listened to the nurse attempt to reach her father over and over again. Muller never once asked if she should call Dani's mother; there must have been a note in Dani's file about her absence from Dani's life. Every so often the nurse would pull back the curtain that surrounded the cot and press her ancient, freezing hand to Dani's forehead. This seemed both unscientific and invasive. Plus, Muller smelled vinegary, a distinct and familiar scent that for some reason made Dani think of baseball. Maybe she was delirious. She just wanted to go home. She woke up some time later to the phone ringing and the nurse's hushed, relieved voice. After a moment, Muller scraped back the curtain and announced that Dani's father was waiting for her in a cab in front of the school.

Dani staggered outside, her hot, feverish tears threatening to spill from her eyes with every step. She slid into the backseat of the cab and found Colin.

"Hey," he said. "Good thing Kate made me watch *Ferris Bueller's Day Off* like a billion times."

Dani's laughter pushed the tears up and out of her eyes, and Colin leaned forward to tell the cab driver Dani's address so she had sufficient time to wipe them away before he leaned back again. At her apartment, she stretched out on the couch in the TV room while Colin rifled through the kitchen cabinets and found a can of tomato soup that he dumped into a big yellow serving bowl and heated in the microwave and presented to Dani with a dish towel wrapped around the too-hot porcelain. He forgot to bring a spoon, and Dani didn't ask for one because she wasn't really hungry. Colin might have been a stoner, but she always thought of him as full of thought; now she understood that he was thoughtful as well. She had a few sips of soup straight from the bowl and then set it on the floor. She'd assumed Colin would go back to school, but he didn't make any move to get up from the spot on the rug where he'd planted himself. It did not escape her that he would take any excuse to skip class. Her mind was too fuzzy to come up with anything to say, and she was relieved that he seemed content to just watch television. When he began to roll a joint, Dani wondered if he planned to smoke it right there in her father's apartment. She was surprised to find that she didn't care. The nurse's vinegary scent, she realized suddenly, was sauerkraut. She drifted into a strangely euphoric sleep, the scent of pot and the sound of cartoons on the television the backdrop for her dreams.

It's not the first time that it occurs to Dani that her memory until her early twenties was like a steel trap; since then, it has become catch-and-release. Something important, she feels, is slipping away from her, and she worries that it is her life.

She knows she should go straight back to her apartment and write. She is nearing the climax of her novel—a story about a group of childhood friends at the beach, the death of a charming but reckless twenty-one-year-old boy, and a narrator plagued by secrets. The scenes that she has yet to write are the ones that she cannot seem to get right; they send her back to the beginning; they are the reason she has been writing and rewriting this novel for nearly eight years.

Isn't she allowed one day of leniency after being fired? On her birthday? It's not like she would get any real writing done when she's this hungover. She'll start checking Craigslist for a new job first thing in the morning. Her friend Layla waitresses at a cocktail lounge in Western Addition and has already promised her a free birthday beer. She'll probably treat her to two when she hears about the day Dani has had.

Dani walks to the bus stop on the corner. Later, she'll take a bath, and the sound of the ice cubes rattling around in the glass of bourbon in her hand will provide as much comfort as the skin-hugging warmth of the water. Now she pulls out the novel she took from the store and opens it. When her bus arrives fifteen minutes later, she looks up and then down again at the dog-eared page, vaguely aware that she hasn't read a word.

4

Kate

"Delivery," Lisa says, entering Kate's office. Her usually cheerful assistant doesn't look at Kate as she sets the box on her desk. "I opened it. Sorry," she mumbles and turns quickly to leave. She shuts the door behind her.

Kate eyes the box warily. It's ten o'clock and the sun is already too bright in her small fifteenth-floor office. Even though it has been seven years since college, since she's known anything else, it still feels unnatural to be in an office on a beautiful summer day. The air conditioner is cranked so high that she shivers in her short-sleeved silk blouse. The combination of dazzling sun and frigid forced air makes her feel off-kilter, as if she were coming down with the flu. Or maybe, she thinks—remembering but not really *remembering*, exactly, because it's not like she's forgotten for even one second—it's the baby making her feel this way. *How did this happen?* she asks herself for the one-millionth time. She finds she cannot think about the baby too much, or the room starts to dim; for the first time in years, she cannot envision her future.

She stands and lowers the shade another few inches before lifting one of the cardboard box flaps. Inside, beneath several sheets of silver tissue paper, a shiny white box holds two neat stacks of wedding invitations.

Kate sinks down into her desk chair so heavily that it rolls backward and knocks the wall. She feels terrified and humiliated and lonely, and she needs to tell someone. Her emotions are like trees falling in a forest—she can't be entirely sure she is feeling what she thinks she is feeling unless someone else hears. She shuffles herself back toward the desk, picks up the phone, and dials.

"Hi," Vanessa says, breathing heavily. Kate hears voices in the background.

"Hey. What are you doing?"

"Walking with Lucy on the High Line. Drew and I are going to Estelle's eighty-fifth birthday party next month and I'm determined to fit into this Michael Kors dress I bought before Lucy was born."

"Oh." Without fail, Kate forgets to adequately prepare herself for these conversations with Vanessa. She picks up the phone thinking she will reach Vanessa Dale, and within moments realizes that she is talking to Vanessa Dale Warren, the grown-up version of her best friend. Kate had known that Drew Warren, with his good looks and high-profile friends, was perfect for Vanessa when she first met him. She'd also known that her friendship with Vanessa would change when she married him, and she didn't begrudge Vanessa this—at least, not much. You were supposed to lose yourself in love. Marriage was supposed to be an impenetrable partnership. Naturally your old friendships would change.

"What's going on?" Vanessa asks, huffing and puffing. During puberty, Vanessa's body had done one of those insane, seemingly overnight metamorphoses from pudgy to curvy, eventually leaving her with the sort of enviable figure that prompted people to describe her as All Woman. Since having Lucy, her body has softened again, as if returning to its natural state. Kate thinks this plumpness makes her even more beautiful (and more approachable too, a trait Kate feels society underrates), but the extra pounds clearly bother her friend.

"Well, I'm officially pathetic," Kate says. "The wedding invitations just arrived and my assistant ran out of my office like they were emitting toxic gas. And she shut the door behind her! Which begs the question: Does she think heartbreak is contagious? Or is it just that she's worried I'm going to cause a scene and she wants to save me from myself?"

Vanessa's breathing quiets as though she is finally slowing down. Maybe she is running her hand down the length of her shiny ponytail. It heartens Kate to picture her friend making this old, familiar gesture.

"Oh, Kate," Vanessa says. "You're not pathetic. Don't say that."

"Well, if I don't say it to you, who am I going to say it to?" She doesn't know why she sounds angry. None of this is Vanessa's fault. She puts her hand on her stomach, which is as flat as ever. Her doctor confirmed that she is about six weeks along. Kate hasn't shared this news with anyone—not Peter, not her parents, not her friends. If she tells someone, the situation will harden into unavoidable reality. She's not quite ready for this.

"At least you didn't send out the invitations," Vanessa says.

"No, but the Save-the-Date cards went out months ago. My parents have started calling everyone to let them know. My dad thinks he can get the Union League to refund our deposit, so there's that. Even the Union League thinks I'm pathetic."

"Stop it."

"Know anyone who wants to buy a wedding dress?"

Vanessa laughs and then abruptly falls quiet.

"It's okay," Kate says. "You can laugh. Humor is allowed."

"Have you spoken to Peter?"

"Yeah." In the eight days since he had broken up with her, Peter had called twice. Each time they spoke, Kate waited for him to admit he had made a huge mistake; each time, she hung up feeling disappointed and heartbroken and foolish all over again. "He just says the same things. He's not changing his mind."

"Do you want him to?" Vanessa asks, surprised. Kate knows what Vanessa wants her to say. Vanessa, with her long black eyelashes and olive-specked eyes and perfect cheekbones, has never been dumped. Her life is a glittering thing: full of love and baby kisses and the magic of New York City.

"Yes," Kate says matter-of-factly. Even though she and Peter had not shared a home, even though they had not been one of those couples that did everything together, they *had* built a life together. The thought of him moving on and eventually marrying someone else makes her want to vomit. And now, of course, there is the baby. Their baby. "I'd take him back if he changed his mind."

"You just need more time. It's all so new." Kate

tries to forgive the distance in Vanessa's voice, reminding herself that Vanessa *is* distant—she's in an entirely different city. "But really," Vanessa continues, "it's better for everyone that he figured this all out now. Before you got married. Before you had kids."

Kate is silent. There was a time when she would not have been able to contain herself and would have now told Vanessa she is pregnant, a time when Vanessa would have questioned Kate's uncharacteristic quiet, a time when Kate might have spent more time analyzing Vanessa's tone. But that time is long gone. Now they are close but not that close. Kate tells herself this is because they're adults, that all women stop spilling out their every secret to one another once they're out of college, that years of e-mails and texts have made it harder for them to really hear each other when they actually speak. But none of this adds up to the whole truth about the space between them.

Even in a normal year—a year when she wasn't pregnant, a year when her fiancé hadn't dumped her—Kate would have been out of sorts right now. It's June, which means the anniversary of Colin's death is approaching. When she was younger, she looked forward to the summer in every other season, but now it is a dark spot in her year, a time she endures with gritted teeth and long runs with Gracie. This is why she had set her wedding date for September—she'd thought it would help her get through the summer, the eighth anniversary of her brother's death, if she had a dangling carrot on which to set her sights. She realizes now that her spike of anxiety as summer approached might be one of the reasons Peter broke up with her when he did.

They'd had a humiliating fight in front of Father Jerry during one of their Pre-Cana meetings four weeks earlier. All Kate had done was set a printout of the detailed plan she had made for their future on the table. Kids, career milestones, bucket list items like visiting her ancestors' castle in Ireland and hiking the Grand Canyon—it was all there, year by year. Peter, not realizing she was serious, had laughed; when he saw she was not kidding, he had sat back on the couch, his mouth hanging open.

"I just don't want any surprises," Kate had said. "Isn't that why we're here?"

After Colin's death Kate had begun to have panic attacks. She would feel them building steam for days, spinning black tornadoes in her chest that sucked the oxygen from her lungs. The only thing that allowed her to catch her breath again was planning, focusing steely-eyed on something other than the past or even the present. She certainly wasn't going to start taking antianxiety medication—not after what happened to Colin.

She directed her laser focus on studying for the LSAT, then her law school classes and law review, then her job search, her billable hours, and, this past year, planning her wedding. *Skate to where the puck is going, not to where it's been,* her father, quoting Wayne Gretzky, had once told her, and it's the best advice she's ever heard. Peter used to *like* how organized she is; they used to compare their daily planners and debate who had neater handwriting. She had told him about the panic attacks that had begun after Colin died, but she had left out part of the story, the part she had never told anyone. Still, she thought he understood.

"You don't want any surprises?" Peter asked. The look on his face told her that he either thought she was insane or he pitied her. It might have been both.

"Any *bad* surprises. You know what I mean, Peter."

Peter swung his gaze to Father Jerry. "She doesn't understand how controlling she is," he said. "I keep telling her to ease up but I don't think she hears me."

Later, on the sidewalk, Kate wanted to dissect what had happened, but Peter told her he was too tired. He went back to his own apartment that night and didn't return her calls, which she must have known would drive her crazy. Crazy enough, in fact, that she'd shown up at his door the next night wearing ridiculous lingerie under a trench coat, her birth control pills forgotten in her rush to catch him in the sliver of time she'd known he would be home between work and his regularly scheduled Thursday poker game.

"Blow the game off," she'd told him, batting her eyelashes so hard that one dislodged into her eye and blurred her vision. "Be spontaneous."

The memory makes her cringe. Of course this was the night she got pregnant. She does something impulsive, and look what happens. Murphy's Law. She shakes her head and pulls herself up to her desk, glancing at her e-mail to ground herself in the present.

"The bunny crackers are all done," Vanessa is saying, half-muffled. "How about a banana?" In the background, Lucy wails.

"Do you want to go?" Kate asks. It still unnerves her that her friend is now someone's mother—has, in fact, devoted her life to being someone's mother. Vanessa, who always seemed destined to live a glamorous, fast-paced life. Kate realizes she envies the life her friend has ended up with—the happy marriage, the embrace of motherhood, the lifeboat of family bobbing through an ever-changing city—more than the life her friend had seemed determined to lead for all those years.

"No, I just need to keep walking. She's fine when we're moving."

"Enough with my sob story. What's new with you guys? How's Lucy?"

"Oh, she's great. She's become very opinionated about what she wears. Every morning is a battle. My parents, of course, say this is karmic retribution. Anyway, our next big thing is tackling potty training so she's ready for preschool in the fall, but I'm starting to wonder if she's too young."

"For potty training or school?"

"Well, both. She's only two. I don't know, the idea of dropping her off and—"

Kate looks down and notices her other phone line is blinking. Lisa cracks open the door and sticks her head in, whispering the name of a senior partner.

"Shoot!" Kate says, interrupting Vanessa. "I have to go. I'm supposed to be on another call right now."

"You called me," Vanessa says coolly.

Kate feels an automatic impulse to acquiesce, to do anything to get back in Vanessa's good graces. But she is an adult and she has a partner-track position at WebsterPrice, the biggest firm in Philadelphia, and she has a few other things on her mind than making sure Vanessa likes her right that second. "Sorry, V," she says. "I'll call you later."

* * *

That night, Kate takes Gracie on a long walk. When they reach Twelfth Street, Gracie turns and looks over her shoulder, tail wagging, eyes bright and sure. "Not today, Gracie," Kate says. "We're not visiting him today." Kate has always spoken out loud in full sentences to her dog in the middle of the city, but today she feels self-conscious about it. Her fragility makes her uncomfortable, but it has a familiarity, too, like the biting cold of winter that you only half forget during other seasons.

When they reach her parents' house, the house where she grew up, her mother is on the stoop, locking the front door behind her.

"Oh my goodness, Kate! I was just coming to see you," she says, turning. Kate inherited her mother's frame—all lean limbs and jutting clavicles no matter how many egg salad hoagies they eat. Her mother retired six months earlier from a long career in the marketing department of a pharmaceutical company and, ever since, her outfits seem to be culled from the wardrobes of two different women. Tonight she has paired black exercise leggings with a chiffon-trimmed cardigan and she is carrying an expensive-looking leather tote bag. Kate wishes her mother would just choose one look: the comfortable, sporty retiree or the posh, pulled-together one. This muddle makes her heart hurt.

Gracie bounds forward and snorts joyfully

into Kate's mother's crotch. "You were?" Kate asks.

"Yes. I wanted to see how you were doing. In person."

"Oh, Mom, that's sweet, but don't worry. I'm fine."

Her mother gives her a troubled look and adjusts the purse strap on her shoulder. "What are you doing here then?"

"Gracie wanted an after-dinner treat. And it seemed like a nice night for a walk."

Kate's mother looks up at the pastel-streaked sky and smiles. Kate just manages to resist falling into her arms. "You're right. It's gorgeous. Let's go sit out back."

The house is narrow and warm. The efforts of a professional decorator had been obscured long ago by additions of lamps and bookcases and family photos in mismatched frames. There is Colin in his lacrosse pads, stick resting on his shoulder. There are Kate and Colin on their first day of fourth grade, Kate in Laura Ashley, Colin in Polo. Kate can still feel the weight of her overstuffed backpack. Colin is everywhere here; her mother will never take these photos down. Still, as the years tick by, new photos of Kate will outnumber old ones of Colin, the house shifting in small ways, evolving over time in accordance with no plan at all.

Unclipping Gracie's leash, Kate hears the *thunk* of her father setting a beer bottle down on a TV table in the den. It's a house in which you never have to ask where anyone is—if you stop and listen, it's possible to detect the location of every person presently under the roof. Was that why Colin was always leaving? Was he seeking privacy the only place he could find it—away from these small, cramped rooms? It's tempting to believe, for a moment, that this intimacy she has always loved, this ability to predict what you will find around every corner, is the very thing that had driven her brother away. It is so tempting to believe it could all boil down to one simple thing: a too-small house.

Her mother heads straight to the kitchen for drinks, and Kate and Gracie stop in the den on their way through the house. Her father is doing a crossword puzzle and watching the Phillies. The room smells of Pep O Mint Life Savers and Yuengling, a minty, yeasty, so-wrong-it's-right mix that might as well be her father's signature scent.

"Gracie!" he says, looking up.

Kate laughs. "Hi to you too."

Her father winks at her. "Laundry?"

"Nope," she says. "Just saying hello."

Her father's face clouds, his hand slowing to rest on Gracie's head. "Hello," he says.

* * *

The sandbox in the backyard has been gone so long that the dogwood tree that took its place is now taller than the back wall. Kate and her mother sit across from each other at the table on the small brick patio and drink Arnold Palmers and watch Gracie sniff the mulch between the hostas. If Gracie digs under the rock in the far corner of the flowerbed, will she find Colin's stash of cigarette butts? Or would they have disintegrated by now, leaving all evidence of his habit buried only in Kate's memory?

"We made him part of our family," Kate's mother says, and, for a moment, Kate is confused. "I don't think I'll ever understand."

"Mom." Her parents fell in love as juniors at PFS—her father was on the football team; her mother covered sports for the school newspaper. They married the summer after they graduated from college and that was that. Kate loves a good chick flick as much as the next girl, but she suspects the small, steady flame of her parents' marriage is as close to true romance as exists in the world outside of Hollywood movies.

"I just think he needs to explain himself. It isn't right."

Kate squelches the urge to defend Peter. "His timing has always been terrible," she settles on finally. She doesn't want to say anything she might regret later. What if they get back together?

"His timing! Kate, aren't you angry? You're allowed to be mad at him. *I'm* mad as hell at him."

In the years since Colin's death, Kate's mother has tapped into her anger. This anger is never directed at Colin—to Kate's great relief, death has absolved him. But beware the Society Hill driver who brakes for less than a full three seconds at the stop sign in front of the Harrington home. Junk mail, also, now routinely bears Kate's mother's unchecked wrath, as do solicitors who call during dinner, Comcast technicians, and Republicans. These things have surely always aggravated her, but she now seems incapable of containing her feelings, as though tolerance were a finite well, now dry.

Kate asks herself if she is angry and decides she is not. "I'm just sad," she says, her voice, finally, cracking on the word.

Later, back on the front stoop, her mother hugs her. "Good night, my good girl," she says, reciting an old incantation. "Sleep tight."

Good girl. Kate knows this is how her mother thinks of her, has always thought of her. And for a long time, it was true. Kate was the one who got straight As and set the table and watched PBS with her parents on nights when her brother claimed to be at the movies. Her mother's incantation to her brother was "Good night, sweet boy" and this, in its own way, was also true. Colin was sweet. He was loyal and fun. He was also deceitful and moody and lost.

Her brother had loved Philadelphia at night, his adolescent-boy energy feeding off the dark streets and swinging car lights and disembodied, echoing voices. Kate, on the other hand, feels unnerved by the city after the sun has set. She knows only a fool would believe that her years in the city provide her any sort of protection—anything can happen at any moment to anyone. She hurries toward her apartment, one hand wrapped in Gracie's leash, one hand on her stomach. If her brother were alive, she would have told him about the pregnancy. They told each other everything. Well, almost everything.

"You're seeing someone," Kate remembers blurting out in the kitchen of the Avalon beach house she rented with Vanessa and Dani the summer after their junior year of college. Beach *shack* was a more appropriate term; it was one of the 1950s-era bungalows over the Twenty-First Street Bridge on the bay side of the island that were quickly being purchased and torn down to make room for huge, Hamptons-style shingled homes. The bungalow had two tiny closetless bedrooms that each contained a built-in bunk bed and not a single other piece of furniture; they draped their clothes on chains of hangers that hung vertically down the walls and slept with the doors and windows open and their faces inches from box fans that pushed hot, salty, back-bay air through the house. The fall after they moved out, the bungalow was razed. The following summer, Dani told Kate that a cookie-cutter home with a big white wraparound deck had been squeezed into its footprint. Even if they'd wanted to, they couldn't go back.

That summer before their senior year of college was the first summer the girls didn't stay in Dani's father's beachfront home on Thirty-Eighth Street. They'd pooled their money to rent that bungalow on Twenty-First Street, and they loved it—loved late afternoons sitting on beach chairs at the water's edge, loved biking out on beach cruisers to parties at friends' houses or for too-sweet shots and dancing at the Princeton (it was the first summer they were legally allowed into the island's popular bar), loved feeling the wind on their faces when they rode home at two in the morning, loved sharing a pot of coffee at the rickety kitchen table before heading out to early-morning shifts at Uncle Bill's Pancake House, the Fishin' Pier Grille, and Avalon Coffee. They'd rented the bungalow for what they considered to be their last summer before college ended and official adulthood, with its "real" jobs and responsibilities, began; this had been the plan for as long as any of them could remember and they were finally doing it. And it was every bit as wonderful as they'd hoped it would be, right up until the day it wasn't.

After being put on academic probation twice, Colin had finally been kicked out of Lehigh that spring. He was living at their parents' house in Philadelphia and working as a counselor at PFS's lacrosse camp. He talked about moving to Brooklyn at the end of the summer and taking a job with his friend's family's construction business. Kate couldn't imagine her brother in Brooklyn, couldn't, she realized, feeling traitorous, imagine him holding down a job and paying rent. She was surprised and hurt to learn he had been making plans without telling her. It was this mention of a concrete plan that made her suspect there was a woman in his life.

"Who is she?" Kate pressed her brother. "Why won't you just tell me?"

Colin took a slug of his beer, a bemused look in his eye.

Vanessa and Dani and Tony—a cute friend of Colin's from Lehigh who Kate would have allowed herself to have a crush on if she and her brother hadn't maintained an unspoken agreement about not dating each other's friends—were still at the beach. Kate and Colin had just arrived back at the house, their fair skin tender from a long day under the July sun. They'd cracked open cold beers and sat at the kitchen table, playing a sluggish game of Go Fish. Kate had felt a buzz building behind her temples—she'd had too much sun and her eyes were sensitive to light, making her prone to headaches. The skin on her thighs was mottled and red; she pressed her thumb into her thigh and when she lifted it, a milky white teardrop was left in its place.

"I'm eleven minutes older than you," Kate reminded her brother. Her words were teasing, but her voice revealed the truth—she was frustrated, baffled, and hurt by his silence. She knew he didn't like to be reminded that she'd entered the world first, but it was hard not to feel protective of him. She watched his eyes darken at her words and felt her heart lurch. Colin was mellow right up until the moment he wasn't, when his anger struck you like a sucker punch. The look was gone as quickly as it appeared. He reached across the table to ruffle her hair. He laughed and so she did too, her laughter a Pavlovian response to his.

I'm losing him, she thought, even as she laughed. She'd never had this thought before—not when he'd stolen her father's Camry in high school and slammed it into a traffic light, not when she'd driven to Lehigh to bail him out of jail after a bar fight left him with three broken fingers and a permanent record, not when he'd forgotten to pick up the cake for their mother's fiftieth birthday party and had mumbled to a restaurant full of uncomfortably shifting adults that the cake had been—"you know, unbelievably"—stolen from him at knifepoint as he'd walked down Walnut Street. She didn't fear she was losing him in any of those moments. She feared it only now, when he was sitting across from her, clear-eyed and laughing and . . . in love? *I'm losing him.*

A month later, Colin's body would be found in the grasses that separated the bay from the island mere blocks from where they sat drinking beers and playing cards that afternoon.

Maybe Peter is right. Maybe she should talk to someone about what happened. Maybe it's time to skate to where the puck has been. Maybe then she could convince Peter that she does not think about Colin every single day, that the weight of guilt does not press down on her shoulders, making it difficult to move forward.

Colin. When he'd reached out to ruffle her hair that afternoon in the bungalow, his hand had smelled like cigarette smoke and suntan lotion, a uniquely Colin-in-summertime scent that Kate, when she tries hard enough, as she does right now on an empty city street, can still—will always—smell.

5

Vanessa

Vanessa,
It was a nice surprise to see you pop up on Facebook after so many years. I'll be in New York on Friday. Any chance you're free for drinks?

Jeremy

Jeremy Caldwell's e-mail has played on continual loop in Vanessa's thoughts since it arrived in her in-box that morning. He'd accepted her Facebook "Friend" request a few hours after she'd sent it, and then, for over a week, there'd been no further communication between them. In that time, she'd scoured his Facebook page and learned that he owned a small graphic design firm, lived in Philadelphia, and was, apparently, single.

"Higher!" Lucy squeals. Despite being two,

Lucy still sits in the baby swing, tolerating enclo-
sure because she knows her mother pushes her
higher when she's snug in the bucket seat. It is 10:00
AM, and they are at Bleecker Playground. Vanessa
pushes the swing from the front, unable to pass
up the view of pure delight on her daughter's face.
She holds out her hands, wiggling her fingers in
tickle threat as Lucy swings toward her. Laughter
bubbling up from deep down in her belly, hazel
eyes scrunched up with joy, dark pigtails curling
behind her, Lucy crows, "I'm gonna get you!"

Lucy has recently begun using more pronouns.
This is a developmental milestone: she's asserting
autonomy, recognizing that she and her mother
are not the same person. Vanessa finds the process both fascinating and disconcerting. Her
daughter seems to be gaining an understanding
of herself at the very rate that Vanessa is losing
sight of herself. It's something of a relief that Lucy
still confuses the pronouns, saying, "Carry you!"
when she stretches up her hands to be carried,
and "Snack for you!" when she's hungry.

Vanessa hasn't told Drew about Lucy's new
sentences. He's been working late all week and
hasn't seen his daughter since Sunday. For years,
Vanessa and Drew called each other frequently
throughout the day, just to say "Hi" or to discuss plans for that evening or to say "I love you."
These calls came to a full stop five months ear-

lier when Drew divulged what had happened with Lenora Haysbach. Despite her anger, Vanessa continues having conversations with Drew in her head throughout the day; she could fill a notebook each day with the things she wants to tell him: *Things I Would Tell Drew If I Didn't Want to Kill Him.* They are everyday things—the latest on the new French restaurant under construction two blocks away, Lucy's (and her own, she must not forget her own) delight at the Richard Serra exhibit, the dry cleaner's nearly mystical ability to remove ketchup stains from silk. She hates that this list forms in her head each day, an ever-present reminder that love makes her weak.

"See Gammie today?" Lucy asks, looking up with bright, expectant eyes, a crust of peanut butter at the corner of her lips. They're sitting on the park bench now, having an early lunch.

"Not today, Luce. Gammie is in Philadelphia. But I'm sure she'll come visit again soon. She misses you too much to stay away for long."

Lucy is in love with Vanessa's mother, and Vanessa doesn't blame her: her mother is the sort of woman who seemed born to mother, as in the verb "to mother," the way some seem destined "to lead." Her parents met at an antinuclear protest in D.C. in 1979; Vanessa's mother, a white woman raised by a history professor and a sculptor, had been drawn to Vanessa's black father because of his funny tweed beret and clear singing voice and what she called "his warm, calm, mauve-hued aura." In their wedding pictures, Vanessa's mother is hugely pregnant. They named Vanessa after a genus of butterfly, and few days go by that she doesn't breathe a sigh of relief that she didn't end up saddled with Clover or Sage, her younger sisters' names. These names seem to have tied her sisters more securely to their parents, which was perhaps their intention. Clover, now twenty-three, lives three blocks from home and has a plot in a community garden; Sage, in her third year at Hampshire, sent Lucy a CD of her own covers of Bob Dylan songs for Christmas. Lucy loved the CD; that very afternoon, Vanessa introduced her daughter to the joy to be found in painting your toenails pink.

Sometimes Vanessa thinks the only thing she has in common with her parents is her contemplative nature. She is not talkative like her friend Kate (who often has to be reminded to take a breath) or attention-seeking like Dani (who seemed determined, back when Vanessa knew her, to never have fewer than two pairs of eyes on her at any given moment). Vanessa senses that some people take her quiet for coldness or bitchiness, but she does not think it is either of those things. And in the gallery, actually, she hadn't been quiet at all.

She'd bloomed there, becoming a better version of herself—relaxed, articulate, more prone to smile. That's who she'd been—a gallerist expertly working the room—when she met Drew.

The change that occurred within Vanessa when Lucy was born, the way her focus shifted so entirely to her daughter's health and happiness, shocked Vanessa. Her daughter became her universe; her life would never again be the same. It seems to her that men do not undergo this same sea change; neither her own father nor Drew, both fine, loving fathers, showed any indication that they felt bereft when they did not spend the day with their children. To the contrary, they seemed to interpret "father" as "breadwinner" and became more committed to their careers. Before she became a mother, Vanessa had thought all that stuff about men and women being different was ridiculous; then she had Lucy and became gripped by something primal, biological. This transformation makes her life bigger and smaller all at once. She both pities and envies Drew for not feeling it too.

The cutout children Lucy and her grandmother created are still taped to the window in Lucy's bedroom. During that visit, Vanessa's mother had extracted a cardboard mac 'n' cheese box from the trash, and—exercising her usual restraint by not actually uttering the two thoughts that Vanessa knew were simultaneously running through her mind: *Boxed macaroni and cheese?* and *Shouldn't this be in the recycle bin?*—had snipped the cardboard into darling little children that would have given a Kara Walker piece a run for its money. Her mother made being a mother, in and of itself, into an art form. Whenever Vanessa felt as if she were losing herself in motherhood, she was inevitably chastened by the thought that her mother, on the other hand, had truly *found* herself in the role.

"When we get home, we'll make a beach for the children," Vanessa tells her daughter. "We'll make fishies and seashells and mermaids, okay?"

Lucy's eyes widen. "Yes, Mama! Yes!" she yells, enunciating the word "yes"—a new word in her vocabulary, though "no" has been around for some time now—so clearly that it rings like a bell in Vanessa's ears. Beautiful or not, words are not enough for Lucy and she scrambles to her feet, losing a sandal in the process, and throws her soft, warm arms around her mother's neck and plants a loud kiss on her cheek. Vanessa's heart soars. Her love for her daughter is an enormous, unwieldy thing; it turns her wild with joy and fear. She blinks back tears and pulls Lucy tight to her. *This is everything; this is enough,* she thinks to herself three times, as though the words are a talisman or a mantra that, if repeated with intention in her heart, will become the truth.

* * *

Vanessa catches herself thinking of Jeremy's e-mail throughout the day. She'd prepared herself for the possibility that Jeremy might be angry with her, even all these years later, for cutting him out of her life the way she had. He has every reason to be bitter. In the days after Colin died, she and Dani had packed their things and Kate's too and returned to Philadelphia for the funeral and the remainder of the final, too-hot days of summer in the city, and Vanessa had broken up with Jeremy over the phone. He was upset but sympathetic, suggesting they speak again in a few days. After that conversation, she never returned his calls or e-mails. Eventually, he stopped trying to reach her. Now, despite her callousness all those years ago, she senses forgiveness underlying Jeremy's e-mailed words. Still, she knows she might be reading too much into his brief note.

The last time she kissed Jeremy was on the beach in Avalon in August in the early morning hours following a party. The streets over the island's Twenty-First Street Bridge line a narrow finger of land surrounded by bay and wetlands, and the party's soundtrack of 50 Cent and Black Eyed Peas had carried over the island, buoyed by inlets of water. Everyone had known it would only be a matter of time before an annoyed neighbor called in a noise complaint. When the police finally arrived to break up the party, Vanessa, Jeremy, Dani, Kate, Colin, and ten or so other friends made the long trek to the beach. Dani rode on someone's back, her flip-flops in one hand and a cigarette in the other. Kate and Colin jostled each other and Kate's snorty laughter hooked Vanessa's heart and Dani's too until they all laughed, over nothing and everything—the packed party with its too-loud, Top 40 soundtrack, the police who seemed disappointed to learn that they were all of legal drinking age, this very walk to the beach on a warm, still night. They were twenty-one years old and it was summertime at the beach and their lives—not just in retrospect but even *then*, even while they were living them—felt golden-hued and electrifying, and this was only the beginning. Vanessa doesn't remember much more of that walk from the party to the beach, but she remembers that feeling, that sense of surety about the present and the future that she's never really felt again. And she remembers that last kiss with Jeremy—and its aftermath.

The ocean had glowed silver in the moonlight. The Big Dipper (which Dani, poetically, if inaccurately, called the Three Sisters until Kate corrected her) looked so, well, *big* that Vanessa envisioned its handle as a stray thread she could reach out and pull, unraveling the entire canopy of stars above as easily as a loosely knit cap. Dani, who had the implausible talent of becoming more bright-eyed and charismatic with every drink, immediately launched into an exaggerated re-enactment of Kate attempting to fold herself into the clothes dryer when the police had arrived at the party. (Kate—perhaps the most drunk that Vanessa had ever seen her—had become afraid that if she were issued a citation she would have to include it on her law school applications that fall. She was still traumatized by the night, five summers earlier, when the police had pulled up to a party on Fortieth Street and loaded each and every person in the house, including Kate, Dani, and Vanessa, onto what had by then become known among the island's many underage party-goers as the "Magic Bus"—a converted school bus that the summer-hire cops used to transport herds of high schoolers from parties to the police station. Kate had been furious that the police entered a private home and arrested her despite the fact that she wasn't drinking—even at sixteen she had a strong sense of right and wrong. It turned out she wasn't the only one who saw the injustice in these methods; later, the girls became part of a class action lawsuit that awarded them each five hundred dollars and set Kate off and running on her career path.)

With the group's attention on Dani's antics, Jeremy gestured for Vanessa to follow him over the low fence that separated the beach from the dunes.

At the time, she didn't think anyone noticed when they slipped away. Within moments, she was leaning back in a cool valley of sand between two clumps of beach grass, and Jeremy was stretched beside her, kissing her, his hand cradling her hip, pulling her closer into his warmth, the voices of their friends subsumed by the tide.

The sound of heels on pavement pulls Vanessa to turn and watch as a woman with a swingy red miniskirt and a wristful of gold bangles hurries by the playground, talking excitedly into her cell phone. Nocelli, the gallery where Vanessa used to work, is displaying installations by Dara Freeman now, and while a part of Vanessa is sitting on the park bench in linen pants and a ponytail, another part of her is clicking through the gallery in peep-toe heels and a teal silk shirtdress. She misses the gallery, the buzzy feel of being part of a scene, part of the world that exists outside of motherhood.

Over the holidays, she'd decided she was ready to go back to work. She was going to call Teri—her old boss at Nocelli who had left to start her own gallery—and her other art world contacts and put out feelers for a new position. Lucy was nearing two and entering a more independent phase of life and in the weeks since New Year's Day Vanessa had felt herself blinking, sharpening, as the world outside of their Mommy-and-Me microcosm began shifting back into focus. Her hourglass figure was a softer, fuller version now, but her body, long done with breastfeeding, felt almost like her own again. She could not sleep as deeply as she used to, but she was at least getting seven-hour stretches of rest each night. And Lucy lit up when she saw other children; she'd probably thrive in a small preschool. Excited to tell Drew about the decision she'd finally reached, Vanessa had slathered Grey Poupon on salmon—she prides herself on not being much of a cook—and made a spinach salad. No carbs for her, she was going back to work!

When Drew came home that evening, he beat her to the Big News punch. He'd kissed Lenora Haysbach. It had happened weeks earlier, he told her, at the show's holiday party that Vanessa had missed because their babysitter had canceled on them at the last minute. Lenora was—*is*—a publicist for the show; they still work together; her office is right down the hall from Drew's. They'd kissed while they lingered by the coat-check cubby at the end of a long hall at the end of a long night.

He waited so long to tell her because he didn't want to ruin Christmas. This part infuriates Vanessa nearly as much as the kiss itself. This, and the fact that when she stupidly asked Drew for a play-by-play of exactly what had happened (she'd needed to know what he meant by "kiss," and it quickly became clear that he had not meant "peck" but something far more involved, something that, had they been in high school, they would have described as "making out"), he'd told her that when he finally pulled away, he had apologized to Lenora, saying something absurdly clichéd like, "I'm sorry. I can't do this." He had *apologized* to her! And the fact that he remembered that little tidbit told Vanessa that the kiss had not occurred because he'd had too much to drink.

She feels silly that she is so devastated by the fact that her husband kissed another woman. But she can't help it—she is furious. She doesn't know how she is supposed to move forward and put his betrayal behind her. It had not taken long for Vanessa to start thinking about her ex-boyfriend. Drew's kiss with Lenora consumed her days, and she found that if every time she thought of their kiss, she immediately turned her thoughts to the kisses she'd once shared with Jeremy Caldwell, she felt a little better. Her thoughts about returning to work tangled; she never mentioned her decision. She'd thought she was feeling like herself again, but she was wrong.

At night, once Lucy is in bed, Vanessa and Drew sit on the couch. Drew sends work e-mails from his laptop; his father's evening news program plays on the television in the background. Vanessa still finds it hard to believe Thomas Warren is her father-in-law, her daughter's grandfather. The sight of him on the television screen each night always makes her feel hopeful. She lifts her laptop from the coffee table and checks the calendars of her favorite galleries and museums.

"MoMA's self-portraits exhibit starts in a few weeks," she says. "Maybe we could get a sitter and go one Saturday." This is more than she has offered in months; Jeremy's e-mail is weighing on her conscience, as much as she wishes it wouldn't.

Drew doesn't catch on fast enough; his eyes remain on his computer screen. "Maybe," he says.

Vanessa stiffens. She has begun to wonder if Drew's professed interest in art all those years ago was simply a ploy to get her into bed. The idea that he might have been lying rattles her. Then again, she rarely watches *Estelle*, the show he produces, the success of which has bought this West Village condo that she loves so much, with its dark wood floors and sleek decor and the balcony that she is sure it is only a matter of time before she locks herself out on.

She checks Facebook. "Teri had her baby," she announces to the room.

Not long after Vanessa left her job, her boss, Teri, a quick-talking wisp of a woman with a cap of black hair and clever eyes, had also left Nocelli to start her own gallery. This news had sent a cold shiver of envy through Vanessa even then, when she was as certain as she would ever be that she could not be happy unless she spent her days with her newborn daughter. And then last year, at forty-one, Teri fell in love, married, and became pregnant in quick succession. Vanessa is eager to see how Teri handles these life changes. Though she's never much liked the idea of having a role model (*What is the point of following in someone else's footsteps?*), she supposes she should just allow that Teri holds this position for her.

She tilts the computer screen toward Drew. "A boy," she says. "Luke." It's the usual shot: red-faced, sleeping newborn, swaddled and topped with a hospital-issue striped cap. They have a nearly identical one of Lucy framed in their bedroom.

"Luke," Drew repeats, still not looking up. "Bible or *Star Wars*?"

"*Star Wars*," Vanessa says, thinking of Teri's engineer husband.

"I see."

Vanessa sighs. "I see" is what Drew says when he isn't really listening.

Drew seems to realize his mistake then and turns his head to face her computer screen, his eyes remaining on his own laptop until the last possible moment. He squints at her screen. "The world," he says, the corners of his lips hinting at a smile before he even gets the sentence out, "welcomes another angry raisin."

Drew has a great, infectious laugh. It's boyish and free with a little snickery glint of wickedness that presses right into her, rendering her powerless. Despite how distant she felt only a moment earlier, she can't help it: she's laughing with him now. She hopes he doesn't know that his laughter is her kryptonite. He might, though, because all of a sudden he's scooting closer on the couch.

"I'm kidding!" he says. "You know I love babies."

Vanessa does know this. She also knows the exact direction his thoughts are heading. She'd heard that pregnant women often dream of their babies, but when she was pregnant with Lucy, she had been tormented by dream after dream of Colin—the dull cast to his blue eyes when he lay in a hospital bed after wrecking his father's car; the dazed grin he released after scoring a game-winning goal, as though stunned by his own ability; his hands curled into rigid fists as a fire lapped at the night sky behind him—and would wake up frantic and nauseated, pinned by guilt. It wasn't the first time that thoughts of Colin kept her up at night, but those dreams were particularly relentless. She'd spent her entire pregnancy with ashen circles under her eyes.

"I'm thinking of getting a drink with an ex-boyfriend," she says. It's effective. Drew shifts back and lifts an eyebrow.

"Oh, yeah? Who?"

"Jeremy Caldwell. I dated him for a summer during college. You've never met him. I haven't seen him in eight years."

Drew runs a hand through his brown curls and smiles. It's no surprise that his dark eyes have come alive. From the very beginning, the passion in their relationship has been fueled in part by their flirtations with others. Vanessa used to experience a shiver of excitement when she felt Drew watching her talk to other men at parties; she felt a sharper thrill—but a thrill nonetheless—watching him do the same with other women. There was a silent connection between them—an understanding, she'd thought, that they would toe the line but not cross it, and their marriage, not to mention their sex life, was more electric for it. She'd really and truly thought they were on the same page. All that time, she'd happily been playing with fire.

"Are you asking my permission?"

"I don't think I need it."

"No," Drew says. "You don't." He looks at her, and it feels like the first time they've made real eye contact in days. For a moment, Vanessa thinks he is going to ask her not to see Jeremy. But he can't ask this. Drew has apologized many times; he is sorry he acted on his attraction to another woman. He thinks he ended things before they went too far, but Vanessa is not sure she agrees. The kiss has cooled something in her heart. She does not know how to trust him; she does not know how she will ever feel secure in her marriage again. She cannot forgive him.

The fact of this incident remains so large and tangible that Lenora herself might as well be sitting between them on the couch, the slender fingers of one of her hands resting on Drew's forearm and the other on Vanessa's so they form a human chain. Drew's smile hardens, and he turns back to his computer screen.

"Just don't run away with him," he says without looking over. He laughs, but it's not his real laugh; it's not the laugh that lassoes her heart.

Late that night, she slips out of bed, walks down the hall, and curling up in a corner of the living room couch, calls her first, and perhaps last, true friend.

"Hey, V," Kate answers. "What are you doing up so late? Everything okay?"

"I can't sleep. Did I wake you?"

"I'm at the office, working on a brief. But I'm glad you called. I could use a break."

"Tell me about it," Vanessa says. "It's been a

long day." She knows she should not feel defensive about leaving her career, but sometimes when she talks to Kate, she cannot help but feel there is a hint of judgment there, a subtle establishment of a hierarchy of busyness.

"*Every* day is a long day," Kate says. "But what else am I going to do? Working keeps my mind off my crappy personal life."

They fall silent after this. Vanessa still can't believe Peter broke up with Kate. He always struck Vanessa as overly analytical and a bit dull, but who thinks any man is worthy of her best friend? She had at least been sure he would not hurt Kate, who, despite wearing her emotions on her sleeve, is the smartest person Vanessa knows, full of endearing, self-deprecating humor, and more loyal than anyone—certainly not Vanessa and now as it turns out, not Peter either—deserves.

"Sorry," Kate says. "Too honest?"

"A smidge," Vanessa says, laughing. "Could you sugarcoat your loneliness a little, please? It's depressing."

Kate laughs. "I'll work on it."

Vanessa lies back and tucks a throw pillow under her head. She looks at the white ceiling, the recessed lights that allow noise to seep down from the floor above, and thinks of her husband and daughter asleep elsewhere in the apartment. There is something clandestine about this phone call, about being awake when her family is asleep, and she thinks of all the nights in high school when she would sneak downstairs, press the kitchen phone to her ear, and whisper to boy-friends.

"Do you ever think about Quakerism?" she asks.

"What?" Kate laughs. Vanessa hears papers being shuffled in the background. "I'll have whatever you're having."

"We went to a Quaker school. It isn't the craziest question."

"Um, yeah, Vanessa, it kind of is. *That's* what you think about when you think about high school? Quakerism? I feel like the whole Quaker thing was kind of an afterthought at PFS. All I really remember is being bored to tears during Friends Meeting. Who thought it was a good idea to force a bunch of kids to be silent for an hour?"

"George Fox."

"Who?"

Of course Quakerism isn't what Kate remembers about school. She'd been like a horse in blinders; a glimpse of anything other than textbooks and her field hockey stick would have thrown her off course. Anyway, the Harringtons were Catholic and had probably subtly trained Kate to ignore the religious aspects of PFS. After Drew told her what happened with Lenora, Vanessa had spent a few Sunday mornings at the Fifteenth Street

Meetinghouse in the East Village. It was the first time she'd been to Meeting since she left Philadelphia for college. Sitting on those different but familiar meetinghouse benches, alone in the crowd, had steadied her, but the experience had released old, hard memories too.

"Catholics go to confession, right?" she asks.

"In theory," Kate says. "I'm lapsed. Like, really lapsed. Seriously, how much wine have you had?"

"I'm just thinking out loud. Catholics talk to a priest because they need a conduit to God, right? But Quakers believe that God is inside each of us. So does that mean it's enough to just *think* about the things you've done, and feel bad about them, but not actually tell anyone? If you're thinking about them, isn't that like telling God?"

"I don't know." Kate's voice sounds distant, and Vanessa wonders if she is really listening or if she is working. "Vanessa, I—" she begins, but Vanessa interrupts her.

"Jeremy Caldwell e-mailed me."

It takes Kate a beat to respond. "Jeremy Caldwell? Whoa. Whatever happened to him?"

"I don't really know. We just connected on Facebook. He wants to meet for a drink on Friday, but I don't think I should."

"He knows you're married, doesn't he?"

"Yes." At least, she assumes he does. Her relationship status is on her Facebook page.

"So what's the big deal?"

Vanessa sighs. "I guess there isn't one."

"Just as long as you don't start doing that thing you always used to do."

Vanessa knows what Kate is going to say. She clenches her jaw.

"The grass is not always greener," Kate says. "Don't start pining for something that isn't nearly as great as what you already have."

Vanessa wonders now if the thin tone of Kate's voice isn't distraction or distance, but sadness. "I won't," she says. It was wrong, selfish even, to have called Kate. She thinks of her friend sitting in an empty office building in the middle of the night, putting off the moment when she has to go home to an empty apartment that still, undoubtedly, shows signs of a relationship that was supposed to last forever. She knows that Kate has struggled with loneliness since Colin's death, and now another man she loves has left her without warning.

"How are you, really, Kate?"

"I'm pretty awful." The words rush out of Kate like breath she'd been holding. "You think you know someone and then it turns out they haven't been honest with you. The person you're supposed to be closest to in the world."

Vanessa's heart begins to thwap around her chest like a wet towel in a dryer. She thinks of the last time she saw Colin alive. His eyes had appeared murky—part reflection of the bay, part hopelessness, and part, as it turned out, drugs.

"Have you told Dani what happened with Peter?" she asks, trying to steer her thoughts away from Colin.

"Not yet. You know Dani—she never picks up her phone."

Vanessa feels a wave of anger, surprising in its size, swell within her. "She should call you back. You're a better friend to her than she is to you."

"It's okay," Kate says, but her voice sounds strained. "We'll always be as close as we've always been—it really doesn't matter whether or not we talk."

Objectively, Vanessa knows that this statement is ridiculous—how can Kate say she is close with Dani when she hasn't even told her that her fiancé called off their engagement? Still, she understands what Kate means. *What you love will always be with you.* It's a line from one of Lucy's favorite books; Vanessa hasn't been able to get it out of her head for months.

"Anyway," Kate says, clearing her throat, "I should go. But, really, why not see Jeremy? You're a happily married woman."

Dani would not have been so encouraging. She would have said that Vanessa was opening a can of worms by seeing Jeremy again. She would have told her she should not see him unless she was prepared for her whole life to change.

After she hangs up, Vanessa looks through the window. Even this late, the city is too bright for the sky to reveal its stars, but she knows that if she drove just a few miles into New Jersey, the stars would appear, like a reward for leaving her life behind.

I'd love to see you, she e-mails Jeremy. *Let me know when and where.*

When the sound of sirens had grown louder than the sound of waves rolling and breaking against the sand, Vanessa pulled back from Jeremy. They looked at each other for a moment, smiling, before scrambling to their feet. It was illegal to be in the dunes and it occurred to Vanessa that some over-zealous homeowner had called the cops on them. It wasn't until she was standing that she caught sight of the flames that leaped into the sky, the smoke that billowed upward, blocking the stars.

Colin, Vanessa thought immediately. Her entire body began to quiver. *What have you done?*

Jeremy grabbed her hand and they followed a line of depression between two hills of dunes, their bare feet sinking into the sand. Vanessa felt something break the skin of her heel but she didn't slow her pace until they reached the low fence that separated the dunes from the beach.

She looked down as she stepped over the fence and when she looked up, Colin stood before her. His eyes were wild as they searched her face and his chest heaved; his hands were curled into fists. When Vanessa dropped Jeremy's hand and took a step toward Colin, he backed away. Behind him, three flashlights bobbed by the water's edge. Vanessa could make out a group of people throwing sand on the fire. It was a lifeguard stand, she realized now, engulfed in flame. When she looked back at Colin, his eyes were still on her face. She did not need to know it would be one of the last times he ever looked at her for his face to burn into her memory.

"Run!" he said. And she did.

6

Dani

Dani awakens and shrinks farther below the covers of her bed in the same moment, as though the morning might stop being the morning if she sleeps through it. She'd been dreaming about the bay in Avalon, reeds snakelike around her ankles, a blue sky hazy with heat, but now light falls against the bed in a long, glinting knife-edge, cutting through the covers and into her sleep. She swallows. She fell asleep without brushing her teeth and her tongue feels thickly coated, the back of her teeth fuzzy.

She reaches one arm out from under the covers and pats the desk that doubles as her nightstand, trying to locate her phone. The corner of the desk overhangs the bed; every night she goes to bed sure that at some point she will roll over in her sleep and impale herself on this point, goug-

ing an eyeball, and every morning she is slightly
unnerved to find herself unharmed. She locates
her phone and draws it under the covers. She has
spent two weeks e-mailing her résumé to book-
stores and cafés and has not received a single response. If she doesn't hear good news today, she
will tell her roommates that Layla, her bartender
friend, is looking to rent a room and is willing to
take over her portion of the lease. And then she
will call her father and begin packing.

Under the dark tent of covers, the glow of the
phone hurts her eyes. The night before, she and Rachel and Macy had swallowed codeine that Macy
had left over from a knee injury and then drunk
two and a half bottles of red wine before meeting
Rachel's bandmates at Hobson's Choice on Haight
Street. Almost immediately upon walking into
the bar, Dani saw sparks in the corners of her
vision. Maybe it was the unrelentingly red walls.
Or the band's bassist's ear-stabbing Texas twang.
Or the fact that it had been two weeks since she'd
been fired and she hadn't managed to write the final scenes of her novel. There were any number of
reasons why her body might have finally decided
to put its foot down. She'd finished her beer and,
squinting, staggered out of the bar. On the sidewalk, a bearded man with a pit bull and a wild
look in his eye had grabbed her arm so tightly
that her jacket had ripped when she pulled away.

She'd run the seven blocks back to her apartment half-blind.

The sparks are gone now, replaced by the decidedly more mundane ache of a hangover. Dani peers at her phone, scrolling through her new e-mails. There are no responses to her job applications. She is going to have to call her father. He'll be disappointed, but he'll get over it. She is his only child; they are each other's only family. He won't admit it to her, but he'll probably be happy to have her at home again. They share the same sense of humor, the same enjoyment of a good time—Dani knows he doesn't strive for this sort of lasting companionship with the women he dates. Not that she is comparing—or competing. That would be weird.

The phone vibrates in her hands. It's Vanessa. She can't remember the last time Vanessa called. Dani burrows her head back into the pillow, deciding not to answer. Then she changes her mind.

"Hello?" she says, wincing at the croaky sound of her voice. Vanessa, who Dani now thinks of as Mombot, likely arose with the sun. She probably had an early-morning latte and a Pilates class and then popped into an art exhibit on her way to a play date with some gorgeous, high-style friend and her gorgeous, highly styled toddler. Dani can't remember the last time she actually spoke with Vanessa, but she gets enough pieces of information filtered through Kate to believe that both of them now securely inhabit an adult world of which Dani is not sure she will ever be a member. If only all of those English teachers at PFS and writing professors at Brown hadn't insisted she was *talented*, maybe by now, in this final year of her twenties, she would have an actual career. Being irritated with herself for having these self-pitying thoughts does not, unfortunately, stop her from having them. They just keep coming.

"Dani? It's Vanessa."

"Hey, V. How are you?"

"I'm fine. Are you sick?"

"I'm just waking up. It's only nine here."

The line is silent for a moment. "So you're not sick."

"No, Vanessa, I'm not sick." Dani tries to decipher Vanessa's tone. Aggression? Exasperation? Certainly not concern.

"Then why haven't you called Kate back? She's been leaving you voice mails for weeks, hasn't she?"

Dani's thoughts race. Sure, she'd missed a few calls from Kate, but that was the way their relationship always worked: Kate called three times for every one time Dani picked up. If she answered the phone every time Kate wanted to talk, she'd never do anything else. Besides, Dani hated talking on the phone; it was awkward, even with her closest friend. She felt anxious without the visual signals of when it was her turn to talk and her turn to listen, so she usually just let Kate rattle on for half an hour before cutting her off. But now, with Vanessa's accusatory tone—*that was it: accusation! She should have known*—in her ear, the thought of Kate waiting for her to call brings a familiar feeling of guilt, and a new feeling of worry.

"Is she okay?" Dani asks.

"She's . . . she's fine. But you should call her back."

Dani releases a sharp breath. Clearly, Vanessa knows something, which means . . . what? Kate is not fine? She realizes that Kate and Vanessa are in better contact with each other than she is with either of them, and she hates that this makes her feel insecure. She used to be the one who brought them together, who kept them laughing, who ensured Vanessa's outfits got wrinkled every once in a while and that uptight Kate skipped a class now and then so they could sit in the park and share a clove cigarette.

"Vanessa, what's going on? You can't just call me for the first time in who knows how long and then not tell me why you're calling. You're freaking me out."

"I'm calling to tell you to call Kate. That's why I'm calling."

"But why?"

Vanessa is silent. Dani hears a hollow screeching noise in the background, metal grinding against metal.

"What is that God-awful noise? Where are you?"

"It's a swing. I'm at the playground with Lucy. I'm convinced men design playgrounds to drive women crazy so men can feel justified when they cheat on them."

"Ouch. Searing commentary from the sandbox analyst."

"That's me," Vanessa says, sighing. "Reporting live from the jungle gym." In the background, the metal chain continues screeching.

"So what's going on with Kate?"

"Don't tell her I told you," Vanessa says.

"Told me *what*?"

"Peter called off the wedding."

Dani pushes herself up in bed. "What? What happened?"

"I don't know. I don't think Kate really knows. Or at least she's not telling me. You know Kate— she has the most amazing way of yammering on for hours on end without actually saying much."

"I'll call her today."

"Good."

"I fucking hate Peter."

"Me too," Vanessa says.

Poor Kate. Her friend's inherent optimism makes Dani think of a flag high up on a pole, something that starts out noble but over time, exposed to all of the elements of the world, fades and tatters. *Who knows?* she thinks. *Maybe being the daughter of a good marriage fucks you up nearly as much as being the daughter of a bad one.* Kate had once told Dani that her earliest memory was of walking downstairs after having a nightmare and spotting her parents sitting side by side on the couch, holding hands while they watched TV. In Kate's memory, seeing them together was enough to reassure her that all was right in the world; she'd returned to bed without even letting them know she was awake. Dani's earliest memory is of her parents fighting. She doesn't remember what they were fighting about, just that the air between them was as sharp and stinging as wind gathering speed between two buildings in winter. She remembers standing there, shivering, while she watched them fight. When her mother finally stormed away, she walked right past Dani as though, already, she could not see her.

"What about Vegas?" Dani asks.

"Canceled. Have you checked your e-mail lately?"

Dani now remembers seeing an e-mail from Kate with "Bachelorette Party" in the subject line.

She'd ignored it, figuring it was just Kate being Kate, micromanaging the details.

"I guess the upside is we don't have to spend a weekend with her boring law school friends," Dani says. She'll call the airline and switch her ticket to Philadelphia instead, which will save her the mortification of asking her father to pay for her airfare. It won't stop her from feeling like she's limping home with her tail tucked between her legs, but it's something. She does not even consider telling Vanessa about this development.

"So what have you been doing out there?" Vanessa asks. "The San Francisco writer thing? Poetry readings at City Lights? Love-ins with hot, artsy men?"

"Ha," Dani says, her mood souring. She feels like a fraud. And, just as sharply, she wants a drink. Anything to bury this feeling.

"Are you dating—"

"I have to go," Dani says. She doesn't mean to cut Vanessa off, but she needs to hang up the phone. The longer they talk, the better chance there is that Vanessa will bring up the things she accused Dani of after Colin died—the accusations that forever changed their friendship. Dani can't bear the thought of Vanessa apologizing. Or not apologizing. She can't bear the thought of either, and both possibilities have been circling stealthily since this conversation began, flashing like sharks' fins. "Thanks for letting me know about Kate," she says. She hangs up without remembering to wait until Vanessa says good-bye.

Rachel is lying on the couch, her legs draped over one of its threadworn arms. Smoke rises in a steady stream from the joint that dangles from her fingers. She is small but strong with muscular arms sticking out from her white tank top and a pixie cut that, today, is pink. She is studying her toenails and scraping her slightly bucked front teeth with the pointer finger of her free hand.

"Thank God you're alive," Rachel says and takes a long drag off the joint.

"Did I disappear last night? Sorry." Dani's stomach has been in knots since hanging up with Vanessa, but the musky smell of pot has a calming effect. She sinks down into one of the chairs across from the couch and holds out her hand. They share everything here—the soy milk in the fridge, the bath-dropped paperbacks littering the coffee table, the drugs.

Rachel curls the joint into the cup of her hand, away from Dani. "Are you going to work today?"

"No," Dani says. "Why?"

"It's laced."

"With what?"

"I don't know," Rachel says and moves her gaze slowly back to her toes, "but it is."

When Dani was twenty-two years old and fresh out of college like Rachel, she too could be found lying on a couch drinking and doing drugs in the middle of any given Monday. Now she is twenty-nine, and she is still here. How is it possible she is still here? How is it possible she is twenty-nine? It's time she moved on to somewhere new, even if that somewhere new is really somewhere old.

"I was fired," she tells Rachel. "Two weeks ago. I'm moving home. But don't worry, I found someone who will take over my part of the lease. You'll like her. She's like us."

Rachel stares at her, blinking. "That sucks," she says finally and passes the joint to Dani's waiting hand.

Dani spends the day wandering the city, attempting to commit the San Francisco streets to memory. It's the twentieth of June, which means tomorrow is the official start of summer, and yet the air here is cold and damp and she is wearing a puffy down vest and a long knit scarf and strange little John Lennon sunglasses that no one in this part of town thinks are strange at all. She is so desperately tired of being cold.

The pastel houses that she passes fit snugly together like saltwater taffy lined up in a box; she's traveled all the way across the country and still she views the world in the context of Jersey Shore candies. Maybe this is why she fell in love with San Francisco in the first place: the air, in places, smells of salt and tides; gulls sit beside pigeons on thick black phone lines that zigzag their way through the Inner Sunset toward Ocean Beach; paint peels from homes in strips of yellow and green; San Francisco and the island that holds Avalon are both seven miles long, ringed by beach and bay. She walks the streets as though in a dream, like walking through a soft-focus watercolor of the city instead of through the city itself.

She orders a beer at Fireside on Irving. At the end of the bar, two old ladies with faded Irish accents are talking about their kids or maybe their grandkids.

"Bill never picks up the phone," the one wearing a ginger-colored wig says. "I think he's living with Karen."

The white-haired one tells the bartender she could be a model. "You have the figure," she says.

"Oh, maybe," the bartender says, clearly pleased. "I'm not healthy enough though. I smoke and I drink."

The old lady thinks for a minute, taking a dainty sip of her beer. "Maybe you're better off here then," she says.

Dani pulls her laptop from her bag and opens it on the bar. One of the many disturbing realizations she has made over the years she has been writing this book is that Colin is remarkably hard to write about, and not for the obvious reasons. She always believed she knew him well—she still believes this, actually, despite the fact that on the page his personality, his essence, is a slippery thing, difficult to pin down. He has become an enigma. Or maybe he was always this way, even for those who knew him best, perhaps even for his twin sister. Anyway, next to front-row, straight-A, people-pleaser Kate, what could Colin do but fade into the background? He filled the role that he felt was left for him. Kate's brightness made Colin seem shadowed; Colin's hazy edges only made Kate appear crisper. They defined each other, the personality of one throwing the other into relief.

Dani thinks of the policemen knocking on their door that Sunday morning eight years earlier, grasping the citation Colin had received for setting fire to a lifeguard stand during a party on the beach two nights earlier. He'd spent Friday night in a holding cell and was in a sour mood all of Saturday, getting into a rare fight with Kate on the beach that afternoon, upsetting her so much that she had run away in tears. Later, he and Dani had sat side by side at the Princeton's bar, drinking through their hangovers. And then, the next morning, there were cops on the doorstep.

Dani had stared at them. Even without their

solemn expressions, their appearance at the bungalow would have made her anxious. Already the sky seemed low and heavy with heat. A blanket of humidity wrapped itself around her as soon as she opened the door, making it difficult to breathe.

"Is this where Colin Harrington was staying?" one of the officers asked, holding out Colin's citation. It was wet and ripped, the writing blurred. A huge white gull landed on the stones in front of the house. It stopped and eyed her and then opened its beak. Its cry—half scream, half laugh— echoed in the street.

A terrible tingling sensation had spread through Dani's fingertips, a feeling that flares again, sharp and painful, whenever she tries, as she does now, to give words and chronology and meaning to everything that happened.

The old ladies are talking about the price of their teeth, which leads them to discuss the week's sales at the grocery store.

"I'll go to Safeway with you," the ginger-wigged one says.

"I'm very drunk," the white-haired one replies.

Dani follows them, stubbing her toe hard against the door as she stumbles onto the sidewalk. The ginger-haired lady looks over her shoulder and makes a tsking noise with her tongue; the white-haired one gives Dani a sympathetic smile and offers a shaky, pale hand. Dani thanks her and hobbles off in the opposite direction, toward the ocean.

She pulls out her cell phone and calls Kate's office line. She won't remember what they talk about, or the offer she makes to her oldest friend. But she will eventually recall that a plane flew over the city as they spoke, pulling a long white banner ad through a suddenly blue sky, reminding her of the prop planes that pace the vivid summer sky along Avalon's coast, advertising ten-dollar beer buckets at Jack's Place and dollar wings at the Princeton. And she'll remember the sound of Kate's voice, ringing with loneliness, familiar and haunting.

Late that afternoon, Dani finds herself sprawled on the couch, her legs dangling over its arm, in nearly the exact position in which she had found Rachel that morning. She wipes at the saliva that has crusted at the corner of her mouth and swings her legs so that she is sitting upright. For a moment, she remembers only the feeling of smoke burning her throat, her chest filling and emptying, and she is confused that she is now on the couch and Rachel has disappeared. Then she realizes that hours have passed; she has wandered the city, sat in a bar. The light that fills the apartment has the still, dust-speckled quality of late-afternoon sun. She detects a low hum of electronics and appliances. Dani is the only one of the four people who live in this apartment who is not working right now.

There is a text message from Kate on her cell phone.

> *V is in! Avalon instead of Vegas—just the 3 of us. Thanks, D. Exactly what I need. Maybe what we all need?*

Dani lowers the cell phone. *Avalon? Vanessa?* Now she remembers calling Kate—the sound of Kate's voice, the plane in the sky, the smell of salt carried on the breeze. They must have talked about Peter. Had she suggested that the three of them spend the upcoming Fourth of July weekend that they'd blocked off for Vegas at her father's house in Avalon instead? Dani winces at the thought. This is the solace she offered her best friend? A trip to the place where her twin brother died; the place where their friendship had been sealed and then fractured?

She can't imagine sitting on the beach with Kate and Vanessa again. She does not think either of them has been back to Avalon since Colin died. Dani has; Avalon is now a bittersweet place for her—sweet because it is where she soaks in a blend of humidity and sun that does not exist in San Francisco, and sweet too because it is a place where she spends a rare, happily wine-sodden weekend with her father, away from the overtly sexual gaze of his latest girlfriend. Bitter, because it is a place haunted by ghosts—the ghost of Colin, the ghost of her friendship with Vanessa, the ghost of the girl she was, a girl full of fire, a girl who never once doubted that the best was ahead.

Dani reads Kate's text again. *Exactly what I need. Maybe what we all need?* What does she mean by that? Had Dani told her that she'd been fired and that she was moving home? As much as Dani is mortified by this thought, she is more concerned by the nagging sense that Kate is referring to something else entirely—something about the friendship between the three of them. The *we* of them. Kate, ever the peacemaker, wants their friendship to be the way it once was, but Dani knows this can't happen, not really, because they don't know the truth about Colin's death. If they did, they would never speak to her again.

7

Kate

Kate sits on one of the long benches in the central hall of Thirtieth Street Station, a soft pretzel in one hand and an enormous cup of Auntie Anne's lemonade in the other. The benches remind her of Friends Meeting at PFS, that cruelly silent ritual with the power to bend and stretch time, making your mind fall through trapdoors of fantasy and memory, kneading an hour out to an insufferable length. Kate, a little guiltily, always thought of that hour as the seventh circle of hell. Even now, she can't sit on a bench without experiencing a shudder of dread. Give her an armchair any day. A nice comfy sofa with a few throw pillows. And someone to talk to, of course.

She looks down at the pretzel in her hand and thinks *Howdy, partner*. Then she takes a big bite. Peter talks to his food too. *G'morning, lovely*, he'd said once, early in their relationship, when Kate set an omelet in front of him. She'd spun around, delighted, and then realized he was talking to the eggs. This realization had made her feel even more delighted, so much so that she'd laughed out loud and had to explain it to him. *We both talk to our food!*

This is her second enormous cup of lemonade—it's been her one pregnancy craving for weeks. She has taken one trip to the bathroom and can already feel her bladder beginning to pinch again. She arrived at the train terminal at 4:00 PM—an hour earlier than Vanessa's train was due to arrive—because she was too distracted by thoughts of the upcoming weekend, and the promise of lemonade at the train station, to sit at her desk any longer. Her office was nearly empty anyway. It's the Friday before a holiday weekend—Monday is the Fourth of July—and everyone has left for the shore.

Kate almost never leaves work early. She loves her job, loves the precision of the law. Sure, the interpretation of many laws could be argued, but most were fairly cut-and-dried—they delineated a right and a wrong, created a road map, laid out a predictable path of action and consequence. Plus, she has a deep-seated respect for rules and hierarchies, which makes her a perfect fit for a big, bureaucratic firm like WebsterPrice. In high school she'd been respectful of students in the upper classes, even the ones who were only six months older than she, and she'd dutifully kissed up to her senior sorority sisters in college. And now she feels a profound satisfaction with the way first-year lawyers nod at her in the halls of WebsterPrice.

If you love your job so much why don't you marry it? a singsong, little-girl voice trills in her head. Maybe she will. Maybe she'll be one of those women who are married to their jobs. *Is it possible to have a baby and be married to your job?*

If there is anything good to be found in Peter's breaking up with her, it is that she is not on her way to Las Vegas right now. She had wanted her bachelorette party to be a weekend of pizza and chick flicks with her closest friends, but Vanessa had laughed when she'd suggested this.

"It's not your twelfth birthday party, Kate," she'd said. "It's your bachelorette. We should go to Vegas. We can stay at the Palms. I'll make us dinner reservations at Nobu. We can go dancing. You love dancing!"

This was true, but before Kate could respond, Dani had groaned. They were on a three-way conference call, an arrangement that Kate had regretted almost immediately. Vanessa and Dani were her matron of honor and maid of honor, respectively, and Kate had felt a responsibility to moderate their conversations. She had forced them back into direct contact, but she knew she could not force them to get along. She did not understood the exact *why* of their falling out, but she knew the *when* down to the day. Dani had told her that Vanessa cut her out of her life because of some comment Dani made about not liking her boyfriend at the time, a guy named Jeremy Caldwell. Vanessa told Kate they'd fought about all the clothes Dani had borrowed from Vanessa and had managed to somehow ruin over the course of that summer in Avalon before their final year of college. Kate had never believed these incidents would have been enough to drive her friends apart; she felt sure their fight had had something to do with Colin. As soon as she pieced this together, she stopped hunting for answers, deciding she did not want to know.

"Bachelorette parties aren't one-size-fits-all, Vanessa," Dani was saying. "Just because you went to Vegas for yours doesn't mean Kate should go for hers."

"What do you know about my bachelorette party?" Vanessa responded. "You weren't there."

Kate closed her eyes and leaned back in her office chair. She knew that tone. Vanessa was moments away from falling into aggressive silence. It was remarkable how she could wield silence like a weapon; if Quakers weren't opposed to violence, Kate would have sworn Vanessa had honed this skill during her double dose of weekly Meeting in childhood.

"I had to move apartments that weekend, Vanessa," Dani said. "If I could have been at your bachelorette party, I would have been there. And P.S., your wedding was years ago. I think it's time to relinquish your bridezilla tiara."

Kate knew that Vanessa had never believed Dani's excuse for missing her bachelorette party. Kate herself thought the whole truth was far more complicated than Dani let on. She might have had to move that weekend, but more importantly, Dani could not afford to go to Las Vegas. Dani had grown up the wealthiest of all three of them, living with her father in a penthouse apartment on Rittenhouse Square, but now she was the one who was perpetually strapped for cash. Dani would never admit this was the reason she didn't go to Vanessa's party, just like she would never call her father and ask if he would cover the party's cost—she had too much pride. *Dignity*, Kate thought, amending her hasty adjudication. "Pride" was an ungenerous word. Still, she worried about her friend. Dani was the most ambitious person Kate knew and yet she appeared to have no plans—a dangerous combination, it seemed to her.

"I'm not really a big sushi fan," Kate said, trying to get the conversation back on track. "I know we're all supposed to love it because it's so healthy and hip, but I'm just not into it. It's so—raw. I feel like I'm chewing listeria. And Vegas will be ridiculously hot in July. You know my skin. It would be just my luck to end up with third-degree burns two months before the wedding. Philly is so quiet in July—I'm sure we could get dinner reservations anywhere in the city—"

"Tell the truth: Are you becoming agoraphobic?" Dani asked, cutting her off. "When was the last time you left Philadelphia?"

"Forget Philly, when's the last time you left your *apartment*?" Vanessa asked. "Are we going to show up there and find a bunch of rotisserie chickens under your bed—"

"—like Brittany Murphy's character in *Girl, Interrupted*?" Dani finished, laughing.

Of course, Kate thought. Dani and Vanessa were finally in agreement and it was at her expense. For a moment, she felt a flash of the out-of-breath feeling that had overcome her once in middle school when she realized Dani and Vanessa had had a sleepover without her. The memory infuriated her. It had taken Kate, who remained gawky and earnest long after Vanessa became beautiful and Dani became cool, years to feel anything other than relieved that they continued to be friends with her in high school. Eventually, though, Kate had come to understand that her friends were the ones who should have felt grateful—she had always been their mediator, the glue that held them together; without Kate, they might not have remained friends as long as they had. Yet, here she was again, struggling to play catch-up even when discussing her own party.

"*And*," Kate said loudly then, knowing exactly how what she was about to say would make Dani feel, "Vegas is too expensive for some people."

They stopped laughing.

"For your lawyer friends? I doubt that very much," Vanessa said.

"You're reaching now," Dani said. Kate heard the edge in her voice—a half-angry, half-panicked tremble that immediately made Kate wish she could take back what she'd said. But she couldn't take it back; instead, she'd add it to the list of regrets that kept her up at night. This, she reminded herself, was what happened when she lost control: she did things that she regretted. "Vanessa is right. We need to get you out of Philly. Besides, as much as it will kill you to hear this, you're not allowed to plan your own bachelorette party. We're going to Vegas."

Kate felt even worse when Dani called to suggest they not cancel the getaway entirely, but move it to Dani's father's house in Avalon, re-name it a girls' weekend, and disinvite "the riff-raff," by which she meant Kate's college and law school friends.

"We'll watch movies and eat pizza, just like you wanted in the first place," Dani said.

Kate couldn't believe Dani had remembered. She sometimes had the sense that Dani and Va-nessa didn't listen to her as closely as she listened to them, and she felt shamed by Dani's offer. But she was also surprised that Dani was suggesting they go to Avalon. And she was concerned about the slur in Dani's voice, the way her sentences me-andered and then gave way to silence that Kate hurried to fill. Dani was always the most experi-mental of the three of them; in high school and in college she had seemed to approach drugs with the mind-set of both a researcher and an adventurer—she was collecting experiences and having fun. This changed after Colin died; her joy dampened. Even from a distance, Kate sensed this, and it filled her with sadness.

When Dani called, Kate had been sitting in her sweats on the floor beside Gracie, flipping through her daily planner, erasing all of her upcoming wedding appointments. There went Dress Fitting and Cake Tasting. Final Caterer Meeting. Dance Lesson. Marriage License Appointment. She was

penciling in the baby's due date—February 9—
when her phone rang. Though she wasn't very
religious and she certainly wasn't New Age-y, it
struck Kate that Dani's call might be a sign. Peter
wanted her to confront the past, and maybe he
was right. Maybe doing so would prove something to him. She suddenly wished she hadn't
erased all those dates.

"I'd like Vanessa to come," she said. It was important that they were all there when Kate finally
admitted what she'd done to Colin.

Dani was quiet for a moment before agreeing.

"And Gracie," Kate added.

"Who?"

"Gracie. Grace Kelly."

Silence.

"You know," Kate said, suddenly embarrassed.
"My dog."

"Oh, sure," Dani said, and her strange giggle
alarmed Kate. "You, me, Vanessa, and Grace
Kelly. It's a party."

Kate hung up and immediately called Vanessa.
She wasn't sure how she would convince Vanessa
to return to Avalon and was surprised when after
just one short beat of time she had agreed, sounding excited. Maybe, Kate thought, she was finally
ready to bury the hatchet with Dani. Immediately,
Kate had texted Dani to let her know Vanessa was

on board, successfully finalizing the plans before Dani's buzz wore off and she realized what she had done.

Kate attempts to smooth the wrinkles on the blue seersucker sundress she had changed into in the bathroom at her office. She had bought the sundress with Vegas in mind, but now that she is sitting on a bench in Thirtieth Street Station, she realizes that the dress is far more suited to a weekend at the beach than a raucous night in Vegas, and she is relieved to be in a position of feeling appropriately attired instead of the opposite.

She takes a long drink of lemonade. Any minute now, Vanessa will appear at the top of the escalator of Track Three. Soon afterward, they will pick up Dani at the airport. And then they will all drive to Avalon. Kate wipes her hands, damp from the sweating lemonade cup, on a napkin and then folds the napkin again and again until it is a tiny, perfect square. Then she unfolds it and starts over.

She doesn't like keeping secrets. When she was younger, she would tell her brother about the crushes she had on boys and then beg him not to tell anyone. He never did. As unpredictable as Colin was in nearly every other way, in this he was reassuringly dependable: when Kate told him a secret, he kept it.

On the beach the afternoon before he died, the skin on his shoulders had turned purple in the hot sun. He had never been good at protecting himself. She'd wanted to hand him sunscreen or make him put on a hat, but the look in his eye told her she could not ask him to do anything more. They had walked away from the water's edge and were now standing in the wide, desolate swath of dry sand that flanked the dunes. Kate could feel Dani and Vanessa's inquisitive gazes on her back. She tried to make her posture relaxed, but the sand was like smoldering ash below her feet and she shifted from foot to foot, her body tense with anguish and actual pain.

"When is the court date?" she asked.

"I don't know yet." The flat quality of his voice broke Kate's heart. The dunes throbbed with the rhythmic song of cicadas. It was as though they were speaking for Colin—his own Greek chorus.

"What's the worst that can happen?" She was afraid for him. She had no idea what the legal repercussions were for lighting a lifeguard stand on fire. What would another mark on his record do to his life, already a muddled thing, an unclear path?

"I don't know that either," he said. "But I'm sure it's going to be expensive."

"I'll help you."

"How?"

"I'm not sure, but I will."

Colin shrugged. "I'll be fine, Kate. Trust me. I've done worse."

Kate felt herself on the verge of tears. She could not face the resignation in his eyes for one more moment. She turned and ran down to the water, her skin burning.

Kate shifts on the train terminal bench and lets her hand rest on her stomach. She worries the pain she feels when she endures these memories is harmful for the baby.

I'm going to be a single mother, she thinks. The knowledge that countless women have raised babies on their own doesn't make her any less freaked out. This baby will bring chaos to her ordered life. Who will watch the baby while she works? A nanny? Her mother? Kate shakes her head at the thought of telling her parents she is pregnant. It does not matter that she is twenty-nine years old—a grown woman. It does not matter how many seasons of *16 and Pregnant* have aired or how many unmarried celebrities have babies—the news that Kate is pregnant will shock her parents, her grandparents, her many aunts and uncles and cousins. The entire situation is surreal to Kate, and the fact that she hasn't told anyone only adds to the sense that it is not really happening.

The train terminal fills with what sounds like a giant bird flapping its wings. The words and numbers on the line of the old-fashioned schedule that displays Vanessa's Acela train from New York spin loudly and finally settle on the word "Arrived." Kate stands, runs her hand down her seersucker dress, and waits for her friend. Soon Vanessa will appear at the top of the escalator, turning heads in a patterned headscarf and fuchsia, floor-skimming sundress, and before Kate has a moment to wonder for the umpteenth time if they would even be friends if they had met in their twenties instead of when they were five, she will realize that she and Vanessa now have something in common as adults. She will be filled with the urge to ask Vanessa questions about being pregnant, about what it is like to be a mother.

They had bought their first tampons together, spoken a rapid Pig Latin–like language they had made up in Vanessa's yard, watched *Sixteen Candles* and *Heathers* and *Shag* and *Reality Bites* and *Almost Famous* together. Their bedrooms had been filled with pictures of one another, a fact that flooded Kate with joy during each and every one of their many sleepovers. They'd driven to parties together, fought and made up and fought and made up over and over again. They'd bought ad space in the back of their senior yearbook and inserted a picture of the three of them with the quote "A million tomorrows shall all pass away, ere I forget all the joys that were mine, today" running along the bottom. It was from a John Denver song. Dani thought the quote was trite and Vanessa thought it was corny, but Kate loved it, and she was the one who had done the layout and collected the money, so she kept it. Because in the end, it might have been trite and it might have been corny, but it was also true: even after all the tomorrows that have come and gone, Kate has never forgotten the joy that was hers during her childhood with Dani and Vanessa, the joy that she felt before she ruined everything.

If she goes to Avalon, if she tells Dani and Vanessa the truth, maybe some of their friendship's magic will return. Maybe she can start to move forward, and maybe this will make Peter love her again. She can't decide if she should feel humiliated that she is trying to change so a man will love her or if she should feel strong for being able to acknowledge that she needs to change. Kate shifts in her flip-flops, watching and waiting for Vanessa to appear. She is resolved, but uneasy—nervous, but also relieved. She's needed to tell someone everything for so long.

8

Vanessa

Vanessa sits on the train and feels her face grow warm as she considers what she is about to do. Outside, the landscape slowly shifts from industrial, smokestack New Jersey to lush, green, summertime New Jersey. It's so easy to forget that the world outside of Manhattan is this vibrant, always such a surprise to see the full trees and big blue sky. It had been almost impossibly difficult to leave Lucy an hour earlier, but as the train hurtles south, she feels her mood shifting, her stomach fluttering with excitement.

Two weeks earlier, her mood had also steadily improved as she sat in a cab on her way to meet Jeremy Caldwell. She had felt enormously guilty leaving Lucy with a babysitter, but as the cab had sped uptown beneath a stream of green lights, she'd stared through the window at the bustling streets and felt, for a moment, like an animal loosed in its natural habitat. She wondered if New York City might be an element of the marrow in her bones. Being on her own in the city reminded her of when she first arrived there at the age of eighteen, when just walking down the street had been enough to make her heart hum in anticipation of what might happen next.

Jeremy had been sitting at a table by the window of the Breslin Bar on Twenty-Ninth Street; she'd seen him before she even walked inside. He was familiar but virtually a stranger, and realizing this had made her pulse quicken. She remembered suddenly that they hadn't dated long enough to meet each other's parents; they'd never seen each other's childhood homes; they'd never been together anywhere but Avalon.

He stood from the table to hug her and kiss her cheek—just one kiss, one beat of time. He was taller than Drew and had a hipper, less moneyed look. She'd already decided it was okay to compare them—she'd earned that right.

"You're exactly the same," he said, holding her bare elbows for a moment before releasing her. She'd worn a black cotton dress that stopped a couple of inches above her knees and a multi-tiered necklace of hammered gold and large, jewel-toned stones. The necklace was nice but the dress was basically a long tank top and she wore simple leather sandals—she had spent time ensuring she looked effortlessly good.

"You are too," she said.

Jeremy's hair was shorn so maybe he was starting to bald, but other than that he really did look the same. There was something sly and a little hawkish about his dark, close-set eyes and, unlike in his Facebook photograph, he now had the shadow of scruff on his jaw. She remembered how drawn she had been to him when she first saw him at that party eight years earlier, how he'd looked at her hungrily and had seemed a little dangerous, and how he'd surprised her by turning out to be affectionate and sensitive, a romantic.

She glanced around the bar. It was floor-to-ceiling wood, an upscale English pub feel. "Not bad," she said, sliding into her seat.

Jeremy gazed at her, his face settling into a smile. The look in his eye was unreadable. "Tell me everything," he said.

She laughed. When a waiter approached, they ordered gin and tonics without taking their eyes off each other. Already it was clear: the chemistry between them was still there.

"So," he said, leaning across the table.

"So," she said, not leaning away. She had to work to keep her hands in her lap, away from his buzzed hair.

"Do you still talk about Cindy Sherman like she's your best friend?"

Vanessa rewarded his memory with a throaty laugh. Cindy Sherman, one of the most famous photographers in the world, has spent her career exploring how women are portrayed in art and media, and the role of women in society. Her photographs have always deeply affected Vanessa; when she looks at one, she finds it very hard to look away. "We *are* best friends," Vanessa answered. "She just doesn't know it yet."

"Maybe you'll represent her one day."

"Maybe," she said. "Or maybe I'll find the *next* Cindy Sherman."

"Even better," he agreed. "How did you feel about that campaign she did with MAC Cosmetics?"

It occurred to her that he was purposefully steering their conversation away from more personal topics, and she felt grateful. She was aware too that this set the tone for the meeting—if there was nothing between them, they could have easily discussed her husband. She had wondered if she should apologize for the way she had extracted herself from their relationship eight years earlier, but now that Jeremy was there in front of her, she had the distinct sense that he neither expected nor desired an apology. Discussing the past would anchor them, and it was clear that, for the moment at least, they both wanted to move with the current.

"I loved that campaign," she said. "I thought it was a perfect fit."

"You didn't think she was selling out?"

"Not at all."

He smiled. "Cindy Sherman can do no wrong."

"No wrong," Vanessa repeated, smiling back at him. "And eventually, I'll tell her so myself." She liked how certain she sounded when she said this.

"I can't tell you," Jeremy said, "how happy it makes me to hear you're still stalking artists."

Their drinks arrived and they clinked them together before taking sips.

"Congratulations on your design firm," she said. "I looked it up."

"Thanks." He told her about his clients, a mix of small businesses and artists and musicians who wanted websites that represented their essence on their best day. They spoke easily; the whole time, his eyes never stopped moving over her. She'd thought she would be nervous, that the attraction between them would make her feel uneasy; instead she felt calm. This was fun. She'd always been good at flirting. She'd missed it.

And then, after they'd been talking for twenty, maybe thirty minutes, he said, "But, you know, work isn't everything." He took a drink and then set the glass down again. He hesitated for a moment, turning the glass in his hand. Vanessa swallowed. "You're married."

"Yes." Vanessa came very close to mentioning Lucy and felt something twist inside of her. It didn't seem fair that she felt guilty. Had Drew felt this same weight, this sense of responsibility at that holiday party? She doubted it. She forced herself to think of Drew and Lenora kissing and told herself, *Just because you are a mother does not mean you are not entitled to feel rage.* And then: *Just because you are a mother does not mean you are not entitled to feel desire.*

"You crushed the hearts of hundreds of ex-boyfriends with that news." His tone was still light, but she could see he was watching her closely.

"Hundreds?" She laughed. "Why, Jeremy, whatever are you implying?"

He laughed. "That's not what I meant."

"Quality over quantity," she said. "That's always been my motto."

"Seize the day," Jeremy said quietly. "That's always been mine." And then he stretched his arm across the table and pressed his palm to her cheek and she felt herself tilting her head so that it rested in his hand. She wasn't really all that surprised by his boldness. Still, she held her breath. She needed, she realized, to decide just how far she planned to take this. She shifted, ever so slightly, and Jeremy withdrew his hand, a small, not unappealing smirk on his face.

She took three sips of her drink, one right after the other. Her cheek felt warm. It seemed impossible that he could not hear how loudly her heart was beating, but she'd learned, over her years at the gallery, that she had a strong poker face. She took a deep breath and noticed that he had a small silver scar at the end of one of his eyebrows.

"What happened?" she asked, tapping her own eyebrow. She was relieved to hear her voice was steady.

"A car accident. When I was nine."

So she'd either forgotten about this scar, or she'd never noticed it the first time around. Something about this made her feel nearly as unsettled as his touch had.

"I forget," he said. "Do you have any scars?"

So here they were, already, speaking about each other's bodies, considering all that was hidden by their clothes. "Yes," she said. Her instinct not to clarify her words has always attracted men, who assume, because they find her beautiful, that she must also be coy.

Jeremy touched the scar in his eyebrow with the pad of his thumb. "This is my oldest," he said. "I have more recent ones."

Vanessa sensed they were circling fraught territory. He might have been on the verge of asking her something—why she'd dumped him so suddenly eight years earlier, why she'd never called or e-mailed, why it seemed she'd never looked back. It occurred to her that he, too, could have more than one reason for wanting to see her—she had broken his heart, and he could break her marriage. She used to be good at reading people's intentions, and now she worried she was out of practice.

She glanced at her watch. "I should get going," she said.

"So soon?" Jeremy looked startled. She wondered what his expectations for their meeting had been. She stood and he gazed up at her for a moment before standing and kissing her cheek. He held her elbows as he had when she'd first walked in, not releasing her.

"I take it back," he said, studying her. "You don't look the same."

For a moment, she was afraid he was going to insult her. *Here it is,* she thought. *The truth.* It had been eight years. Who knew what he saw when he looked at her?

"You're more beautiful," he said.

She released her breath, laughing. "And you're smoother," she said.

"Let's do this again."

"Maybe."

"Think about it." He smiled, running one thumb along the curve of her elbow, and then let her go.

When she arrives at Thirtieth Street Station in Philadelphia, Vanessa sees Kate before Kate sees Vanessa. Kate is wearing a wrinkled sundress and seems to be reading something in her hand that Vanessa realizes, as she approaches, is in fact a napkin.

"Hi!" Kate says, looking up. She stuffs the napkin into her shoulder bag and throws her thin arms around Vanessa. Kate hugs with the ferocity of a child; her smile is wide. "It's so good to see you."

"You too," Vanessa says, hugging her back. Kate has the sort of kind, expressive face that draws people to her. Her lips are set in a slight smile even when her face is at rest, giving the impression that she is sure something good is about to happen and she is waiting, ready to be proved right. And then, always, Kate starts talking.

"We have an hour to kill before Dani's flight gets in. What should we do? Are you hungry? We could eat. Or we could get coffee. We could stay here or walk toward University City or drive somewhere. I brought my car. We'll have to pick up Gracie later. I hope that's okay. Is that all you brought? My bag is twice as big. You've always been such a good packer."

Vanessa knows Kate isn't talking so much because she is nervous; it's just what she does. For the first time since Vanessa left Lucy hours earlier, she feels a sense of calm spreading through her. Kate always has this effect on her—not on the phone, but in person. Everything else might change, but she knows she can depend on Kate always being Kate. As Dani used to say, a Kate is a Kate is a Kate.

Kate drives a hunter green Volvo which, it seems to Vanessa, is basically Kate in car form. They end up at Capogiro in University City. After trying six flavors, Kate orders a large cup of Thai coconut milk gelato. Vanessa orders a small iced coffee and adds a splash of nonfat milk.

They sit at a table on the sidewalk. The shop blocks the late afternoon sun but the air is damp with heat even in the shade. Vanessa tucks the length of her ponytail into her headscarf and feels the slightest breeze against her shoulder blades. Kate extracts a package of antibacterial cloths from her purse and wipes down the table. She has always been a germaphobe. When they lived together in Avalon that summer before their senior year of college, Kate bought a new kitchen sponge at Hoy's Five and Ten every week.

"Thank you so much for coming," Kate says. "I know it might not be high up on your list to spend the weekend with Dani. How are you feeling about seeing her?"

"You don't need to thank me," she says, skirting the question. She will never get used to the idea that Kate and Dani have remained in contact when she herself barely talks to Dani. She used to be the one who held them all together—she smoothed things over whenever one of Dani's snide jokes hurt Kate's feelings; she convinced Dani to include Kate even when they both knew she could sometimes be a wet blanket. "Anyway, we should be talking about how *you* are feeling."

Kate takes a huge bite of her gelato. "Well, I still feel like my life has a Peter-size hole in it, if that's what you're asking."

"It's only been a few weeks," Vanessa says. "It will get better."

"I hope so. I don't think I could handle it getting worse."

"Of course you could, but it's not going to." Kate is one of the strongest people Vanessa knows, and yet she continually underestimates herself. *Fake it till you make it*, Vanessa is always advising her friend. But Kate is an open book.

"I know finding a guy isn't the be-all and end-all," Kate says. "I'm not waiting for my Prince Charming. You know I'm not like that."

Vanessa cocks an eyebrow and fails to suppress a laugh. "You're not looking for Prince Charming? Kate. You named your dog after Grace Kelly. She *literally* married a prince."

"I named her that because they're both blondes from Philadelphia."

Vanessa laughs and Kate smiles, flushing.

"Okay, so I want to share my life with someone," Kate says, throwing her hands up. "Sue me. And now I have to start all over. I have to go on first dates. I have to be the single girl at other people's weddings. It feels like I'm starting from scratch, just when I thought the cake was already baked and I was about to dig in." Kate looks down at her nearly empty gelato cup and the color in her cheeks drains away, her pale skin suddenly taking on a yellow cast. She looks up at Vanessa and swallows. "Sorry."

"It's the start of our girls' trip," Vanessa says, shrugging. "Anything goes."

"I promise I won't talk about Peter all weekend."

"You can talk about anything you want. It's just us."

Kate gives her an uncharacteristically tight smile and excuses herself to use the bathroom. As soon as she leaves, Vanessa can't help it, her thoughts turn to Jeremy and the status update he'd left on Facebook in the days after they met for drinks. She feels a sharp, new version of an old, familiar feeling.

* * *

The night Colin died, Jeremy and Vanessa had seen him swimming in the bay. They told this to the police the next morning. This is what Vanessa never told anyone: after Jeremy fell asleep in her bed, she sneaked out of the bungalow and walked, barefoot, back to where Colin was still swimming. The island was quiet; the air was still; the houses lining the bay were darkened. She peeled off her tank top and shorts and dove off the public dock and swam toward Colin. He pulled her arms around his neck and kissed her. And then she broke his heart.

"What's the deal with you and Jeremy?" he'd asked as she treaded water in front of him, putting distance between them.

Colin had kissed her for the first time when she was home from college for spring break in March—he was living at home by then. He'd visited her in New York every couple of weeks for months afterward; they'd spent their time together lying in Vanessa's bed, ordering Chinese food and ignoring the vibrant pull of the city around them. Their attraction to each other had been simmering below the surface for years, but was it possible that they loved each other? A part of Vanessa hoped this was the case, even as she suspected it was not. But if they loved each other, then the relationship wasn't just physical, wasn't just the thrill of the illicit, the inevitable consummation of a flirtation that had started years earlier, and Kate might forgive them.

The cracks in their relationship revealed themselves when Colin began talking about moving to New York. As he started devising plans to work at a friend's construction company in Brooklyn, Vanessa realized she could not picture him in her New York life. He walked too slowly for New York sidewalks. His favorite sound was a bottle of beer being opened; he had told her this. When she thought about Colin, she thought about the huge crush she'd had on him in high school, back when all the girls were chasing him and the fact that they could not be together made her pulse quicken every time they locked eyes. When he began to talk about moving to New York, she realized that she saw Colin in her past, but not her future.

"I want to be in a relationship I can tell my best friends about," she said by way of answering his question. She was already itching for the conversation to be over. She wanted to run back to the bungalow and press her body against Jeremy's. She'd told Jeremy that Colin was a troubled ex-boyfriend (a secret one at that—Kate and Dani did not know they had dated), and that they had to be sensitive of his feelings and tone down their affection for each other when he was visiting. She and Colin had never talked about being in an exclusive relationship; still, she knew what she was doing with Jeremy was unfair to him, that the fact that their relationship was a secret put him at a disadvantage because he could not be openly jealous or angry.

"So let's tell them about us," Colin said.

"Kate would never forgive me."

"Sure she would. Forgiveness is what she does best."

"Colin." Her teeth had begun to chatter. She was tiring of treading water in the cold bay. The small slapping noises they made as they swam disturbed the dark, tranquil air around them, echoing and carrying across the water.

"Are you sleeping with him?"

She was not really surprised by this question; still, she did not realize how she was going to respond until the words were already out of her mouth. "I think I might love him," she said.

Colin pushed at the water between them, sending it rippling toward her. "You barely know him," he muttered. He released a vague smile that made Vanessa look away, angry. He was stoned. She realized they were having two different conversations—her sober one, and his high one. Her parents liked to smoke pot too and so the drug had never held any allure for her—it seemed to paint a glaze over people she loved, making them unreachable. Nothing about the act seemed rebellious or fun or potentially enlighten-

ing to her; it seemed cowardly. She felt sorry for
Colin. He'd found the thing that defined him, the
thing that allowed him to snag the spotlight from
his sister, and it was fucking up.

"I love him," she said. She realized now that
the best thing for Colin would be a clean break.
She'd tried to protect his pride by letting their
relationship slowly fade into memory, but this
plan had not worked. He had to understand it
was really, truly over between them. "Jeremy is
a grown-up."

"A grown-up dating a college girl. That's not
creepy at all."

"At least one of us is in college, Colin. This is
life! We're not kids anymore. Jeremy knows that.
He's not running around setting fire to lifeguard
stands."

He stared at her. "And I am?"

Despite warning her to run at the beach party
on Friday, Colin had been caught by the police
and was held in Avalon's makeshift jail cell until he was sober. It had taken all night. Vanessa
pieced together that he had seen her sneak off to
the dunes with Jeremy and in anger had set fire to
the lifeguard stand. What she didn't understand
was why he had allowed himself to be caught. He
had been the fastest boy on the lacrosse field at
PFS; he should have easily outrun the police. She
thought he was sabotaging himself, yet another

of his habits that used to seem complicated and endearing and now seemed cowardly.

"What were you thinking?" Vanessa asked. She was trying to keep her toes from skimming the bay's spongy floor. "It's not funny, you know. Setting a fire? That's serious. What if someone had been hurt? You could go to jail."

Vanessa felt as if she were the only one who saw how serious Colin's drinking and drug use had become. Kate was either in denial or truly could not tell when he was high. Dani thought it was no big deal; she would invoke the Youth Clause, saying there was no other time in their lives when there was practically a societal mandate to party. Vanessa suspected the real reason Dani didn't want to intervene was that her own house contained too much glass for stone throwing.

Colin sank slowly below the water, watching her even as the salty bay met his open eyes. Vanessa winced.

"Colin . . ." she said, but he was already under. She felt the water churning around her legs as he swam away. When he resurfaced, he was fifteen feet away in the middle of the channel.

"So go," he said.

And she had, just like that, feeling—it pained her to remember this—relieved.

When she had lain back down beside Jeremy, the bed creaked beneath her. She had felt sure that

at any moment Jeremy would reach over and pull
her toward him, his fingers moving over her body
until they sank into her wet hair and he opened
his eyes, startled, wondering where, and with
whom, she had been. But this never happened.
Jeremy had just kept sleeping while Vanessa lay
beside him, her greatest concern whether her long
hair would dry in the thick, humid air.

"Really," Kate says as they drive toward the airport, "how are you feeling about seeing Dani?"
When she looks out of the corner of her eye at
Vanessa, the car tires crunch loudly over the line
of ridged pavement along the side of the highway.
Kate jerks the wheel to bring the car back into the
lane, glancing in the rearview mirror as Gracie
fumbles to regain her footing in the backseat.
They'd picked up Kate's dog before heading to
the airport and almost immediately the car had
begun smelling, bizarrely, like a fish tank.

   Kate is a truly terrible driver. You would think
someone as responsible as Kate would be a good
driver, but she is the worst. Driving and love
seem to be the two areas in which she is incapable of gaining any sort of competency. How can
someone be so smart and so successful and so incapable of finding love? It seems like a horrible
cliché to Vanessa that she has a husband and no

career, and her friend has a career and no husband. Of course, neither of them is particularly happy these days. Maybe that, too, is a cliché.

"We'll probably try to kill each other," Vanessa says without thinking. "But what's a girls' weekend without a little homicide?" She stares at the road, dismayed by what she has just said, but Kate releases one of her horsey, snorting laughs and the car shudders. Dani and Vanessa used to insist on sitting in the backseat when Kate drove—which was often, because they usually roped her into being the designated driver. They'd gasp and bite their hands, exaggerating their terror every time Kate hit the brake or pulled the wheel. Kate once crashed her car pulling into a repair shop where she had an appointment to fix the bumper she'd dented in a previous accident. The new damage cost thousands more than the old. Neither of those Harrington kids should have been allowed behind the wheel, ever.

Adele's "Someone Like You" is playing on the radio. Vanessa can't seem to escape this song, though she knows she shouldn't take it personally—the song is playing everywhere, whether she's listening or not.

We were born and raised in a summer haze,
bound by the surprise of our glory days.

"Just what you need," Vanessa says, wincing, "A breakup song."

Kate grins and turns up the volume. Vanessa holds her breath, willing Kate to keep both hands on the wheel. They take the exit for the airport. Vanessa decides that she will hug Dani and then get back into the front seat of the car and leave Dani to share the backseat with the dog.

I'll be in Avalon over Fourth of July weekend, Jeremy had posted to Facebook a few days after they'd met for drinks. *Who else is going?*

As though by fate, Kate had called Vanessa to relay Dani's invitation only hours later. Vanessa had not thought that going to Avalon was a good idea; she doubted that it would help mend her friend's broken heart to be in the place where her brother died. But since Jeremy was going to be there—and because she had the impression that seeing him again might finally give her some clarity about what she should do—she had said yes. Now that she sees Dani standing on the sidewalk outside of baggage claim, her stomach twists. Dani is a ferreter of truth, an anecdote collector, a relentless observer. Vanessa tightens the knot on her headscarf, preparing herself as best she can.

9

Dani

"The actual Jersey Shore should sue the *Jersey Shore* television show for slander," Dani says as she pulls the door of Kate's car shut behind her. "As though we weren't already fighting an uphill publicity battle, now my roommates in San Francisco are convinced I'm going to spend the long weekend clubbing with beefy guys in tank tops."

"Your roommates watch *Jersey Shore*?" Vanessa asks, turning around from the front passenger seat. They'd hugged on the airport sidewalk, Kate's gaze as subtle as a high beam. Vanessa is undoubtedly now envisioning Dani and her slacker roommates sitting around watching *Jersey Shore* marathons. Dani is sure she doesn't let Lucy watch TV—they probably spend their afternoons wandering the Met and organizing fundraisers for a fancy preschool that serves organic kale as a

snack and has uniforms made by some hip designer. Despite this image, she reluctantly admits
to herself that Vanessa doesn't look much like
a Mombot. She looks like Vanessa, crazily patterned headscarf, gorgeous bone structure, and
all. That knowing look in her eye, both intelligent
and sensual—has Dani captured that in her book?
Vanessa's face seems a little drawn, but this could
be age—she is, after all, three years and one baby
older than the last time Dani saw her—or, more
likely, wariness. Dani doesn't blame her for being
guarded. The fight they had after Colin died feels
both like ancient history and as if it happened
yesterday.

"It doesn't matter if they actually watch it. The
show is pervasive," Dani says. "That's the problem."

"Who cares," Kate says, shrugging. "We know
the truth about *our* Jersey Shore so who cares what
the rest of the world thinks? More sand for us."

If the car didn't smell like Grace Kelly—
"Howdy, Princess," Dani had said when she
hopped in beside the wildly panting dog—and if
Dani didn't already know that Kate had had this
car forever, she might have thought Kate had just
driven it off the lot. The pale gray floor mats are
stain-free, the pockets on the backs of the front
seats empty. The windshield is so clear Dani
can barely see it. No one is really this painstak-

ingly tidy without being on medication for obsessive compulsive disorder, and Dani is certain the only pills Kate takes are Vitamin C and birth control. She has long suspected that Kate is outwardly neat but secretly messy. She has a theory that everyone has at least three out-of-character quirks—for Kate, bad driving is one of them, and Dani is sure she harbors a couple other surprising tendencies. (Kate and Vanessa would probably never guess that Dani, for example, who loathes shopping, collects drinking glasses from garage sales. She likes the feel of a new glass in her hand. She just does. Also, she has a soft spot for the various singing and dance competitions that dominate prime-time programming. All of those untalented, semi-talented, and extremely talented people sharing the same supersized dream? They pluck like crazy on Dani's stiff old heartstrings.) Dani wonders if somewhere in Kate's tidy apartment there is a closet filled to the brim with decades-old hotel toiletries and assorted polyester jumpsuits, capes, and thigh-high stockings from the unfortunately themed costume parties of yesteryear. All of the detritus that evades organization.

The Walt Whitman Bridge looms suddenly large, an inch or two shy of the side of the car.

"Holy shit, Kate," Dani cries. "I can't believe we're letting you drive. Pull. Over. Right. Now."

"You should have been in the car when she was driving through the city. It was terrifying," Vanessa says. Her eyes are glued to the road.

"Pipe down, you two. It's my car and I'm driving. Besides," Kate says as they exit the bridge, "look at that! We made it to New Jersey."

The trees in New Jersey are lush in a showgirl way that makes every tree in San Francisco seem pale and sickly by comparison. The back windows of the car are cracked for Gracie and the air that seeps in is so warm and sweet that Dani wishes she could swallow it.

Warmth. Finally. When she had walked out of the airport in Philadelphia, the air had immediately draped itself around her, producing within her a feeling that these days she most often equates with a drink. She used to make rules for herself: drinking only after 4:00 PM; drugs only on the weekend. But it was so easy to find exceptions—drinking before four was okay on the weekend; drugs were okay on weekdays when she didn't work because those were basically her weekend—that eventually she no longer saw the point in having rules. Only luck and maybe something in her DNA has kept her habits casual for so long. Lately, Dani has begun to feel a stronger pull—desire becoming need. Her luck, it seems, is running out.

There is an Altoids tin of OxyContin in her bag

that Rachel gave her as a good-bye present. When Dani's plane had hit turbulence over the middle of the country and her throat had gone dry and her skin had begun pricking uncomfortably, she'd managed to stop herself from reaching inside her bag for those pills by focusing on the book she was reading—*Faithful Place* by Tana French. She'd just kept reading, turning page after page until she was no longer sitting on that surely doomed plane and had instead disappeared entirely into someone else's world.

But now that she's thinking of those pills again, it's hard to stop. She looks out the car window. They're moving slowly thanks to holiday-weekend traffic. She still has little memory of suggesting this trip to Kate, but she finds that she's not unhappy to be on these familiar roads, headed to Avalon. When people ask her where she is from, she says Philadelphia, but when she thinks of the word "home," she thinks of Avalon. That much has not changed.

Kate seems to be talking even more than usual—she's been discussing her mother's new obsession with some exercise called Zumba for most of the time they've been on the Garden State Parkway—and Dani suspects this is due to the weirdness between Vanessa and herself. Kate has always quivered like a tuning fork at the slightest hint of tension. Vanessa occasionally makes a noise to indicate she's listening, but she's gazing out the side window, and it's clear she isn't really engaged. *How does Vanessa's husband handle her silences?* Hopefully, he prods at her until she snaps open like a clam. *If he doesn't,* Dani thinks, *they're in trouble.*

She has a flash of déjà vu. It happens to her a lot—the sudden sense that what is happening has already happened. *How many times have the three of us driven down this stretch of road together?*

"How's writing, Dani?" Kate asks.

"Horrendous," she answers. She's never been anything but forthright about how hard, and necessary, writing is for her. "There hasn't been a book this bad since the last one I tried to write."

Kate laughs. "I don't believe you for a second. You're a great writer."

"Just own it," Vanessa says, sounding distracted. "Be authoritative."

The retort on the tip of Dani's tongue is that she despises advice, but it occurs to her that this Vanessa is a diminished version of the Vanessa who was once her friend. It's possible that Vanessa is no longer a capable adversary, and nobody likes a bully. "I don't like authoritative people," she says instead. "I don't buy what they're selling."

"You're so San Francisco," Kate says.

"We should have known you'd end up there," Vanessa says.

"Exit Thirteen," Dani says, looking out the window. "We're here."

Kate shuts off the music when they turn onto the causeway that cuts through the wetlands, connecting the mainland to Avalon. They lower their windows all the way, and the car fills with thick, salty air. Gracie sticks her quivering brown nose out the window, her eyes narrowed to contented, contemplative slits. The sky still holds the Technicolor streaks of sunset, and the bay glows pink where it snakes between patches of bright green marsh grass. Vanessa points to a heron, dark and hunchbacked, perched at the top of a pole in the middle of a wide channel.

"Summer," Dani says, mostly to herself. She sticks her arm out of the window and lets her hand rise and fall on the wind.

She doesn't have to direct Kate despite the fact that Kate hasn't been here in eight years. They turn right off Dune Drive at Thirty-Eighth Street and head toward the beach. The house is the closest one to the dunes, a handsome, white shingled rectangle of a house with two layers of decks running the length of its longer, beach-facing side. Something within Dani flutters when she sees it. The lower deck is in near-constant shade, blocked from the sun by the deck above and the wild tangle of shrubs and grasses and low trees that make up the stretch of dunes that separates the house from the beach. The upper deck looks out over the dunes to an expansive view of the beach and the ocean. On a clear night you can see the lights of the Wildwood Ferris wheel, ten miles down the coast and on another island entirely. The bedrooms upstairs are the best place to get a cool ocean breeze when the air conditioner is off. The bedrooms downstairs are the ones that are easiest to sneak out of without anyone upstairs hearing a thing.

The tires crunch over sand-blown pavement as Kate slows the car to a stop. Dani's father's Mercedes is parked in the driveway.

"What's he doing here?" Dani wonders aloud.

"You told him we were coming, didn't you?" Vanessa asks.

"Of course," Dani says. "Just park in the street."

Grace Kelly scrambles out of the car and takes a piss so long you would have thought she'd been cooped up all day instead of less than two hours. They pull their luggage from the trunk and pile it on the sidewalk. Kate has brought an incredibly large bag of expensive-looking dog food. Either Gracie somehow shares her owner's remarkable metabolism—doubtful, given the rolls of pudge around the dog's shoulders—or Kate is doing her usual disaster planning. The night is darkening; the sound of the ocean is distant even though it's close. As they're shutting the trunk, the light beside the front door of the house turns on, adding a glow to the gray street. Dani glances toward the light, and the door opens.

"Hello!" her father calls. The hinges on the screen door whine. Her father is short and fit with smooth, tan skin and a full head of silver hair. Dani grins at him. He strides down the stairs and is on the sidewalk in a moment, wrapping her in a hug. They haven't seen each other since she was in Philadelphia around Christmas—they're Jewish, but they buy a tree each year. They decorate it with strings of tacky turquoise lights and a collection of antique glass ornaments they found at a flea market one year when Dani was in middle school. They drink a couple of fancy bottles of wine that her father purchases for the occasion and stay up late watching Hitchcock DVDs. The next day they sleep late and finally, around noon, eat mountains of cinnamon French toast, her father's lone culinary trick, just the two of them.

"Welcome," he says, grinning. He looks beyond her and waves to Kate and Vanessa. "You're all here. All the summer girls."

"Hi, Dr. Lowenstein," Kate and Vanessa say in unison. They look at each other and laugh. Gracie nearly tackles Dani's father and he grins, wiping off the slobber she's left on his cheek.

"Hey, now," he says. "Buy me a drink first."

Gracie bounds past him and through the open doorway. He grabs a few of their bags and turns back toward the house. Dani follows. Her father is wearing shorts and a linen button-down shirt that she recognizes and a large gold watch that she does not. His feet are bare. She had not anticipated having to tell him in person that she is moving home. She won't bring it up in front of Vanessa, that much is certain. Maybe she won't bring it up at all—he'll piece the news together himself when her boxes start arriving in Philadelphia. As she passes his car, she realizes it's not the same sand-colored Mercedes he was driving the last time she was home; it's the same color, but this one is a bit smaller and has a soft convertible top. Dani has not owned a car since she sold the Jeep her father had bought her in high school to her coke-dealing landlord when she lived in Chicago five years earlier.

"Dad," she says as they step inside. "What are you doing here?"

"In my house?" he asks.

"Is this one of those 'senior moments'? You remember I asked if we could have the house this weekend, right?"

He laughs. "I remember. We've been down all

week, but don't worry, we're leaving now. Back to Philly on the hottest weekend of the summer so far, and a holiday weekend, to boot. I must really like you."

Dani is still hung up two sentences back. "We?"

"We," her father repeats, shoving his hands into the pockets of his khaki shorts. "Susanna?" he calls up the stairs. "Suz?"

Dani glances back to where Kate and Vanessa are standing awkwardly just inside the door. Gracie is wildly sniffing everything in sight; the sound of her toenails against the tile floor is manic.

"I'm here," a woman—Suz, presumably—says, hurrying down the stairs. She looks about ten years older than Dani and wears a white cotton tunic that hits her legs midthigh. It's one of those tunics that are of ambiguous clothing category— dress? beach cover-up? nightgown? She does not seem embarrassed to be caught without pants, so Dani rules out shirt.

Suz stops when she reaches the bottom landing of the stairs and takes a dramatic breath as though she has been in a huge hurry and now needs to compose herself. The landing is still one foot above the entryway floor level so she is looking down on them. She tucks her chin-length auburn hair behind her ears, like someone who is pretending to be nervous. Then she descends the final step.

"You must be Dani," she says, extending her hand. "I'm Susanna. Suz. Whichever."

Dani shakes her hand. "Hi," she says. She raises her eyebrows at her father, waiting for an explanation. Her mind is racing. Her father has had countless girlfriends over the course of Dani's life—some while he was still married to her mother, many more since their divorce—but he has never brought one of them to Avalon. In Philadelphia, Dani expects to find a gold tube of lipstick that has rolled behind the toilet, or almond milk in the fridge, or a pink wool blazer tainting everything else in the hall closet with its suffocating rose scent, but the Avalon house belongs only to Dani and her father. They grill fish together on the upstairs deck and watch movies with their feet up on the ottoman and ride beach cruisers for soft-serve cones at Avalon Freeze, standing in line with the little kids. The Avalon house is where he chaperoned the activities of Dani and Kate and Vanessa for two weeks every summer, just a single dad and three growing girls, no girlfriend in sight.

Now, watching her father reach his arm around Suz, Dani feels like an idiot. *Of course he brings women here.* All these years, he's been bringing women here. Just not when she and her friends were there.

"Hi, girls," Suz says, smiling at Kate and Vanessa. "I'm so sorry we're still here. This probably isn't how you expected your girls' weekend to start. You girls are going to have so much fun! I'm so jealous. I haven't had a girls' weekend in ages!" Dani hopes that Kate and Vanessa are noting how many times Suz says the word "girls" so they can discuss it later. "We just wanted to make sure the house was in tip-top shape for you girls before we got out of your hair. And I really wanted to meet you, Dani. And . . ." Suz pauses, widening her eyes as she bites her lip. She looks over at Dani's father.

Dani's father clears his throat. "And," he says. "And—" He looks at Dani, glances at Vanessa and Kate, and then back at Dani. "And we wanted to tell you the news in person, Dani."

The news? Dani thinks, but even as she is thinking the words she is noticing the ring on Suz's finger. A huge diamond. Unmissable, unmistakable.

"Oh," she says.

"I asked Susanna to marry me and she said yes."

Dani almost never cries, so at first she is confused by her blurred vision. The silence that follows feels interminable.

"Mark," Suz says quietly. "We're not even in the living room. We could have had them come in first, offered them a drink."

Dani hears Kate step up behind her and feels the weight of her hand on her shoulder. But then

she hears Kate, still by the door, saying "Congratulations" in a tight voice. Dani looks beside her
and sees that it is Vanessa's hand on her shoulder;
it is Vanessa who will not fill the awkward silence
with a polite expression. She should have known
she could count on Vanessa for solidarity in the
delivery of silent treatment.

"*Ankthadavaka ouyadavaka*," Dani says loudly
and quickly to Vanessa. Suz looks at Dani's father,
her mouth open. Dani and Vanessa and Kate developed DaVaKa in elementary school—a hybrid
of Pig Latin and the first letters of their names.
The key, they'd decided, was to speak so quickly
that no one outside of the three of them stood a
chance of interpretation. Four of them, actually.
Colin had figured it out the first time he heard
them, putting a momentary damper on their
chatter with one word: "*syeadavaka*." *Easy*.

"*Ouryadavaka Elcomewadavaka*," Vanessa says
now, quietly but just as quickly. *You're welcome*.

"Ladies," Dani's father says. "English, please."

Dani swallows. She wills her eyes to dry and
they obey. "Suz," she says in the one language she
knows her father's fiancée will understand. "I'll
take that drink."

10

Kate

"We're going out," Dani announces after Dr. Lowenstein and Susanna leave.

"Where to?" Vanessa asks without hesitation.

"Hang on," Kate says. "I thought we were going to stay in and watch movies." Dani is clearly upset and already a little drunk. Kate feels awful for her. What was her father thinking, breaking the news of his engagement in front of them? For such a successful, charming man, he has always struck Kate as insensitive, treating Dani more like a buddy than a daughter.

"Kate," Dani says, exasperated, doing that thing she does where she ruffles her own blond hair and then it falls, despite her best efforts, right back into pin-straight place. Kate is sitting on the couch and Dani is pacing in front of her. She is thinner than Kate has ever seen her and there is a dull cast to her skin. Still, her brown eyes are shining and she talks as loudly as ever, emphasizing her words with her small, expressive hands. "My dad just told me he is getting married."

"I can't believe he dropped the news like that," Kate says. Dr. Lowenstein and Suz had slunk out of the house twenty minutes earlier. From the nervous, darting look in her eye, Kate suspected Suz thought the "girls" were on the verge of rioting. "He never even mentioned her before?"

Dani shakes her head. She takes a slug of whiskey, which Kate can smell from five feet away. She wishes they could just stay in. She's ready to beg, if it comes to that. "Well," she says, "my fiancé just told me we're *not* getting married." She meant the line to be self-deprecating and funny, but to her disappointment, she sounds petulant. She's usually the one who will agree to anything if she thinks it will cheer someone up, so now Vanessa and Dani are peering at her, confused. She feels her face reddening. She'd planned to tell them about Colin that night, she'd been amped up and jittery the entire car ride down thinking about how they would take her confession, but she can't tell them everything *now*, not when Dani is dealing with her own stuff and halfway drunk.

And then Vanessa says, "I still have feelings for Jeremy Caldwell."

Kate feels her mouth drop. Dani stops pacing.

They both stare at Vanessa. She's sitting on one of the stools at the kitchen counter, across the room from the couch. She takes a demure sip of her wine. Dani drops down beside Kate on the couch and laughs. It's not a nice sound. "We're all fucked," she says.

"What are you talking about?" Kate asks. She remembers Jeremy following Vanessa around like a puppy that summer eight years earlier. She'd worried no one would ever look at her the way Jeremy looked at Vanessa, but when she'd mentioned how sweet they were together to Dani, Dani had given their relationship three weeks tops before Vanessa became bored and moved on to the next challenge. It took a little longer than three weeks, but not much. "What about Drew?" Kate asks.

"Drew and I are having problems."

Kate wonders if having such dramatic looks makes Vanessa more prone to *be* dramatic. "Since when?" she demands.

"What? You don't believe me?" Vanessa asks. "*You're* the one who said I should meet Jeremy for a drink."

"You're encouraging this?" Dani asks. She sounds delighted. Even drunk, she has a way of asking questions that makes Kate feel like she is taking notes, like there is a good chance this conversation will end up in print some day, all her

inadequacies exposed in a row like granny pant-
ies pinned to a clothesline.

"No, of course not!" she says. She points a finger
at Vanessa. "*You* didn't tell me the whole story."

Vanessa shrugs and takes another sip of wine.
Her composure disturbs Kate. She has everything
Kate wants and it's not enough for her. Vanessa
once told her that early in their marriage she
and Drew had stayed in bed for a whole day
and watched the entire first season of *Mad Men*
on DVD, drinking martinis and eating deviled
eggs. It sounded sophisticated and fun—like the
most romantic thing in the world (though she did
take a moment to consider how long the smell of
eggs must have lingered in the air). When Kate
had suggested the idea to Peter, he had given her
a funny look and reminded her of his Sunday
morning basketball game with his law school
buddies. *No,* she had said, agreeing. *You can't miss
that.* She'd been disappointed but felt she could
hardly fault someone for believing in the sanctity
of schedules. You can't dislike the very thing you
love about someone, the very thing you have in
common. If she disliked him for it, she'd have to
dislike herself too.

"We definitely don't have enough alcohol for
this conversation," Dani says. She sounds relieved. Dani can turn almost any situation into a

reason to go to a bar. "Let's get out of here. We can take the beach cruisers."

"Where to?" Vanessa asks again. "The Princeton?" Where they are going is important to her in a way Kate will never understand. To Kate, the question is simply: Stay in or go out? Her irritation is starting to feel unwieldy.

"Why don't we just stay here?" she says again. "I brought a bottle of chardonnay. We can sit on the deck, listen to the ocean, have a glass of wine. It will be relaxing." Already, it's come to this: she's begging. She doesn't care. The last thing she wants to do is stand in a crowded bar and pretend to be able to hear her friends. Her feet hurt and she is tired. She looks around the living room, which has been redecorated since she was here last. It's still luxurious and peaceful, with blond wood floors and light-colored furniture and a large unframed painting defined only by a few sweeping gray brushstrokes—she'll have to ask Vanessa how she is supposed to feel about that—but it turns out the new white couch is much more comfortable than the old white couch, and all Kate wants to do is stretch out on it and watch a movie. The house is spotless—Dr. Lowenstein must have a very thorough housekeeper; even the baseboards are clean, Kate has already noticed—and this makes her happy. She sees a photograph of Dani and her father in a silver frame on the mantel. Next to it is a photo of Dani, Vanessa, and Kate sitting on a lifeguard stand in their bathing suits with their arms around one another's shoulders, the dunes and the house in the background. The picture was taken in eighth grade, a fact Kate knows because Vanessa's cheekbones are still obscured by baby fat, Dani's chest is as flat as a board, and her own huge smile is marred by the metallic blur of braces.

"I want a martini. Did you bring the ingredients for that?" Dani asks.

Kate looks at Dani but does not answer. Dani is wearing a threadbare black T-shirt with a hole in the shoulder, black leggings, and black flip-flops, and not a single swipe of makeup. It's a variation of the same outfit she has worn every time Kate has seen her since college. By the end of tomorrow, Kate knows, the dull quality of her friend's skin will be gone, replaced by a bronze glow. Her hair, already the color of straw, will whiten in the sun and her eyelashes will pale, making her amber eyes appear darker, flashier. Looks mean little to Dani—she is the least vain person that Kate knows—but it has to be pretty easy to not care about your looks when you look the way Dani does wearing what most of Kate's work associates would consider very old pajamas.

"She wants to stay in," Vanessa says to Dani. She unsnaps the large gold buckle on her woven leather clutch, peers into the bag, and pulls out a tiny pot of cantaloupe-colored lip gloss. It's a color that should not look good on anyone, a shade that Kate would barely have glanced at in the lineup at Sephora. She already knows how it will look on Vanessa.

"Of course she does," Dani says. "But you and I both know the only thing that is going to make her feel better is finding someone new."

"I'm right here," Kate says. "Hello."

"Hello," they say. Vanessa rubs the gloss over her lips, and they become as full and shiny and attention-hogging as a supermodel's. Kate manages to stop herself from asking to try the lip gloss, and this feels like an accomplishment.

"Well, you're wrong," she says. "I don't want to find someone new. Not yet, at least. Maybe after the wedding."

Vanessa stops rubbing her lips. "What wedding?"

"*Our* wedding. The wedding Peter and I were supposed to have. It wouldn't feel right to start dating someone new before then."

Dani sighs. It's her "this-is-worse-than-we-thought" sigh. "We know you don't *want* someone new right now," Dani says. "But trust me, staying home is not going to make you feel better."

"Dani's right," Vanessa says. "We should go out. Just for a couple of drinks."

"We'll have the Meg Ryan movie marathon tomorrow night," Dani says. "I promise."

Kate looks back and forth between her friends.
They are exasperating and selfish, but they have
always been this way and she has always loved
them and she is not going to stop now, or ever.
She realized this a long time ago, and the knowledge has become a touchstone that brings her
comfort. They will never leave her life because
she will never allow them to.

"'We can *have* a good time,'" Kate says in the
nasally drawl of an uptight Southern debutante,
"'but we *cannot* be wild.'" Dani and Vanessa
grin, relieved. It's one of their favorite lines from
Shag, a movie about best friends letting loose in
Myrtle Beach the summer before they leave for
college. Kate had given each of them a copy as
a high school graduation gift and during their
freshman year at college they would three-way
call each other and watch the movie simultaneously, each in separate dorm rooms and cities.
Kate missed her friends so much that year; it had
been a stubborn sadness, a steady whine that
sometimes felt like a soundtrack, setting the tone
for her adult life.

Pedaling down Dune Drive on a red beach cruiser,
Dani ahead of her and Vanessa behind her, is a
transporting experience. The night is quiet; the

air on her face is soft; her hair streams behind her; the stars above are as brilliant as stars in a children's book. They could be nine years old, or fifteen, or twenty-one; they've ridden bikes down Dune Drive at all of those ages and all of the ones in between. There must have been so much more to those summers, but what she remembers are the two weeks she spent in Avalon with Dani and Vanessa—two weeks that always went by too quickly, but that in memory stretch to fill an entire season.

She has never been to Avalon in winter. Dani periodically suggested off-season visits throughout high school and even college, but Kate always declined. She knows that Vanessa brought Kyle, one of her high school boyfriends, to Dani's father's house one night in the middle of winter, slipping the key from its hiding place under a rock beside the garage door. Vanessa told her parents that she was sleeping at Kate's house that night and asked Kate to intercept any calls that came in on their house line. She also asked Kate not to tell Dani, an omission that did not sit right with Kate. She had felt trapped—if she told Dani, she would break Vanessa's trust; if she kept the secret, she would break Dani's. She had kept the secret and then she sat by the phone all night, worried that Vanessa's parents would call—and wondering what secrets Vanessa and Dani kept between themselves.

Kate realizes now that she had never wanted to see Avalon in the hushed grip of winter because she had worried that doing so would take away some of its magic. How optimistic, to think that cold air would be the thing to complicate her feelings for the place. She lived more than twenty years without losing anyone, not a grandparent or an uncle or so much as a neighbor. She'd had no idea. All those fast, lucky years.

She and Vanessa stop their bikes at a traffic light. Dani whizzes ahead of them, eliciting a long honk from a Range Rover. Dani raises her middle finger into the air without a glance back.

"You're going to get a ticket!" Kate calls.

Dani shrugs but slows down. When Kate and Vanessa reach her, she turns on her bike seat so she is sitting sidesaddle, the wheels still spinning as though pedaled by an invisible rider. "If you get arrested for biking under the influence, does your driver's license get suspended?" she asks Kate.

"I have no idea." People are always asking her criminal law questions. It's possible that no one, not even her closest friends, listens when she tells them about her job. She practices civil litigation, mostly intellectual property cases. But people always question her about criminal law. It's enough to make her think everyone she knows—maybe everyone, period—is just one bad decision away from criminal activity. She's glad the laws exist. *Clearly,* she thinks, *we need them.*

It's not until they are almost to the Princeton that Kate remembers to question if she should be on a bike in her condition. She then becomes so consumed with the thought that she might hurt her baby that she can no longer think about the possibility that she might meet someone new, someone who is not at all like Peter, someone who is not her ex-fiancé or the father of her child. She does not think about meeting someone new even one more time before the moment, an hour later, when she does.

To Kate's relief, a table on the patio opens up just as they arrive. She sinks into the cushioned seat and cleans the table with an antibacterial wipe from her bag, ignoring the look Dani gives her. She knows, she knows: she's crazy. *News flash: this is not news.*

The Princeton has been remodeled since Kate was here last and is nearly unrecognizable. What used to be a dark, airless dive bar and liquor shop is now brightened by a wall of windows opening onto a patio spruced up with square-edged, contemporary furniture and a complicated cocktail menu. Kate orders a hamburger and a glass of wine. She figures she'll take one or two tiny sips of the wine and then claim a headache. Or maybe she'll take it with her to the bathroom and dump it into the toilet. It doesn't really matter. She's never been much of a drinker, and her friends aren't likely to suspect anything. She plans to tell them about the baby, but she finds she's not quite ready yet. Not tonight, at least. She's not prepared to confront the reality of her situation at a bar; no amount of hip new furniture can make the Princeton the ideal spot to reveal you are with child.

Dani seems to be attempting to pull the waitress to the table, drinks in hand, through aggressive staring alone. Vanessa is texting. Kate wonders how Gracie is doing all alone at the house. Ever since she found out she was pregnant, she has felt more protective of her dog, and more attached. She'd blinked back tears when she knelt down and pressed her cheek to Gracie's thick neck before they left for the bar twenty minutes earlier, inhaling her earthy scent, not caring about the hairs she knew she would find on her dress when she pulled away. She does not know what she would do if anything were to happen to her dog.

Vanessa glances up from her phone at Kate. "Sorry," she says. "Just making sure Lucy's bedtime went smoothly."

"Nice try," Dani says, tearing her gaze from the waitress's back. "We know you're really texting Jeremy Caldwell."

She is teasing, but Vanessa is clearly annoyed. They've always known exactly how to push each other's buttons; this bothers Kate on more than one level. "I shouldn't have said anything to you," Vanessa says.

"Oh, V, I'm only kidding. Lighten up," Dani says loudly as the waitress returns and sets their drinks on the table. Kate is in the habit of not conversing in front of waiters, and it makes her uncomfortable that Dani is continuing this conversation as though a perfect stranger weren't standing six inches from her shoulder.

"Should I start a tab?" the waitress asks. Her chest is mauve with sunburn.

"Yes," Dani says and drains a third of her martini. She makes no move to find her wallet. Vanessa rolls her eyes, opens her purse, and hands the waitress a credit card.

When the waitress walks away, Kate releases her breath. "We should have stayed home," Kate says. "It's pretty hard to fight when you're watching a movie."

To her surprise, Vanessa and Dani laugh. "We could do it," Vanessa says at the exact moment Dani says, "We'd find a way."

Before Kate realizes what she is doing, she has taken a long drink of wine. She holds the chardonnay in her mouth, cheeks full, unsure what to do.

"What's the matter?" Dani asks. "Is it awful?"

"It's the house chardonnay at the Princeton," Vanessa says. "Of course it's awful."

Kate swallows. "It's fine," she says, inadvertently pressing her hand to her belly. *Sorry, baby*, she thinks. It's the first time she has addressed her thoughts directly to the baby and the act stuns her. She gives her belly a discreet pat.

"Well, *salud*, then," Dani says, holding up her glass. "To the Princeton's fine wine."

Kate first notices him watching her when she walks by the bar on her way to the restroom. He is leaning against the bar, talking to the guy on the stool beside him, and he doesn't take his eyes off Kate even when she meets his gaze. He smiles and raises his beer. From a distance, his eyes look dark, but she will later see that they are in fact a deep shade of blue. For a guy that gangly and young looking, he is impressively confident. Kate smiles back without thinking and then drops her eyes to the floor, embarrassed. His smile is disarmingly sweet and she carries it with her all the way to the bathroom.

Two girls are standing in front of the sink talking about a fire on the beach. Kate hurries into a bathroom stall.

"John set the thirty-pack box on *fire*," one of the girls is saying. "I didn't think he'd actually do it."

"He's lucky he didn't get hurt," the other girl says.

"He *did!* He has a huge blister on his thumb now."

They break into laughter, and the bathroom fills with the pulse of music as they pull the door open. The door swings shut and Kate is left alone in the quiet with her racing heart.

She has found it helps, in moments like this one, to focus on making a list. She lists the things she remembers about Colin, testing herself. She and Dani and Vanessa used to lie on their stomachs on the public dock at Fifty-Third Street and pull nets through the water, catching tiny fish and the occasional crab. That is what this list-making exercise feels like: she snags some memories, but many others evade her. She worries that the memories that flit out of reach as quickly as they appear—the darkest and the most luminous ones—are the important ones; she's left with random, ordinary memories—the slowest and dumbest. Still, the task steadies her.

1. Colin would watch anything on television, even the girlie nighttime soaps Kate favored. She always waited for him to ask her to change the channel, and he never did.

2. He loved all candy, but especially lemon drops. His jeans had a faded little rectangle

in the front right pocket where he kept a box of them.

3. He had borderline Dumbo ears. In pre-school, the teacher told their parents that Kate had developed a habit of grabbing Colin's ear and tilting his head as if she were pouring water out of a teakettle. (He grew his hair to hide them in high school.)

4. In middle school, as a gag, he switched all of the gift tags on their Christmas presents. It turned out to add to the fun, so he did it every year for the rest of his life.

5. Even when he was angry, he was quiet. Their grandmother once asked him if the cat stole his tongue and gave it to Kate, and the line swiftly evolved into a famous fam-ily joke, nubby with use: *What's the matter, Colin? Kate got your tongue?*

When she gets back to the table, Dani and Va-nessa have moved on to shots, and Dani hands her one as she sits down. They don't notice that she dumps it over her shoulder, dousing the pot-ted plant in the corner of the patio.

"Let's dance," Vanessa says. She is drunk, her eyes liquid. There are two empty shot glasses and an empty martini glass in front of her. The color-ful scarf that was once tied around her head is now around her waist. Her long hair is pulled up in a high, slick bun, and large gold disc earrings sway against her neck when she talks. It seems as if every guy in the bar is looking toward their table. *What would that be like?* Kate wonders. *To have your pick?*

"Yes," Dani cries. "No one dances in San Fran-cisco. The hipster police arrest you if you do more than bob your head."

Kate has never heard Dani speak ill of San Francisco. It makes her happy to hear that the city across the country hasn't completely won over her friend. She lets them pull her onto the dance floor. They all love to dance. The music's bass is thunderous—*Stupid loud!* Dani yells, thrilled—and Kate feels it move her body, buoying her. Dani does her ridiculous hands-on-knees dance move, an act that looks like one of the Three Stooges doing hip-hop. Kate laughs so hard her eyes get misty. Vanessa does her sexy little shimmy. Kate is about to do the African Anteater ritual from *Can't Buy Me Love* when a hand cups her hip and she spins around.

It's the guy from the bar, the lanky one with the confidence, and he's smiling that smile again. He can't be older than twenty-three or twenty-four. "Can I dance with you?" he asks. At least, that's

what Kate assumes he asks; the music is too loud
to hear much of anything else.

Kate looks at Dani and Vanessa. They are already dancing with the guy's friends. Vanessa's
eyes are shut and her palms are up in the air and
she is shaking her hips. Dani grins at Kate and
wags her eyebrows over the shoulder of the guy's
friend. Kate wishes she were drunk.

She turns back toward the guy, and he takes
this as a sign that she will dance with him. He
puts his hands on her hips, dancing so close to
her that she smells his minty soap and feels his
smooth cheek brush her ear. She can't remember dancing like this with Peter. They must have,
but she can't remember when. They had danced
together at countless weddings—lately, in fact,
it seemed all they did together was dance at
weddings—but never like this.

"I'm pregnant," she says now, knowing the guy
she's dancing with won't hear her. It is the first
time she has told anyone. He pulls back and grins.

"I'm Gabe," he yells. Maybe he's not even in his
twenties, she thinks. A decent fake ID is all he
needs to be there.

"Kate," she yells and regrets it immediately.
She has always wanted to tell some guy in a bar
a fake name—Coral, she'd decided—and now it's
too late and she's having a baby and she'll prob-

ably never have another chance. She could have laughed about this moment with Dani and Vanessa later—*I told him my name was Coral!*—but now that will never happen.

"Where are you staying?" Gabe yells.

"Thirty-Eighth Street on the beach," Kate says and then bites her lip. Again with the honesty. She doesn't even know this guy.

He yells something else. Kate is fairly sure he is saying that he likes her freckles. Her face grows warm. "Where are you from?" he yells. No one is from Avalon.

"Philly," she yells.

"Me too."

Avalon is no Vegas. These guys you dance with—they're probably your neighbors back home. Or the sons of your firm's senior partners. She's not sure if this makes it better or worse that she told him her real name. She turns back to her friends.

It's too hot! she mouths. She pulls at the neck of her sundress and waves at her face, pantomiming being overheated. They point toward the patio. She nods and looks at Gabe. She wants to explain that this weekend is about her and her friends, not meeting guys, but then she remembers that he is probably already thinking about the next girl he will dance with. She gives him a small, awkward wave and follows her friends outside.

* * *

By the time Kate snakes her way through the dance floor and pushes the door open to the patio, a group of guys has already offered up their table to Vanessa and Dani. It's in this moment, when she sees they're both literally swaying, that Kate realizes just how drunk they are. Dani looks as if she might slide off her chair. Vanessa's eyelids are heavy and have a bit too much shine, and she's glaring at Dani. Kate's stomach flips. Vanessa, usually reserved, is a fight-picker when she's drunk, and Dani, drunk or sober, is always up for sparring. Kate hurries over to the table and suggests they go across the street to Circle Pizza.

"No! You have to get back out there," Dani says.

"Out where?"

"The dance floor. That guy was super into you."

"That guy probably isn't even old enough to be here."

"So what?" Dani says. "He's cute."

"I'm not interested." The thought of having to bike all the way home, worrying the whole way about the baby, is elbowing its way through the crowd of thoughts in her mind. She thinks she should probably just start walking now, but she can't, of course, leave her friends.

Dani shrugs. "Maybe it's for the best. It was a little weird. He kind of looked like—*ow!*" Dani bends over to rub her shin, glaring at Vanessa.

"Like who?" Kate asks. Vanessa is shaking her head at Dani. *Colin.* That's what Dani was going to say. Gabe doesn't look a thing like Colin—*not a thing*—but she knows that's where Dani was headed. This is the first time Colin has come up. They look everywhere but at one another.

"Shut up, Dani," Vanessa says finally.

"It's okay," Kate says. "But you're crazy. He doesn't look anything like Colin."

"So then, what is it?" Dani asks. The elbow she's leaning on slips off the tabletop. "You're single," she says, righting herself. "He's cute. Live a little!"

The last time Dani said this to her, Kate got so drunk she did something she will regret for the rest of her life. She will never, ever go down that road again. But this is exactly what Peter wants her to do, isn't it? He wants her to remember how to lose control. Kate had only told Peter a version of the truth about what happened to Colin. This, she knows, is as much an indication of a problem between them as anything.

Dani drinks from a plastic cup.

"Was that cup here when you sat down?" Kate asks, feeling a wave of nausea. Kate knows Dani is hurting from her father's announcement, but her drinking seems compulsive. Who knows whose lips last touched that cup? It constantly amazes her how oblivious people are to the real danger presented by invisible germs.

Dani looks down into the cup and then back at Kate. She picks up the cup and drinks the entire thing.

"That's disgusting," Vanessa says.

"No," Dani says. "It's vodka."

A waitress appears and sets down three shots. "These are from those guys," she says, hiking her thumb in the direction of the group of guys who had given up the table. They are huddled by the door of the bar and one of them is rocking back and forth on his heels like the wolf in one of the Saturday morning cartoons Kate and Colin used to watch.

"Perfect," Dani says. "Let's invite them over."

"No," Kate and Vanessa say in unison.

"They're not for you, Vanessa. You're married, remember? They're for Kate."

Vanessa narrows her eyes.

"Thanks, but no thanks," Kate says. "Let's talk about what we're going to do tomorrow. Bagel sandwiches from Avalon Coffee? Then hit the beach around ten? Wawa hoagies for lunch? What should we have for dinner?" This attempt at redirection is futile. She can see that Vanessa does not even hear her.

"I *remember* I'm married, Dani," she says. Her eyes are slits now, and Kate doubts she is seeing much of anything. "You don't have to remind me."

"Well, what's the deal with Jeremy Caldwell

then? You dated him for all of five seconds a few thousand eons ago and now, what? You think he's The One Who Got Away?"

"Dani," Kate says.

"It's fine, Kate. Let her say what she wants. I'd love to hear Dani's thoughts about love. This should be fascinating." She's leaning forward on the table. Her face is a little slack. This is as close to ugly as Vanessa gets.

Kate groans.

"I'm not talking about love," Dani says. "I'm talking about marriage."

"Marriage! That's the one thing you know less about than love. You've never even been the *child* of a successful marriage."

"And now Lucy won't be either," Dani says.

Vanessa gasps.

"Oh my God, you guys, stop it!" Kate says. "You're both drunk. Let's all just take a breath."

Without breaking eye contact with Vanessa, Dani reaches across the table, grabs the shot glass that is in front of Kate, lifts it to her lips, and drains it.

"Why? Why is she taking Drew's side?" Vanessa mumbles to Kate. Her hair has started to escape from its bun. "She doesn't even know him. She doesn't even know what happened."

"So what happened?" Dani asks, except it sounds more like "sowahapin?"

"Yeah," Kate says. She can't help herself. "What happened?"

Vanessa's gaze drops down to the table. "He cheated on me."

"What?" Kate can't believe it. "Drew slept with someone? Who? When?"

"He kissed someone," Vanessa says.

Kate is stunned. All this time she thought her friend had, if not a perfect marriage, at least a strong one. Even though Vanessa is drunk, Kate can see that she is embarrassed by the situation, the turn her relationship has taken. Kate reaches out and squeezes her hand.

"Oh," Dani says. Kate cringes at her tone—she sounds disappointed and a little bored. But then Dani lays her head down on the table and Kate wonders if she even meant to speak at all.

"No, not '*Oh*,'" Vanessa says. She pulls her hand from Kate's and sticks her finger into the air. "Not '*Oh*.' He's my husband and he kissed another woman. We're married. He's not allowed to do that." She starts to cry and Kate tries to put her arms around her, but Vanessa shakes her off. "Whatever, Kate. You wouldn't understand."

Vanessa is going to forget she even made this comment, but it's going to stay with Kate forever, and this pisses Kate off.

Vanessa peers at her and her face softens. "I'm sorry. That came out wrong."

"Maybe," Kate says, "but you meant it. You think Dani and I are the same—that neither of us could make a relationship stick if we tried."

Dani lifts her head and releases a bleary grin. "I never try!" she says, and then lays her head back down.

Vanessa stares at her and opens her mouth to respond but all that comes out is an enormous, sickly sounding hiccup. She looks as if she is about to vomit.

Kate has no idea how any of them are going to find their way home.

11

Vanessa

The next morning, Dani trudges into the kitchen wearing the same black T-shirt she wore the day before, the one she flew across the country in and got drunk in and slept in. Somewhere in the back of her mind, Vanessa had wondered if Dani still wore the same outfit for days on end, and now she has the answer. She has the urge to demand that Dani take a shower, the way she would if Drew came home smelling of sweat after a steamy ride in an un-air-conditioned bus.

Dani eyes her warily and lifts her hand in greeting.

"Morning," Vanessa says. They fought last night, but she cannot remember why. She thinks it was about Jeremy Caldwell. Or Dani's father? She has no idea why she would think this; it doesn't make any sense. She had thought she might run into Jeremy at the Princeton, but she hadn't. Or had she? She would remember at least that much, wouldn't she?

"You made coffee," Dani says. Her voice is croaky. She stands in front of the coffeepot, holding an empty mug, blinking. Vanessa wonders if she is still drunk.

"I did," she says.

Dani fills her mug and then sits beside Vanessa on a stool at the breakfast bar. Behind them, a wall of sliding doors is open to the deck, and the sky is so bright that the beach seems almost white below it. The ocean shimmers flat and silver like a mirror. Dani's father's house is so beautiful, so comfortably elegant, that it takes Vanessa's breath away. Looking around, she wonders how much of Dr. Lowenstein's taste—and the time she spent in this house and his equally well-curated condo in Rittenhouse Square—is to thank for sparking her interest in art and design. She thinks of her own apartment, the foundation of Dr. Lowenstein–esque creams and contemporary furniture that she has layered with intensely colored textiles collected during her travels with Drew. If her parents had owned this beach house, they would have filled it with mismatched furniture collected at thrift stores and garage sales; decorating would have been a chore for them, a necessary evil to ensure they had a surface on which to play Scrabble.

Spinning her stool slowly back to the breakfast bar, Vanessa realizes this is the first time she and Dani have been alone together, sober, in eight years. She takes a sip of her coffee and when she lowers it, she sees that her knuckles are nearly white.

"Where's Kate?" Dani asks, as though reading her thoughts.

"Out for a walk with Gracie. Two walks, actually. She returned to tell me what a beautiful day it is and then she went back out."

Dani squints over her shoulder at the beach and turns back to look down into her coffee. "So beautiful it makes me want to vomit."

Vanessa laughs despite feeling certain that she and Dani are still fighting about something—something *new* at least, though this does little to reassure her. "Coffee first, beach later," she says. The day stretches out in front of her—no snacks to pack or toys to straighten or swings to push, just a day on the beach.

Downstairs, the screen door opens and shuts. They hear flip-flops being kicked off and Gracie's nails clattering against the floor. Then Kate is stomping up the stairs, taking them two at a time. When she reaches the top, her cheeks are pink and her chest is heaving. Gracie loudly laps water from a bowl on the floor and then splays out on the kitchen tile with a groan. Without lifting her chin from the floor, the dog looks up at Vanessa, one eyebrow raised, her tail thumping slowly.

"Were you running?" Vanessa asks Kate. "In flip-flops?" It seems to her that Kate has two speeds: zero (when she's spread out on a couch—any couch will do—watching a movie or sleeping) and sixty (the rest of the time).

"No, just walking. I picked up breakfast." She looks back and forth between them in a way that makes Vanessa and Dani look at each other and shrug. Their fight last night must have been pretty bad because Kate is clearly relieved to find them sitting side by side, their hands far from each other's throats. Kate digs into a white paper bag and pulls out two wrapped bagel sandwiches. Her peppiness is a little annoying. *How is she not hungover?* Vanessa can't remember how many shots they did the night before; she lost track at three. "I didn't get you one, Dani," Kate says, handing Vanessa a sandwich.

"I don't want one," Dani says. Vanessa can tell she too finds the sight of Kate all freshly scrubbed and full of energy annoying.

"I know," Kate says. "That's why I didn't get you one." Dani never eats breakfast. She says her brain isn't capable of sending her jaw "the chew signal" until at least 11:00 AM. This has been the case for as long as they've known her—she used to arrive at school and immediately hand Kate the cereal bar that her father insisted she put in her bag.

"Hello there!" Kate says to her bagel sandwich, unwrapping it. She takes an enormous bite, and then another before she's even swallowed the first.

"My God, woman, slow down," Dani says. She really does sound disgusted. The contrast between the grayish circles below her eyes and the greenish tint of the rest of her face is getting starker by the minute.

"Eating delicately is for wussies," Kate says through a mouthful of bagel. Vanessa and Dani laugh. "It's almost time to go to the beach," she says, as though there's some plan to which they've all agreed. Leave it to Kate to have a plan for their lazy beach weekend. "Dani, does your dad have extra tags?" The beaches aren't free in Avalon—Dani's father always bought a bunch of season passes at the beginning of each summer so the girls never had to buy their own.

Dani nods. "In the basket next to the coffeepot."

The beach. Bathing suits. Vanessa looks down at the bagel sandwich. She's only had a couple of bites, but she wraps it back up and puts it in the fridge. When she turns around, Dani is watching her in a way that drives her crazy; it's a look that's half judgment and half recording device. Vanessa has never read Dani's book, but she suspects if she did, she would find a caricature of herself in its pages: a biracial, married, former gallerist with a wandering eye and an obsession with trivial subjects like weight and clothes. Victoria, maybe. Or Veronica. The thought makes her deeply uncomfortable. Angry, even.

"What?" Vanessa asks, glaring at Dani.

"Nothing," Dani says, then adds, "Crunch crack." When they were sixteen, Kate accidentally drove over Dani's bike in the driveway of the beach house. She'd come running into the house, crying and babbling in her particular Kate way about how she'd had no idea the bike was even there until she ran over it and heard "crunch crack." Ever since, it's what they say when someone says or does something that seems to come out of nowhere or that one of them feels is unjustified.

"How's Lucy?" Kate asks, always ready to change the subject at the first whiff of tension.

"Good. I checked in this morning and . . ." She trails off. She is hesitant to talk too much about Lucy with them. Kate wants a child someday and now that Peter has broken up with her, who knows when that will happen? Vanessa has no idea if Dani wants to be a mother; they've never discussed it. How strange that the two women who used to know her best now understand so little about her life—the world of motherhood. "They're going to the playground."

Dani stands and stretches. "And I'm going to take a shower." She leaves Vanessa and Kate alone in the kitchen and walks out onto the deck. They can hear her footsteps on the outside staircase. Dani only uses the outside shower in Avalon.

"I'm glad Lucy and Drew are having fun," Kate says. Vanessa senses something off in her tone. She knows that Kate has had a little crush on her husband ever since the night Vanessa introduced them and Drew wore a Vineyard Vines tie with tiny black Labradors all over it. Kate's pale cheeks had immediately brightened into pink starbursts. She probably would have liked Drew even without that tie; few boys failed to spellbind her. That summer before their senior year of college, Kate had attended to Colin's Lehigh friends like a hostess at a cocktail party in the 1950s, clearing empty beer cans and offering bowls of pretzels. And Vanessa still remembers the look in her eye when Vanessa mentioned, during the wedding shower that Kate threw for her in Philadelphia, that she would never cook meat for her future husband. Kate had pressed her lips together in a way that Vanessa knew meant she was appalled. But Vanessa is a pescetarian—she hasn't eaten meat since the day her mother brought those chickens home to live in their yard—and she's not going to cook meat for anyone. Ever. Kate, on the other hand, is allergic to shellfish but would probably cook bouillabaisse for a man. She'd probably eat it, too, in the hope that he would hold her hand on the way to the hospital.

A snort of laughter cuts through the air. Vanessa looks over, and Kate points at the kitchen counter, her eyes crinkled and glistening as her shoulders shake. In the fruit bowl, someone has suggestively rearranged a banana and two oranges. *Dani*. She used to do this all the time when they were growing up—in all of their homes, the school cafeteria, even the nursing home where they sang holiday carols in middle school. No fruit bowl was safe. Vanessa is surprised by the force of her own laughter. She can't seem to stop it. She and Kate laugh together, a fresh wave building each time their laughter seems on the verge of lagging.

Her phone vibrates on the counter and her heart skitters when she sees it's a text from Jeremy Caldwell. She picks up the phone, covering its face with her hand. "I'm going to take a quick shower too," she says. "And then the beach, I promise."

Kate is still smiling. "I'll be out on the deck," she says, "waiting for you slugs."

Vanessa sits on the edge of the bathtub and looks at her phone. *When can we get together?* Jeremy's text reads. She scrolls up and is surprised to see that he is writing in response to a text she sent him at 2:00 AM that morning. *I'm in Avalon*, she'd written. *Staying at Dani's house.* It is a small relief to see that, even drunk, she is a woman of few words.

The air in the bathroom moves, and though she knows it's just a breeze through the open window, she feels the presence of Lenora Haysbach. She met Lenora once, months before she and Drew kissed at that party, when she'd brought Lucy to the show's studio in Hell's Kitchen to meet Drew for lunch. Lenora was fresh out of college and an unremarkable shade of pretty—highlighted blond hair, athletic build, a string of pearls at her neck that she'd probably put on in the hope it would make her look sophisticated. Those pearls only made her look prudish, like an uptight twenty-two-year-old. Not at all Drew's type. Vanessa had not felt even the slightest twinge of concern when Drew introduced them. Later, after the "indiscretion" (Drew's word), when Vanessa pressed her husband for more information, she learned that Lenora was bright and ambitious and had a dry sense of humor that made her a favorite with craft services. She'd felt plenty of twinges then—one for "bright" and one for "ambitious" and another for "humor."

In the shower, Vanessa's thoughts turn to Lucy. Whenever her daughter takes a bath, she says the word "shampoo" over and over again, laughing her sudden bubbling laugh. Vanessa's stomach roils with guilt and hangover. She misses Lucy so much it makes the air feel thin in her lungs. She hopes her daughter isn't missing her. She hopes Lucy is happy in the moment and is not thinking about what—or who—is missing.

Did she remind Drew that Lucy was not allowed to bring her rings into her crib? Her daughter was obsessed with a stack of tiny rubber rings that the dentist had given her during her recent first visit to his office—a horrible reward for a small child given that they could so easily be swallowed, but Lucy loved them. She would wear them to bed if no one stopped her, two pastel rings on each chubby thumb, the danger of which causes Vanessa's chest to clench. She makes a mental note to text a reminder to Drew and wonders what other critical details of Lucy's care she had forgotten to share.

So here she is, alone at last, thinking only of her daughter. When she is with Lucy, she fantasizes about having a weekend to herself; when she is away from Lucy, she misses her so much it takes her breath away. She no longer expects to feel completely comfortable in either world. It's been this way since the day Lucy was born; this is motherhood. Even as she has these thoughts, Vanessa hears the voice of Dani arguing that this inability to feel satisfied in the present moment is not in fact Vanessa-as-Mother, this is simply Vanessa. Period.

She jumps when she hears the door click open. "V?" It's Kate.

"We're not knocking?" Vanessa peeks around the shower curtain and sees that Kate is blinking back tears. "Oh, Kate. What's wrong? Hang on." She turns off the shower, wraps herself in a towel, and pulls back the curtain.

"I was sitting out on the deck by myself and I . . ." Kate begins and then stops, biting her lip to keep herself from crying. She seems to have lost her train of thought and Vanessa gives her a moment to see if she'll find it. "It's just," Kate says, sinking onto the toilet seat, "everything." She rubs her knees, looking all of ten years old with her skinny legs sticking out from her khaki shorts and her bikini straps tied behind her neck and her sunglasses tucked like a headband into her humidity-crimped hair. That summer before their senior year of college they had worn sunglasses every waking hour, surprised to find them perched on their heads, still holding back their hair hours after the sun had set.

"I know it must be hard for you to be here," Vanessa says. Last night, or at least the part of last night that Vanessa remembers, Kate had seemed in a strange mood—swinging from nervous chatter to periods of quiet so unusual that Vanessa had almost wondered if she was about to fall asleep. It's the first time she's seen Kate since Peter broke up with her, and her friend is dealing with the emotions of being back in Avalon on top of everything else. Vanessa worries that the combined weight of these things is too much to bear. "I'm still not sure this was the best idea," she says.

Kate nods without looking up from her knees. "Do you remember that movie *Sliding Doors?* I keep thinking about it. I keep thinking one version of me is in Philadelphia planning a wedding to Peter and one version of me is here in Avalon, brokenhearted."

Kate is obsessed with romantic movies. Vanessa wonders if she should remind her that these movies are for entertainment; they're not meant to mirror life. Peter probably isn't going to show up outside her window holding a boom box.

"Technically," Vanessa says, "one of you would be in Vegas right now."

"Well, that's true. I'd rather be here."

"Even with what happened to Colin?" These words just come out. Kate looks up from her knees and stares at Vanessa. "I'm sorry," Vanessa says. "I shouldn't have said that."

Kate blinks and reanimates. "It's fine. I'm glad you said it. We're allowed to talk about Colin. People are so terrified to say his name to me— like they're afraid to remind me he existed. Like

I've forgotten. Like I don't think about him every single day and still manage to function."

Vanessa does not say anything. Losing a twin must be like losing a piece of yourself. It would be like losing Lucy—a thought she barely allows herself to have, her heart aching for the pain her friend will forever carry. She has an urge to track Peter down and yell at him for breaking her friend's heart. Vanessa knows how to take someone down a notch; this skill is coiled neatly inside of her, stealthy and patient, ever ready to strike.

"Anyway," Kate says, "the answer is yes. Even with what happened to Colin, I'm glad we're in Avalon. He did something incredibly selfish and stupid, but he doesn't get to ruin this place for us. For me. I love it here." Vanessa can hear the crack in her voice. It sounds to her as if Kate is trying to convince herself of something. Vanessa is proud of her for trying—it's a valiant effort.

She pulls Kate from the toilet and puts her hands on her shoulders. "Let's go to the beach," she says. "Get a little tan on that ghostly lawyer skin."

Kate looks in the mirror and frowns. "I don't tan. I freckle."

"I know," Vanessa says.

They are on the beach all of fifteen minutes before Dani runs back inside to throw up. When she finally returns, she is wearing an enormous pink sun hat that must belong to Susanna because it certainly doesn't belong to any of them. Vanessa still can't believe Dani's father is planning to marry that woman. She can't imagine growing up the way Dani did, knowing her mother was out there somewhere with another family, pretending Dani didn't exist. What kind of mother did that to her daughter? The whole thing makes her blood boil. As much as Dani puts up a good front with her barbed jokes and armor of black, all you have to do is look at her when she is reading to see the truth. She reads like a starving person who has been handed a plate of food, her big Bambi eyes quivering over the page.

"Well, that was embarrassing," Dani says as she drops down into her beach chair. They had found their old chairs hanging from hooks in the back of the garage as though they had hung them there the day before and not eight years earlier. Rainbow stripes for Dani, pastel stripes for Kate, and solid turquoise for Vanessa.

"It happens," Vanessa says. She doesn't feel so hot herself.

"I'm never going to drink that much again," Dani says. Vanessa and Kate both laugh. "No, seriously. I'm over feeling like shit."

Vanessa and Kate exchange a glance. "Okay," Kate says. "Good for you."

"And I'm going to the library later. To write. I know we're supposed to be on vacation, but I need to get some work done so I feel like less of a waste of life."

"That's fine," Kate says. "Vanessa and I will shop for dinner."

"Or take a nap," Vanessa says and closes her eyes. It's generous of Kate to pretend she believes Dani when she says she's not going to drink that much again, but they all know the truth.

When it gets so hot their bodies shimmer with sweat, they move their beach chairs to the water's edge and sink their feet into the chill of the ocean. Vanessa is relieved to realize that she still loves Avalon despite its being the place where Colin died. She has been to more beautiful places— Paris, Bali, her honeymoon in Greece—but no place makes her feel the way she does here. The ocean sparkles below the high sun, and the lull of tumbling waves makes her sleepy. She is overtaken by languid happiness.

"Kate?" a guy says, approaching barefoot. His trunks are slung low on his narrow hips. "We met last night, remember? I'm Gabe."

"Gabe!" Kate leaps to her feet. Once she is standing she seems to immediately regret the decision and looks around awkwardly.

"Hey," Vanessa says, saving her.

"Hey," Kate echoes, remembering herself. "What are you doing here, Gabe?"

Repeating someone's name isn't the worst flirting strategy, but Kate has always overdone it. Vanessa wishes she would push her shoulders back. Kate is so much prettier than she gives herself credit for. Vanessa would kill for her long legs, her lovely collarbones—she'd know just how to show them off.

"I'm sitting down on Thirtieth Street with my friends," Gabe says. "I thought I'd try to find you. I remembered you said you were staying on this beach."

"She did, did she?" Dani says.

"This is Dani and Vanessa," Kate says.

"Hey," Gabe says again. Vanessa lifts her hand in a tepid wave. He might be only five or six years younger than they are, but he somehow seems like an entirely different species. He probably passed out fully clothed on the couch of a rental house the night before and had a beer with breakfast. Age aside, he's tall and thin and has a kind, pensive face and he's probably just Kate's type. He makes Vanessa itchy with boredom.

Gabe looks at Kate, shielding his eyes even though he's wearing sunglasses. "Want to go for a walk?"

"Sure." Kate grabs her shorts off the back of her chair and pulls them on. "See you guys later," she says. From the back, with her bikini straps dangling down her back and her hair up in a ponytail, she could be any teenager on the beach. She has the most identifiable walk Vanessa has ever seen—a flat-footed, rolling, slightly turned-out walk, her arms loose at her sides. A skinny-girl walk. A tomboy walk. Vanessa could spot her a mile away.

"Go, Kate, go," Dani says, finally laughing.

"She's not really interested in him, is she?"

"Who cares? If it gets her mind off Peter, it's a good thing."

Vanessa isn't so sure about this, but before she has time to respond, a woman comes traipsing down the beach toward them, waving. It takes Vanessa a moment to realize it is Ginny Kimble, a girl they first met playing skeeball in the arcade, one of three small businesses that made up Avalon's rinky-dink boardwalk, when they were twelve. A summer friend—Vanessa can't even remember where she was from. She hasn't seen her since the last time she was in Avalon. This is the problem with sitting by the water's edge—everyone you know will see you. The thought that Jeremy is somewhere on this island, that he might show up at any moment, makes her feel unsettled. She wonders how she should respond to his text, how long this will go on, where it's headed. Maybe she won't write him back at all;

she'll end this all right now, using silence as her response. Even as she has this thought, she knows it is not what she is going to do.

"I thought it was you two!" Ginny says, bending over to kiss them on the cheeks before sitting in the sand next to Vanessa's chair. She looks as if she's walked out of a John Currin painting, all red hair and boobs and creamy skin that must be slathered with a thick layer of invisible sunscreen. "I just saw Kate making googly eyes with some college kid. Scandalous! I haven't seen you guys in ages. What's going on?"

They catch one another up on where they are living and with whom. Dani says she works in a bookstore, and Vanessa says she stays home with her two-year-old. It's clear that both answers disappoint Ginny and it bothers Vanessa that this stings. Then Ginny brightens. She looks at Vanessa, a smile on her full lips.

"You know what's so funny?"

Vanessa looks at her, knowing whatever she is about to say won't be funny at all. "What?"

"Remember that guy you used to date? Jeremy Caldwell? I dated him after you did. We went out a few times in Philly."

Vanessa feels her throat tighten.

"That's hilarious," Dani says.

Ginny waves her hand in front of her. "Oh, you know how Philly is—everyone dates everyone. I swear, it's the worst city in America for singles. I kind of hate it. Anyway," she says, "the funny part is Jeremy. That guy is a terrible kisser! He's such a stud that you think he'd be, like, the best kisser ever, but he's the worst! I mean, *the worst*! I always wanted to track you down, Vanessa, so we could laugh about it."

It is clear to Vanessa that Jeremy broke Ginny's heart. Still, she's pissed. Jeremy is a great kisser. Just the thought of their kisses makes her mind go a little fuzzy.

"Jeremy is a great kisser," she says.

Ginny and Dani are both silent. Maybe it was the cool tone of her voice. Or maybe it was the fact that she used the present tense—Jeremy *is* a great kisser. So Drew kissed Lenora and Jeremy kissed Ginny. The two incidents are not remotely connected, but still Vanessa feels enraged. She's dying for a glass of water. Why didn't they bring water?

"I don't trust people who hate their home-towns," Dani states after Ginny finally gets the hint and saunters off. "How can they not be even the teensiest bit nostalgic? They're just one ther-apy session away from being diagnosed bat-shit crazy."

"You're so judgmental," Vanessa snaps, and then immediately regrets it. Dani isn't the one she is frustrated with right now. And after the things she accused Dani of eight years ago, she has no grounds to call anyone else judgmental. She holds her breath, waiting for Dani to bring up that fight, realizing she's basically chummed the waters.

But Dani just shrugs. "Show me someone who isn't judgmental, and I'll show you someone without a pulse."

Vanessa laughs, relieved. "It's good to see you're the same ray of sunshine you've always been."

"Haven't changed a bit," Dani says. She begins to absently flick the top of a tube of sunscreen open and shut.

"That's not necessarily a bad thing," Vanessa says. "Sometimes I don't even recognize myself."

Dani stops flicking the sunscreen top and looks at her. "I recognize you," she says. "You're in there."

Vanessa is unnerved by how much Dani's small kindness affects her.

"So," Dani says. "Jeremy is a great kisser, huh?"

"He was. Years ago." She pushes her sunglasses up onto her head and Dani does the same with hers. They squint at each other. Until this moment, Vanessa hadn't known if Dani remembered what she had told them about Drew's infidelity the night before—she herself barely remembers telling them. "I saw him a couple of weeks ago for the first time since we broke up," she says. "Nothing happened. We just talked."

Dani drops her sunglasses back over her eyes

and begins to rub suntan lotion onto her legs. "What do you want to happen?"

Vanessa thinks of Jeremy's hand cupping her face, of Drew and Lenora's kiss. "I honestly don't know," she says.

"Well, is this a revenge thing or is this a real-feelings thing?" Dani asks.

"I'm not sure it's an either-or situation."

"I think it probably is," Dani says. "But what do I know?" She snaps the top back on the lotion and tosses it into her beach bag. "So when did Drew kiss that woman?"

"At a holiday party in December." She thinks Dani might say something about the many men Vanessa should not have kissed but had anyway. She looks down the beach for Kate, hoping she'll be back soon.

Dani says, "What a fucking asshole."

Vanessa releases her breath and laughs. Still, it seems to her that Dani is going easy on her, and something about this makes her sad. Dani has turned her face up to the sun now; her eyes are closed. When Vanessa's phone buzzes, she pulls it from her bag and sees that Jeremy is calling. Dani stirs and Vanessa drops the phone back into her bag, unanswered, as Dani moans, "It feels so good to be warm for once."

She sounds so genuinely satisfied with the *weather* that Vanessa isn't sure if she should resent her or feel sorry for her. *What must it be like to be Dani, with no one to think about but herself?*

"This," Dani intones, "is the summer of our discontent."

Vanessa scoops wet sand on her big toe and flicks it toward Dani. It lands on the side of her leg with a thwap. "You're not allowed to quote Dickens on the beach."

"It's Shakespeare. And I was misquoting so it's okay."

"Nothing is okay," Vanessa says.

Dani turns her head to look at Vanessa. "Crunch crack," she says after a moment, but softly.

12

Dani

The Avalon Public Library is sun washed and silent. The building is only six years old, and its presence still surprises Dani every time she drives by; she expects the island to look exactly the same year after year despite being confronted every summer by the huge new homes that have sprung up over the winter and the increasingly chic boutiques and restaurants multiplying along Dune Drive. It irritates her that these changes always surprise her, that she never learns, never sufficiently braces herself for the passage of time.

She can't remember when she was last in a library. She walks around the hushed space until she spots an electrical outlet near a table in a relatively dark corner. Her laptop's whir fills the corner she has staked, its sickly drone satisfying for once. *If you build it*, she thinks, *I will bring my crappy laptop.*

The air conditioning makes the blond hairs on her bare forearms stand up. She takes a sip of the hot coffee she smuggled in behind her laptop bag and looks at the librarian standing by the rack of paperbacks near the library's entrance. Her heavy arms are deeply tanned, speckled with age, and her hair is a bubble of white, a scoop of vanilla atop a brown waffle cone. *A year-round resident,* Dani thinks, and then: *This is my rock bottom.* It's an optimistic thought. Things cannot get worse. She is unemployed, adrift, unaccomplished, miserably hungover, and now, she thinks, allowing herself a bit more melodrama—orphaned. First her mother started over with a new family, and now her father is doing the same. She is not the only woman with staying power in her father's life. She has to make room for *Suz.*

That morning, as she was hunched over a toilet, puking, she was relieved to be alone in the house. She would never have such privacy in her father's condo. It was one thing to feel this way—to be this way—when she was thousands of miles away from anyone she had known longer than a year or two and another thing entirely to be this way in front of Kate and Vanessa in Avalon and possibly her father and *Suz* in Philadelphia. She'd decided, as she'd pressed her forehead to the white marble bathroom floor, that she was done with drinking that much. And that if she ever wants to look herself in the mirror again, she'd better finish her damn novel.

There is nothing new about either declaration.

Still, she has surprised herself by not taking even one of the OxyContin pills from the tin that Rachel gave her as a send-off present. Which isn't to say she isn't thinking about them. Being high gives her a warm, sleepy peace, a sense that everything is okay, or at least that nothing matters. Without pills or alcohol, there is no guarantee she'll ever feel that way again.

Case in point: on her walk to the library, her father had called and she'd suddenly felt so upset she could not bring herself to answer the call. Now, sitting in front of her open laptop, she listens to his voice mail. *Dani*, her father says. *I forgot to tell you the beach tags are by the coffeepot. I'm sorry. Call when you have a second.*

The beach tags are always by the coffeepot; the beach tags are not why he called. Suz might be behind this oblique apology, but she might not. Directness has never been Dani's father's strong suit. The summer after her parents divorced, he bought the house in Avalon. He never mentioned his ex-wife. On the rare occasions when Dani brought her up, the word "Mom" sounded strange to her; it was an odd bubble of a word, more like a sound effect than the name for the woman who had birthed her. *Kapow! Bam! Mom!*

The first time Dani returned to Avalon after Colin died was early in June of the following summer. Her father brought down a bottle of cabernet sauvignon that Dani knew he'd been saving for years. He could not give her a mother, but he could give her a beach house. He could not bring back Colin, but he could bring her a hundred-dollar bottle of wine. He did the best he could. This is what Dani always told herself.

That first night, they sat on the deck and drank the cabernet with grilled tuna steaks and a salad. Her father did not say anything as he clinked his glass against hers at the start of the meal. Dani had just graduated from Brown and would move to Boston in ten days.

"You could clean boats," her father said as the meal wound down. They were discussing what else, besides writing, she would do in Boston.

"Or birds," Dani responded. "Nobody likes a dirty bird."

Her father refilled their wineglasses. "Or you could teach Chinese."

"I don't know Chinese."

"Didn't you take Chinese at Brown?"

Dani thought for a moment. "I ate cheese at Brown. Is that what you're thinking of?"

"Yes," her father said, unable to keep a straight face. "It must be. Unfortunately, Boston's once-strong cheese industry is now floundering."

"Still, I could be a cheesemonger. I'm sure Boston has mongers. It's a very Colonial word."

"Mongering is sales. Do you consider yourself a people person?"

"I don't mind people who share my interests."

"Cheese?"

"Cheese."

"Well, then, you could always work with mice."

"For the last time, Dad, I'm not going to be a scientist."

Her father sighed, feigning exasperation. "My daughter, the writer. If only you had an imagination."

They could go on like this for hours, and they did, working their way through another bottle of less expensive wine. When the sky turned pink, the bugs descended; by the time the sky darkened to a sheet of bedazzled navy, the bugs were gone. The cicadas sang and the ocean tumbled and somewhere down the street a screen door slammed. Sometime before midnight, her father stood, steady as ever on his feet, and, bowing to an imaginary crowd, said, "And that, folks, is that. Don't forget to have your ticket validated on the way out." Colin was dead and still, somehow, another summer had begun. After her father went to bed, Dani sat by herself and cried, and then she didn't again for a very long time.

* * *

It's risky to try to write while surrounded by books. Her propensity is to pull one from the shelf and drop herself into someone else's story.

A man enters the library. "Hi, Joyce," he says, waving to the librarian. "Hello there, Sam," Joyce says back. She tucks her vanilla hair behind her ear and smiles at him like a woman half her age. Sam heads in Dani's direction, but his step falters when he sees her.

"Did I take your spot?" Dani calls out. The librarian and the only other two patrons in the library all stop what they are doing to look over at her.

Sam shakes his head. "No," he says, and smiles. He turns and settles at a table in the center of the room, pulling a laptop and a few books from his bag. Dani can't read their spines.

If she were Kate, Vanessa even, this is when she would start daydreaming. This man named Sam is attractive—if you like that sort of thing. He is wearing cargo shorts and a short-sleeved, button-down shirt in a faded blue shade that perfectly matches the slice of sky Dani can see through the library windows. He has sensitive eyes and a clean-cut, old-fashioned face that reminds her of the poster of Hemingway that had hung in her high school English teacher's classroom. That poster was *Tiger Beat* Hemingway—young, rosy-cheeked, Paris Hemingway, years before the ladies' man mustache or swarthy, mountain-man beard entered the equation. Happy Hemingway. Hemingway Lite.

The writer's job is to tell the truth. Ms. Dougherty's solemn intonation had made even Hemingway quotes sound like lines from fortune cookies. She'd taken the poster down after Dani raised her hand one day and asked if it was prudent to idolize, in a roomful of hormonal, angst-ridden teen-agers, an alcoholic who had committed suicide. Ms. Dougherty had probably rehung the poster above her bed.

To Dani, Happy Hemingway—Sam—is just some guy who is probably a lot like a lot of other guys. She doesn't think in terms of fairy-tale end-ings or fate. She likes sex and she likes men, but she is not looking for a life partner. It's not that she is itching to die alone, but she wants to do more than some guy in the library.

She is aware that she is the only one of the three of them—Kate, Vanessa, and herself—who is not focused on coupling and procreating. She knows this makes her a rare twenty-nine-year-old fe-male. She does not anticipate ever having to leave work early to care for a sick child or having to quit a high-powered job because she needs work-life balance. She should probably use this power for good and break a glass ceiling or two. She should run a Fortune 500 company or do something to further womankind. She feels embarrassed by the small life she has led, her perpetually unfinished novel, and her string of failed jobs. She is so far from where she thought she would be.

Joyce the librarian is making a beeline for Sam's table. "Working on your lesson plan already, Sam?" she asks in the drippiest whisper Dani has ever heard (she can't help it, she's carrying that ice cream metaphor now). "It's only July."

"Summer school," he answers. "I have a few lucky kids who will be rereading *The Call of the Wild* this month."

"They *are* lucky," Joyce says. *To be alone with you*, Dani imagines the sentence continues in Joyce's head. She laughs out loud at her own joke as she is prone, and not at all ashamed, to do. Joyce spins on her heel and peers over her standard-issue librarian bifocals at Dani. Sam looks at Dani too.

"E-mail forward," Dani calls, gesturing toward her computer screen. "Hilarious e-mail forward."

Joyce turns back to Sam. "You'll let me know if I can pull anything for you. I'm dying to sink my teeth into a new research project."

The Call of the Wild. It was Colin's favorite book back when he still read for the fun of it—which meant middle school, before he tried pot for the first time and lost interest in most other ways to pass the time. Dani seems to recall that it is a dog book, which explains why it was Colin's favorite.

Every member of the Harrington family has always been crazy about dogs.

Often when Dani's father was working late, Dani would join the Harringtons for dinner. She loved these nights—these glimpses into the life of a normal family, a family with married parents and a sibling. They would usually eat out, the addition of Dani the only excuse Kate's mother needed to plead off cooking duty, and at some point as they walked the city streets one member of the family would inevitably spot a dog in the distance—it seemed to Dani they all had extraordinary vision—and yell out something like, "Beagle-Weimaraner!" Then they would wait as the dog approached and sometimes another family member would amend the original call with "Beagle-schnauzer!" or the like and they would eventually anoint a winner when the dog was close enough to make a fair call about its breeding. The amazing thing was that they never disagreed about this final call. That whole family, Colin included, saw eye to eye on dog breeds, if nothing else.

A year after Colin died, the Harrington's golden retriever, Melly, died too. Kate said her father didn't leave his bedroom for an entire day. Mr. and Mrs. Harrington never got another dog. It felt strange going over to their house now, and not just because of the void created by Colin's death. They were a dog family without a dog.

Kate adopted Grace Kelly from a shelter while she was in law school. Dani still remembers the voice-mail message Kate left her announcing this news. *I got a dog!* Kate had said, and then added about one hundred more superfluous words to the message. Listening to Kate's voice, Dani had experienced a sharp pang in her chest. It would have been understandable—Dani, for one, would certainly have understood—if losing Colin had made it hard for Kate to love, but instead losing Colin seemed to make her love harder, with more ferocity.

Her brave, brave friend, Kate.

What if all of those people who had told Dani that the best was ahead of her were wrong? What if childhood is like summer—the time when life is at its lush peak, before everything begins to wither and fall?

She remembers watching Colin and Kate talk on the beach the day after the fire eight years earlier. Their conversation seemed fraught with tension; Colin's arms were crossed and Kate bit at her fingernails, hopping from foot to foot on the hot sand. *Colin,* Dani thought, watching them, *of all the dumb things you've done, this might be the dumb-*

est. Why had he set fire to that lifeguard stand? It was like asking herself why birds fly. Colin sabotaged himself because it was in his nature to do so. Of all people, Dani should have understood this. But even though Dani made questionable decisions when it came to partying, it seemed that her future was being held secure for her, high above the mess she made in the present. A couple of her Brown writing professors had offered to introduce her to their New York agents— all she had to do was write. Colin had been given no such promises; his present bled into his future, darkening the path. DUIs, fights, failing out of Lehigh, and now, arson.

Kate ran into the water, upset. Dani had started to rise from her towel to follow her when Colin strode up.

"Let's go get a drink," he said.

She glanced over at Vanessa. Jeremy Caldwell was sound asleep, face down on a towel beside her. "I'll make sure Kate is okay," Vanessa said.

Dani looked back at Colin. It had been clear all morning that Kate was upset about the fire and Colin's arrest and now she had yelled at him, reprimanding him. What Colin needed, Dani thought, wasn't another lecture, but for someone to try to understand him, to let him know that he wasn't the only one who made mistakes. With golden child Kate as your twin sister, it was so easy to disappoint. People expected it of him by then. *It's okay,* Dani would tell Colin. *There's still time to be young and stupid.*

She had thought she was so wise. She had been glad she could be there, understanding Colin when he needed to be understood.

"Let's go," she said.

They rode their bikes to the Princeton and sat at the bar facing the part of the cavernous, neon-sign-strewn room that was a liquor store. Colin was silent through much of his first beer. He seemed defeated. She'd chipped away at his mood by doing her well-worn impression of Ms. Antonelli, a math teacher at PFS who had frequently interrupted her class to give Colin a sympathetic shoulder squeeze or to lob a chalkboard eraser in his direction. Dani liked to play Ms. Antonelli as a Southeast Philly Mrs. Robinson. *Colin, jeet yet? Want some wudder? How 'bout an ahrenge? Just show me yer lacrass stick. You know the one.* After a half hour of this, Colin's mood seemed, if not lighter, at least not any heavier.

"So," he said, "what's going on with Vanessa and Jeremy?" Two brunettes in bikinis and flip-flops and not much else showed their IDs and paid for a case of beer at the register near the door.

"She seems really into him," Dani said. "But you know V. She'll like him for a week and then kick him to the curb." Colin took a long sip of his beer, his gaze on the door as it swung shut behind the girls. "Why?" Dani asked. "Jealous?" She tried to make this sound like a joke, but really she had suspected that Colin and Vanessa had had crushes on each other since high school. The thought made her angry. Neither could be trusted with the other's heart—together, they'd self-destruct, taking all of their friendships along with them.

Dani was sure that Kate saw the way Colin and Vanessa looked at each other, though none of them ever brought it up. It must have killed Kate not to discuss it—Dani knew how hard it was for her to keep her thoughts unspoken—but not discussing it kept it from becoming a thing. Dani was grateful for Kate's uncharacteristic restraint. She didn't want any of them to talk about it—words would give it power, and power could shatter them, this family they had created and that Dani needed more than any of them.

She didn't know then that within hours *she* would be the one to shatter them, that in the end there would be no one to blame but herself.

"Sure," Colin said drily. "It's eating me up inside." He finally looked over at Dani and shrugged.

Dani realized that her grip on her beer bottle was tight. She let it loosen. "Three more weeks of summer," she said. What she meant was three more weeks of being in Avalon; three more weeks until she and Kate and Vanessa and Colin went their separate ways. Technically, it would still be summer when Dani went back to Brown for her senior year, but it wouldn't be *summer*.

"The thing about summer," Dani remembers Colin saying then, looking again toward the door in a way that made her wonder what—or who—he was waiting for, "is that there's always another one."

13

Kate

Kate wants to watch *The Kids Are All Right*, but Dani is putting up a fight.

"It got rave reviews," Kate says.

Dani groans. She has a problem with things that everyone loves. "I'll just read a book if that's what you guys want to watch," she says. Dani is always reading several books at once. It is clear that these fictional worlds appeal to her more than the actual world, and this hurts Kate's feelings.

"It was nominated for an Oscar," Vanessa says. She sounds ambivalent. Vanessa does not have a problem with things everyone loves, but she prefers to be the *first* to love said things. When Kate admits she is surprised Vanessa has not seen *The Kids Are All Right* yet, Vanessa explains that she could not get Drew to agree to it. Something about this admission makes Dani relent, and after popcorn is popped and lights are dimmed, they sink side by side onto the couch with Kate in the middle. Their bare feet form a row on the cushioned ottoman—Kate's and Vanessa's are still sandy despite turns in the outdoor shower.

They don't speak for the length of the movie. They've never been the sort. Even Kate.

By the time the movie is over, the sky outside is full of stars that are visible from the couch. None of them move. Avalon is never silent. The wind rustles the dune grasses, and the waves break in the distance. Gracie lies by the screen door, gnawing loudly on a bully stick and pausing every so often to sniff the breeze.

"Who wants wine?" Kate asks, switching off the television. She is afraid one of them might beg off to bed soon.

"Not me," Dani says. Kate immediately feels bad for offering. She'd forgotten about Dani's resolution.

"I'll have a glass," Vanessa says.

Before Kate can get up from her spot in the middle of the couch, Dani rises and walks toward the kitchen. She returns with two glasses of white wine and hands one to Vanessa and one to Kate. Then she flicks through her father's CDs and inserts one into the stereo. There are at least one hundred CDs on the shelf, but Kate can only remember five ever playing in this house: Gipsy Kings' *Greatest Hits*, Bob Marley's *Legend*, Neil Young's *Harvest Moon*, the Eagles' *Greatest Hits*, and the Grateful Dead's *Skeletons from the Closet*. These are the songs of Avalon, songs that Kate can hardly bear to listen to anywhere else. She feels the skin on her arms prick as Neil Young's plaintive voice fills the living room.

> *She grew up in a small town,*
> *never put her roots down.*
> *Daddy always kept movin', so she did too.*

Dani looks peaked. Even before she speaks, Kate can tell it's more than just the remnant of her hangover.

"*Suz*," Dani says, managing to make the name sound like a curse. "My father is going to marry someone named *Suz*."

"At least she's a girl's girl," Vanessa says. The sound of Dani's laughter meeting Vanessa's has a hard, metallic ring, like a knife sliding against a sharpening rod.

Kate looks down into her wine, unsure of how she ended up with a glass. She places it on the floor; she is not going to have another sip of alcohol for her entire pregnancy. Not even in the final month, which is when she remembers Vanessa telling her that she had started treating herself to a small glass of wine every other day. She had called it medicinal—it was the only thing that soothed her aching back.

Everything Kate knows about pregnancy she has learned from Vanessa and movies. Who will run out to the corner store to buy her ice cream when she wakes up with a craving in the middle of the night? Who will be in the delivery room with her, telling her to breathe? Who will buy her a necklace with her son or daughter's first initial on a charm after the baby is born?

If she didn't long desperately for just one fun night with her best friends, one night of normalcy before she admits that everything is about to change, now would be the perfect time to announce her pregnancy.

"At least your dad seems happy," she says instead.

"Did he seem unhappy before?" Dani asks.

"No," Kate says, "but maybe he was. It's lonely being alone."

"Kate—" Vanessa says.

"*I'm* not lonely," Dani says.

"How is that possible?" Kate asks. "Are you *happy*?"

"I'm not *un*happy."

Neither Kate nor Vanessa says anything.

"'Happiness in intelligent people is the rarest thing I know,'" Dani says.

220   MEG DONOHUE

"Shakespeare again?" Vanessa asks flatly. She takes a long drink of her wine, finishing it, and then exchanges her empty glass for the one Kate had set on the floor. She's in a pensive mood, and Kate hopes she isn't gearing up to pick a fight. She really does not want to be the referee for the entire weekend.

"Hemingway." Dani is silent for a moment and then adds, "There was a guy who looked like him at the library today."

This piques Vanessa's interest. "Oh, *really*?"

"Settle down. He wasn't my type."

"No facial hair?" Kate asks.

"No tongue piercing?" This is Vanessa.

"No Lycra-blend rock-star pants?" Kate continues, rapid-fire.

"No enormous tattoo creeping up his neck?"

"You two are hilarious," Dani says drily, but she can't contain her smile. These reminders of how well they know one another light matches in each of their hearts. Dani *is* lonely. Her father's marriage will only make things worse. Kate hopes she has good friends in San Francisco, friends who joke with her like this, friends she spends time with on couches, watching movies, sober. She knows so little about her friend's life across the country. *I'll go visit,* she tells herself. *While I'm still early enough in my pregnancy that I can fly.*

"Anyway, Kate," Dani says, "we all know who

we should be discussing right now. How was your romantic beach stroll with young Gabriel?"

Kate feels herself blush. She doesn't know what compelled her to agree to a walk with Gabe when he asked. The easiest answer is that it felt good to be wanted by someone. She had been curious too—what did he see in her? Of all the girls in the Princeton the night before, why had he sought her out? Why had he come to find her on the beach today? As they walked, he told her he had just graduated from Penn, where he had studied history. She told him she'd majored in history at Penn seven years earlier. The revelation of her age had no discernible effect on him. He is starting a research fellowship at the Center for Law and Social Policy in D.C. in the fall.

Kate had studied him, wanting to make sure that Dani was wrong, that he didn't look anything like Colin. And he didn't. But of course even just the possibility that he might seemed a bit like sacrilege to Kate—no one looks like Colin. Maybe in the eyes, there was a hint of resemblance, but that was it. And even there . . . no. Colin's blue eyes had a stormy cast while Gabe's are clear.

Gabe told her his family had been coming to Avalon forever, but his last name—Dorrey—was not familiar. They both remember getting bubble-gum ice cream with rainbow jimmies at Dippy Don's, back when Dippy Don's existed. Gabe also runs along the Schuylkill River in Philly on Sunday mornings; they'd probably run right by each other more than once. His mother breeds Bernese mountain dogs in Mount Airy—she'd trained his favorite dog, Teddy, to drop his Penn acceptance letter into his lap four years earlier. As he told her this story, Gabe plucked a piece of smoky green sea glass the size of a quarter from a tangle of seaweed at their feet. When he handed it to her, their fingers touched and Kate's heart flipped. She hadn't seen sea glass in Avalon since she was a kid. The glass is in the middle drawer of the bureau in her room downstairs now, next to a bottle of prenatal vitamins.

"He's sweet," Kate says, "but he's twenty-two. He just graduated from college."

"He looks even younger than that," Vanessa says.

"So what?" Dani says. "If we were guys, we'd be high-fiving one another right now."

Kate holds up her hand and Dani smacks it. "Feel better?" she asks.

"That depends. Are you going to bang him?"

"Dani!"

"What? I think a good summer shag is just what the doctor ordered."

"No," Kate says. "It's not."

"Maybe Dani's on to something," Vanessa says. "You don't have to have sex with him, but why don't you guys go out for a drink? He could be a great distraction. You don't have anyone to answer to, Kate. You're free to do whatever you want."

Vanessa takes a long sip of wine, locking eyes with Kate over the glass. Her skin glows with the day's sun; her eyelashes are long and thick and dark even without mascara; her oversize tortoise-shell sunglasses are still perched between her hairline and her high ponytail. She looks like a movie star. It occurs to Kate that maybe Vanessa is just bored. Kate knows that marriage and a baby do not always equal happiness—just look at Dani's parents—but still, she'd like to believe that Vanessa could be happy if she didn't always want more. She wonders *when* exactly Vanessa started thinking about Jeremy Caldwell again—was it after Drew kissed that woman, or before? Maybe it isn't even a matter of when she started—maybe she had never stopped. Kate wants so badly to believe that marriage and family can work. She decides it's okay to hang on to this idea, despite everything.

"I don't want to do whatever I want," she says. "Doing whatever I want holds no appeal for me at all."

"That doesn't make any sense," Dani says.

"Live a little!" Vanessa says. She has no idea how much Kate hates this expression. "Loosen up!"

"Did Gabe give you his number?" Dani asks. "Let's call him."

"I don't want to," Kate says. She feels testy. It's distressing to think she has nearly a year of these mood swings ahead of her.

Dani is back at the stereo, flipping through the CDs again. She replaces Neil Young with another CD, and spins around, wagging her eyebrows as the opening guitar riffs of Marvin Gaye's "Let's Get It On" blare out of the speakers. Vanessa laughs, and she and Dani begin to gyrate around the rug in front of the couch. They motion for Kate to join them but she doesn't feel like moving. Gracie trots over and nudges her head below Kate's hand and releases a soft, halfhearted woof that blows out her butter-yellow cheeks and sounds like *humph*. Her brown eyes shine.

How will Gracie feel about the baby? Will she chew the baby's toys out of jealousy? Or will she sleep beside the crib, protecting the baby? The room seems to tilt, and Kate closes her eyes. When the music shuts off, Kate opens her eyes to find Dani and Vanessa watching her. Dani is pointing the stereo remote at her, as if she might use it to change Kate's mood. Both of her friends look as if they are trying not to be annoyed. She thinks of Colin—he was always ready to remind her that nobody likes a party pooper. She is glad that her brother can still make her angry; it makes it feel like less time has passed than actually has. A lump forms in her throat. She knows Peter wants her to deal with what happened to Colin, but she decides now, in this moment, that it will be easiest to wade into the secrets, starting in the shallow end and working her way to the deep.

"I'm pregnant," she says.

"Are you sure?" Vanessa asks. She and Dani are sitting on either side of Kate. "Remember that time you thought you had an iron deficiency?"

Kate has a habit of Googling her symptoms—in the case that Vanessa is referring to, bruising easily—and calling her friends with self-diagnoses.

"Or maybe you really are allergic to gluten," Dani says. "Remember when you thought gluten was making you nauseous?"

"And swollen?" Vanessa adds.

"This isn't like those other times," Kate says. "I'm not self-diagnosing. I've been to the doctor. I'm eight weeks pregnant."

"What are you going to do?" Dani asks.

"I'm going to keep it. Her. Him."

"I can't believe Peter broke up with you when you were pregnant," Vanessa says.

"Peter doesn't know. Nobody did until now."

"What? You haven't told him?"

"No."

"Your mother is going to have a heart attack," Dani says.

"That is so not helpful," Vanessa says. Then, turning to Kate, "You're giving her a grandchild. She's going to be thrilled."

There is a chain-gang pop of fireworks outside that ends nearly as quickly as it starts. Gracie sits bolt upright, trembling. Kate strokes her silky ears. *The Fourth of July isn't until Monday, people,* Kate thinks. *How hard is it to stick to a schedule?* She realizes she is biting her bottom lip, her whole mouth screwed over to the side. She does this right before she cries, each and every time. She begins to cry.

"I'm sorry," she says. "I've been crying a lot."

"Don't apologize for having feelings," Vanessa says.

Dani snaps her fingers and points at Kate. "Birth control is your messy closet!"

Kate is familiar with Dani's theory that everyone is hiding something. For years, Dani has been peering into Kate's purse and opening drawers in her kitchen, determined that Kate could not possibly be as meticulous as she appears. *If only,* Kate thinks, *my secret is as innocent as a messy closet or unprotected sex.* "You caught me," she tells Dani. "Every once in a while, I forget to take the pill."

"How are you feeling?" Vanessa asks.

No one has asked her this yet. Kate takes a moment, considering. She wants to say that she is terrified. That she is afraid that if she does not tell Peter soon she will lose him and be single forever. But her friends are looking at her in a way they have never looked at her before, and so she draws herself up a little and says, "Thirsty."

Vanessa nods. "You should drink a lot of water. Carry it around with you all day."

Dani stands. "I'll get you some."

When Dani is in the kitchen, Vanessa leans close to Kate. "You're having a baby!" she whispers. She is drunk, Kate realizes, but still the tears in her eyes are a surprise. "Drew wants us to have another baby."

"Oh, Vanessa. Do *you* want another baby?"

"Someday, but . . ." She shakes her head. "Sorry. I'm not going to hijack this conversation." She's still whispering. "I'm really happy for you. Congratulations!"

Her words sink into Kate and wrap around her heart.

"Well, Kate, thanks a lot," Dani says when she returns from the kitchen and hands her a glass of water. "A career and a baby. Way to make me feel like an overgrown child."

"You're doing it all," Vanessa says. She looks despondent.

"Um," Kate says. "Note you did not list 'husband' in there anywhere."

"Whatever," Vanessa says.

"I'll buy you a vibrator," Dani says, clinking Kate's water glass with her own.

They spend another hour on the couch discussing baby names, Ginny Kimble, and everything they know about the current lives of their old classmates from Philadelphia Friends School. Kate knows the most about their old classmates, so she does most of the talking. Heather O'Donnell, who had gone to Harvard and started her own consulting firm in Boston, stopped working after having her second son and is now pregnant with her *third* child. Matt Gordon, a wiry boy who had seemed incapable of finding shirts that weren't too big and who had never said a word to Dani or Vanessa, but with whom Kate had occasionally studied, is now a Hollywood agent with a reputation for being a cutthroat negotiator. These are the tidbits that are the most fascinating—the people whose lives have turned out so differently from what Kate or her friends might have imagined, revealing, perhaps, just how little they had understood one another. Still, they had all known one another when they were young, and this would always tie them together.

It's after midnight. Vanessa has finished an entire bottle of wine by herself. She lies on the couch, eyes half-lidded, her feet on Kate's lap. Kate would not have pegged Vanessa as the one who would spend most of the weekend drunk. *Maybe this is what motherhood does to you.* The thought, naturally, is troubling.

Dani is sitting on the rug with her back against the ottoman, absentmindedly stroking Gracie, who is stretched on her side in a deep sleep, her exposed ear twitching whenever the breeze picks up. "Peaceful Easy Feeling" is playing on the stereo, as it has a hundred times before. Kate feels a mix of excitement and contentment—the unlikely combination of feelings she only experiences when she is with Dani and Vanessa.

"I can't imagine what they say about me," Dani says without looking up.

"Who?" Kate asks.

"Heather O'Donnell and Matt Gordon, when they're sitting around gossiping about the people they used to know." Dani's hand still rests on Gracie, but she's no longer petting her. "The conversation probably goes something like, 'Kate Harrington? She's a hotshot lawyer at some big firm in Philly. Vanessa Dale? She married the son of Thomas Warren; they live in Manhattan and have a daughter. Dani Lowenstein? Huh. No idea what happened to her.'"

"You just defined me by the man I married and the fact that I have a daughter," Vanessa says. She's speaking slowly, staring at the ceiling and blinking.

Kate is still surprised that Vanessa gave up her job at the gallery when she had Lucy. It's clear she struggles with the decision, and Kate wishes she would talk about it. She's empathetic—she doesn't know who she would be without her job either. She loves working, possibly to an embarrassing degree. When she was still in law school, she and Vanessa would call each other and talk about their days as they walked back to their respective apartments. Vanessa always sounded a little out of breath and excited on those walks home from the gallery; these days she sounds tired, but her voice has a softer quality too. Kate would never tell her friend this, but the excitement in Vanessa's voice as she strode down the streets of New York had made Kate feel a little sad. Vanessa had a new home. She was never coming back to Philly.

"I don't think she's *defining* us," Kate tells Vanessa.

"It *is* a definition, actually," Dani says. Dani has made jokes about her own life choices over the years, but Kate has never heard her sound so melancholy. She finally turns around to face them on the couch. "People sum you up in a sentence, two if you're really interesting. It's the two-cent, gossip version of the whole picture. A dictionary entry versus an encyclopedia. I'm not telling you guys anything you don't know."

"Well, it's up to the listener to know the value

of being a mom," Kate says to Vanessa. "*We* know what an important job it is. You're raising a little girl. What could possibly mean more?" Vanessa shrugs and closes her eyes. Kate turns to Dani. "And you. What's going on with you? You're a California girl. You're writing a novel. You're living the dream. *That's* what people say." Kate thinks for a moment. "Anyway, since when do any of us have to be the brightest star? If you're content in your life, then who cares that no one is sitting around talking about what a genius you turned out to be?"

Dani looks up at her, shaking her head, smiling. "Kate," she says, "you have always been the best therapist money can't buy." Just then, Vanessa releases a soft snore. Kate and Dani laugh.

"You know, I really don't think it would hurt anything to call that Gabe guy," Dani says. "Just for fun."

It's what everyone seems to want from her—to loosen up, to have fun, to not think so much about the future. She just wants them to be happy, and if this is what it takes, she'll do it. "Okay," she says. "I'll call him."

Dani looks surprised. "Are you delirious? Should we go to bed? You're up pretty late for a pregnant lady."

Listening to the Eagles, talking in the rambling way that only time away from the demands of everyday adult life allows, feels like a gift. It makes Kate sad to think of the summers that have come and gone over the past eight years without their meeting up in Avalon for this time together.

"Music is good for babies," Kate says.

For a moment she sees a glimmer of the love Dani feels for her shining in her eyes. It's like the sun peeking out from between clouds, a flash of soul-fortifying warmth, and Kate basks in it. She wishes she could bottle this feeling, take it home in a doggie bag and feast on it later.

"Well, then, we should turn it up," Dani says, pointing the remote in the direction of the stereo. "For the baby."

14

Vanessa

Vanessa stirs, awake but barely. She is wearing the clothes she wore the night before and is stretched out on her stomach, lying diagonally across the queen-size bed. She only vaguely remembers Kate shaking her awake last night, stumbling down the stairs to bed. The room is now full of sun. She wants nothing more than to continue sleeping. If this were a typical Sunday morning in New York, this would be the moment when she would hear Lucy's voice through the monitor. But here, there is only the sound of birds outside the window. Vanessa is so relieved she could cry. She pulls the covers over her head and sinks back into a deep sleep.

An hour later, her phone buzzes. It's Drew.

"Morning," he says.

Vanessa squints. The room is painted a pale shade of yellow. On the wall by the closet are a series of framed photographs of the sun setting over the wetlands. They're schmaltzy, sentimental, and poorly composed; she guesses they were shot by Suz. She hates them. It gives her some satisfaction that Dr. Lowenstein hung them down here in a guest bedroom. He must hate them too, but now he's stuck with them. They're part of the Suz package—the hot sex will only last so long, but the bad photography and huge pink hats are here to stay. She doesn't like to think what else might change around this beautiful house as Susanna makes her mark.

"Hi," she says to her husband. "How's Lucy?"

"Happy as a clam," Drew says. "She went down the slide about eighty times yesterday. She was playing with another little girl. Emma, I think. They seemed to know each other."

Vanessa remembers this little girl and her mother, a willowy woman of ambiguous ethnicity who wears camel-colored sheath dresses and patent leather flats to the park, her hair glossy around her face. Exactly the sort of woman Vanessa would have said was Drew's type, back when she thought she knew his type—back when she thought *she* was his type.

"I'm glad she's having fun," she says. "I miss

her." Why does she sound whiny? Vanessa clears her throat. "Kate is pregnant."

"You're kidding!"

"She's having the baby. On her own." Part of her feels sorry for Kate but, selfishly, she is excited about the possibility of Kate becoming a mother. None of Vanessa's premarriage friends have children yet and most of the mothers she meets in New York are a decade older; it's hard for her to connect with these women, some of whom have built and sold entire companies before having children and say things like, *When I'm on my deathbed, I won't wish I had spent more time at work.* Now she'll have a friend with whom she can speak honestly.

"Wow. How is she doing?"

"She seems okay. I can't believe she's known for weeks and hasn't told me. She might be in denial."

"Well, I guess she has nine months to get used to the idea."

"It takes a lot longer than that," Vanessa says. "It's not just being pregnant. It's her whole life. Everything is going to be different from now on."

The edge in her voice is obvious, but Drew does not acknowledge it. They didn't used to be like this. They used to address the emotional undercurrents of their interactions, call each other out on their occasional sharp tone, and rehash the turns their conversations had taken, pinpointing the places where they had misunderstood each other or hurt each other's feelings. They used to *talk*. Vanessa knows she has pushed them to this point. But he started it.

"Just assure Kate that every once in a while, even in the midst of being a mother, you get a free pass to go away for a long weekend with your best friends and be young again," Drew says. "Everyone gets a break."

These are the things she loves about Drew: he has a habit of circling Vanessa's wrist with his fingers and pulling her toward him to kiss her shoulder when she walks by; he bought an expensive camera the month before their daughter was born and has taken, literally, thousands of surprisingly wonderful photographs of their daughter; he gestures like an Italian when he speaks; he admires strength and beauty, and this makes Vanessa feel strong and beautiful; he has impeccable manners, not the least of which is always refilling everyone else's wineglass before his own; he washes his hands the moment he walks through the door at night because he has an intense fear of bringing germs into their home; he is so handsome that women's eyes are drawn to him when he strides down the street; he loves to travel; he speaks as easily and genuinely with cab drivers as he does with their elderly neighbor, her father, his fraternity brothers from Columbia, and the president of his network; he is himself in every environment, a feat that indicates a bottomless pool of confidence and is deeply, irresistibly sexy. All things considered, it is a long list. But there are times when Vanessa also hates some of these things.

She wants to tell Drew that there is no such thing as a break when you are a mother. And if she needs a break from anything, it's not motherhood, it's *them*, but the shards of their relationship are lodged so deep that she carries them everywhere. She wants to tell him that she hears Lenora on the phone with them, her breath on the line like the phantom roar of the ocean in a conch shell. But they've rehashed this all so many times. What more can he do? He's told her he loves her. He's told her the "indiscretion" was a mistake. He's told Vanessa that he believes in their marriage and he wants to be with her. It's Vanessa's turn now, but she doesn't know what to say. She thinks of Colin, of Jeremy, of all of the paths her life could have taken but didn't. It used to be so easy for her to walk away. Vanessa can't believe she has grown up to be a wife whose husband kissed another woman, a mother who does not know what she wants.

When she finally gets out of bed, Vanessa finds a note from Kate on the counter telling her to

meet them at the beach, and to remember to shut
the screen door behind her when she leaves. She
loads the coffee filter and then sits on the kitchen
floor and pets Gracie while she waits for the coffee to brew. The breeze off the ocean is warm and
she tries to enjoy these moments of dripping coffee and the sweet rise and fall of Gracie's belly
as she breathes, but she has never been a person
who handles waiting well. When a few ounces of
coffee have filled the pot, she pours them over ice
in a glass, sits back on the floor, and drinks. Once
the pot fills again, she adds more ice to her glass
and refills it. This time, she adds two heaping
spoonfuls of sugar. *What the hell,* she thinks. *I'm
on vacation.* She takes the coffee downstairs and
gulps it while she puts on her bikini and a gauzy
olive-green tunic. She looks around the room for
ten minutes before remembering that her sandals
are in the living room. This leisurely pace and the
quiet house make her miss the constant company
of Lucy and at the same time luxuriate in being
alone.

Outside, the heat envelops her. Delicate fila-
ments of cloud thread the cerulean sky along the
coast. She heads down the sandy path that cuts
through the dunes and scans the beach for Kate
and Dani. She remembers how she used to look
for Colin too—the thrill she would get when she
finally spotted him.

In the weeks and months following Colin's death, no one questioned Vanessa about her relationship with him. She broke up with Jeremy and returned to New York, ignoring Jeremy's calls and e-mails. She never told him that she'd been swimming with Colin the night he died, or that the reason she broke up with him was that she was sure Colin's death would cast a shadow over their relationship. She never told anyone else that she'd dated Colin; Jeremy was the only one who knew.

The fact that Colin is no longer alive still throws Vanessa off balance, like the time she was bodysurfing in sixth grade and was pulled into the tumbling curl of a wave and for long, panicky seconds could not figure out which way was up and which way was down. She feels certain that had she not fallen in love with Jeremy, Colin would never have set fire to that lifeguard stand. He would never have been distraught and heartbroken and taken all those drugs. He would be, if not here in Avalon with them right now, then *somewhere* in the world. Alive.

Vanessa watches a pair of beach taggers scan the beach for their next target. They are every beach tag girl in the history of Avalon: tan, bored, unsmiling blondes in tiny shorts. The taggers sit at the entrances to the busier beach blocks and wander through the sand of the less crowded ones. Beach tagging had been a popular summer job, but it had always sounded terrible to Vanessa and her friends. It turned sitting on the beach into a requirement—by the end of the summer, those girls inevitably looked like they wanted to be anywhere but Avalon.

"Did you talk to Drew?" Kate asks as Vanessa unfolds her beach chair. "You must miss Lucy."

Vanessa is about to say something about how nice it is to carry a bag filled with her own things, instead of one brimming with diapers and sippy cups, how nice it is to move at her own pace rather than that of a toddler, but she stops herself. Who wants to hear a mother vent about the trials and tribulations of being a parent? Certainly not the pregnant and the childless. Part of the problem with becoming a mother is that Vanessa feels she has lost what little voice she had; mommy talk is welcome only in such small, specific venues. "I miss Lucy, but I think it's good that I'm getting a little space from Drew," she says, thinking of the anger that had flared within her when Drew implied during their phone conversation that it only takes nine months to adjust to being a mother.

"Do you want to talk about it?" Kate asks.

No, she thinks. But she does. She tells them that Drew and Lenora kissed at the holiday party after months of what Drew referred to as "mild flirtation." She tells them that she has gone to nearly every work function Drew has invited her to since. That she feels if she stays with Drew, she is going to spend the rest of her life trailing him, peering around corners for Lenora Haysbach and the women with the potential to be the *next* Lenora Haysbach. That she cannot see herself doing this, but she also cannot see how she could not.

"No wonder you had a drink with Jeremy Caldwell," Dani says.

Vanessa considers telling them that Jeremy is here now, somewhere on the island, but decides against it.

"How was seeing him again?" Kate asks.

"He's still really good looking."

"So, what?" Kate asks. "You want to kiss him? Even the playing field?"

"I'm not sure," Vanessa says. "That's the problem, I guess."

"Maybe the biggest problem isn't whether or not you want to kiss Jeremy," Kate says, studying her, "but that you're still madly in love with Drew."

Vanessa rolls her eyes at Kate's use of the idiom "madly in love," but she has to admit her choice of words hits close to home. She used to be "in love" and now she's *"madly* in love." This, it seems to her, is a downgrade.

"That's not a problem," Dani says. "If she loves

Drew, problem solved. All he did was kiss someone else. They didn't sleep together."

"Stop saying that," Kate says. "She trusted him.
She put her faith in him. It doesn't make her situation any better if she still loves him."

"Do you?" Dani asks, turning to her. "Do you
still love him?"

Vanessa thinks about how nervous she had
been to introduce Drew to her parents when she
first started dating him. Drew bought his shirts
from a boutique in Nolita; Vanessa's father had
worn the same two suits for twenty years. How
would Drew respond if her mother offered him
one of the pot brownies she indulged in to ease
the pain in her (allegedly) arthritic knee? When
Vanessa finally worked up the courage to bring
Drew home, she had looked around the rooms
where she'd spent so much of her childhood
and felt embarrassed by the clutter, the lack of
restraint, the way the smell of strange, sharp
spices—or, really, who knew what?—lingered
in the air. She spent several long minutes in the
bathroom trying to catch her breath. When she returned to the living room, she found Drew cheer-
fully sipping her father's bitter home-brewed beer
as if it were Dom Pérignon and regaling her parents with a story about how, as a kid, he'd not only
dug up but had *named* the worms for the compost
bin at his parents' house in Connecticut—a story

Vanessa was sure she had never heard before. Her father—accustomed to a house full of girls—had looked so pleased that Vanessa had feared he was on the verge of mussing Drew's hair.

"He's still the person I married," Vanessa says. The problem might be, she realizes, that she is not sure he would say the same about her.

Kate falls asleep reclining in her beach chair, her mouth hanging open. Vanessa envies her. She has not slept that easily, without an ounce of wine in her, since she was pregnant with Lucy. Her own eyelids feel heavy, but she's never been a napper. It is probably for the best. You only feel groggier after napping on the beach, with newly tender, crisped skin below your eyes or behind your knees or on the thin skin of your chest.

A toddler sitting in the sand near them begins to shriek. He throws his body around and stomps his feet, such quintessential toddler moves that they seem like an imitation, or performance art.

The little boy's mother stands next to him with her hands on her hips, frustration pouring off her in waves. "If you cry one more minute, we are going home," she snaps. "The beach is supposed to be fun!"

Vanessa and Dani look at each other and laugh. The mother shoots them a dirty look.

"Sorry," Vanessa says quickly, "it's just—"

"Words to live by!" Dani says.

Vanessa laughs again and the mother turns away. She considers telling the woman that she has her own tantrum-prone toddler at home, she's been in her shoes, but then decides she doesn't feel like it.

"I'm going to head to the library," Dani says.

It occurs to Vanessa that Dani did not have a single glass of wine the previous night. What is it about being in Avalon with Vanessa and Kate that is making her stick to a resolution that Vanessa can only imagine she has broken countless times over the course of her twenties?

"Say hello to Hemingway," she says, and wonders if Dr. Lowenstein's engagement might open Dani to the possibility of love.

It is nearing one o'clock, and Kate is still sleeping. Vanessa rises from her chair, pulls on her green tunic, slings her beach bag over her shoulder, and begins to walk toward the pier. Shells crunch below her feet on the hard, wet sand. Admitting that she still loves Drew makes her feel defeated. The thought of forgiving him feels akin to resigning herself to a life of jealousy, of not being loved, but not forgiving him seems equally unbearable. If Lucy weren't in the picture, this would be less complicated, but she does not even want to linger on the thought of Lucy not being in the picture—a life without Lucy is not a life at all. If she and Drew were to divorce, her daughter would spend some time with her father, away from her, and the fact of this—not being able to read Lucy her bedtime story, to comfort her when she is sad—is unfathomable.

She wishes she knew whether kissing Jeremy Caldwell would help heal her, or break her heart anew.

At the pier, there are a few surfers in the water but the waves are small and round, rolling more than curling. One of the surfers is lying on his back on his board; he might be asleep. It's quiet in the shade under the pier and the sand is cool and damp under her feet; the air smells briny; barnacles dot the pylons like thorns on rose stems. Eight years earlier, Jeremy kissed her under this pier. She can still feel his lips against hers, the way he used to trace her jawline with his thumb.

She pulls her phone from her bag. *How about tomorrow night?* she texts Jeremy and then stands in the shade another minute before walking back toward Kate. She wonders what might have happened between her and Jeremy if that summer had ended differently. If Colin hadn't died and Vanessa hadn't broken up with Jeremy out of guilt and fear, would Avalon have become *their* place? The place where Jeremy proposed? The place where they watched their children and grandchildren experience summer, jumping the waves and playing skeeball and wearing bathing suits from the moment they rolled out of bed until the moment they rolled back in, glowing with happy, sunbaked exhaustion?

She can see this life, and she can see Jeremy, but she still can't, no matter how hard she tries, see herself.

15

Dani

Dani decides to walk to the library. She's not one for exercise, but the chill of San Francisco still hasn't melted entirely and her body craves warmth. She can feel her fingers quivering in the pockets of her shorts. One or two of those Oxy-Contin pills hidden in her luggage would steady her, but she is trying not to think about them. She's amazed by how hard it is to not think of them once she starts—she feels as if one is lodged in her throat, a phantom pill.

Ironically, it was Colin who had given her her first taste of prescription drugs. Ritalin. They had crushed a few pills and snorted them before Friends Meeting during their senior year at PFS. It was a terrible idea, snorting a stimulant before enforced sedentary silence. They had sat side by side, their fingers drumming the cushion on the long wood meeting bench until Dani couldn't stand the silence anymore and rushed out of the auditorium, pushing aside the knees of her seated classmates. She's never much cared about making a scene.

It does not even cross your mind to say no to the drugs people offer you when you are young and the future seems limitless. It is still easy to say yes when you are no longer young but you do not care about your job and you are not in a relationship and you are nowhere near your father or closest friends. A part of her has known that she has been running away from home, hoping the farther she gets, the less she will think about Colin and the opportunities she has wasted. But it's only now, walking to the Avalon library with her fingers trembling in the pockets of her shorts, that it occurs to her she might also have been running toward addiction. Without anyone who cares about her around, she has been free to destroy herself.

I'm too smart for this, she thinks. And: *I used to be fearless.*

Vanessa used to be fearless too—with her bold outfits and that way she walked the halls of PFS as if she owned the place, that quiet way she had of looking around as if she were sizing everything up and finding it all lacking. She was catnip for boys. They couldn't resist her and she crushed them, one by one, a trail of broken hearts through high school and college. Something important seems missing in Vanessa now; the old Vanessa would not have had such a tough time deciding whether to break away from or forge ahead with her marriage. Then again, the old Vanessa would have been the one doing the inappropriate hallway groping.

Kate was never fearless, not really. That summer before their senior year of college, when Seth, a meathead lifeguard who had flirted lazily with Kate for weeks, teasing her in a way that had never sat right with Dani, ended up hooking up with another girl right in front of her, Kate had slipped out of the party and run back to the bungalow without saying a word to anyone. Dani and Vanessa had found her sobbing on her bed. If it were up to Kate, she would have cried herself to sleep and that would have been the end of it, but Vanessa was hell-bent on revenge, and Dani liked nothing more than strategic mischief. The next day, they went to Sylvester's Fish Market and convinced Kate to buy the biggest, stinkiest fish there. They left Pepé, as Dani had dubbed the fish, on the bungalow's sunny front stoop all day where, as intended, he became significantly more pungent. Later, under the cover of darkness, the three of them sneaked up to Seth's Jeep Wrangler.

"Go ahead," Dani whispered.

Kate's eyes had widened. "Me? I can't!"

"Yes, you can!" Dani and Vanessa had said together, but Kate's fingers were trembling too much to even remove the fish wrapper. She'd looked relieved when Dani had grabbed the package from her, swiftly unwrapped the fish, and wedged him under the backseat of Seth's car. With Pepé ensconced in his new resting place, they all took off in a sprint, so close on one another's heels that when they burst into the bungalow they fell into a pile on the floor, gasping for breath, laughing so hard that tears streamed down their faces.

Now it seems to Dani that Kate has probably turned out to be the bravest of the bunch.

Dani recognizes that her friends are going through difficult times, and she sees that they're each going through these difficulties alone. She wants to help them, but would they want her support if they knew the truth? She has stayed away for years, not wanting to know the answer.

When she gets to the library, she opens her laptop but is immediately stuck.

She has been trying to write this scene—the scene between the party on the beach and the boy floating in the bay—since college. She presses her laptop shut and asks the librarian—Joyce again, as purse lipped and scoop haired as the day before—to keep an eye on it while she steps outside. A sweating can of Diet Coke is anchoring her hands when Sam cruises into the parking lot.

"Nice bike," she says as he leans over to lock it to the rack near the handicap ramp.

"Thanks," he says. "My students tease me about it, but what's the point of living on an island if you're going to drive a car everywhere?"

"You must freeze in the winter."

"I make exceptions," he says, stretching out his hand. "I'm Sam."

"I know. You're Joyce's boyfriend."

He laughs. "I don't usually fall for septuagenarians, but—"

"You make exceptions," Dani finishes. He is not her type, but he is the sort of handsome that transcends type. It disappoints her to learn that she, like the rest of the world, is attracted to a symmetrical face. No wonder passion fizzles, she thinks, foreseeing their end before they even begin.

"I'm Dani," she says.

"Nice to meet you, Dani."

Vanessa once told her that when a man repeats your name, it's because he likes you. Notably, in college Vanessa had a string of boyfriends that she referred to only by names like Mr. Vanilla Latte and Trader Joe and Sports Jacket Guy. Dani had finally told her to knock it off; just because she lived in New York didn't mean she was, or should aspire to become, a character on *Sex and the City*.

"Are you headed in or out?" Sam asks, pulling open the door to the library.

She looks up at him, squinting, trying to determine if her fingers have stopped trembling enough to release the can of soda. "In," she says, deciding, and passes through the open door.

Sam sets his laptop across from hers. At this close range, he looks nothing like Happy Hemingway; he looks like a Sam. She asks him what it is like to live in Avalon year-round, and he tells her it's quiet but beautiful—the island returns more to its island-ness with each passing month. She knows exactly what he means. Dani can tell there is a reason Sam is here; he is running away from something or toward something and she wonders if it is a woman.

"What about you?" he asks. "Where are you from?"

She tells him she is from Philly but lived in San Francisco until she lost her job a month earlier and was forced to give up her apartment. This news is incredibly easy to tell a stranger. She thinks of her own parents meeting, envisioning for the first time how simple it must have been for them to fall in love, to believe that the few things they had in common were enough to last a lifetime. She wonders when she and Sam will have sex, and when they will stop being able to stand each other's company. These two events seem as linked as bookends—the only thing that is unclear is the length of space between them.

"Where did you work?" Sam asks.

"In a bookstore."

He spreads his arms wide and holds up his palms as if he is about to make a great pronouncement. "I love books," he says in a funny booming voice that causes Joyce to stare at them and frown.

Dani laughs. This sudden glint of Sam's inner weirdness intrigues her. "That makes two of us," she says. "But, let's be honest, books are easy to love. They don't hog the bed or bug you for Valentine's Day presents or buy the most expensive thing on the menu."

"Or complain about your taste in music."

"Oh, Sam. Were you a little too country for an ex-girlfriend?"

He grins. "A little too rock and roll."

"With so much crossover music these days, it's a shame you couldn't make it work."

"Well, moving to Avalon didn't help." Sam shuts his laptop, and with it any pretense of working. "Are you just here for the weekend?" he asks.

"I'm not sure," she says. She has been wondering the same thing. Can she really see herself living with her father and Suz? Even if she can, she realizes he might not give her the option. "I was planning on staying with my dad in Philly, but he just told me he's getting married to some woman he'd never even mentioned before. Now I don't know what I'll do." She surprises herself with this admission. Is it Sam or her aching head that is making her behave like this? She looks down at her hands. They have, for the moment, stopped trembling. Still, she does not feel like herself.

Sam offers a sympathetic grimace. "I'm sorry."

"It is what it is. What about you? What brought you to Avalon?"

"My mom retired here after my dad died ten years ago," he tells her. "And then, a couple of years ago, she got sick and I moved here to help her. She passed away last winter."

"Oh, I'm sorry."

"Thanks." He looks past her shoulder for a moment before meeting her gaze again. Then he shrugs. "I was a horrible son for a solid decade. Kept her up nights. I was *that* teenager."

Colin, Dani thinks. Is this a version of who he might have become? A teacher? A good son?

"Will you stay?" she asks.

"I'm committed to teach another year. After that, I might take some time to travel and just see where I land."

He is looking at her in a way that tells Dani he is imagining what it would be like to bring someone like her on this adventure. She pictures him with a tour book and a backpack, drinking a pint in a pub, writing postcards to former students with Avalon addresses, and wonders how long it would take for him to decide she is toxic.

"Thanks for not telling me I'm an asshole," she says.

"You're welcome," he says, laughing. "Why exactly would I say that?"

"Oh, you know, here I am complaining about my father falling in love—" *and your parents are dead*.

Sam smiles. "That doesn't make you an asshole. You're never too old to fear an evil stepmother."

"She doesn't seem that evil, actually," Dani admits.

"Oh. Then maybe you *are* an asshole."

"At least I'm up front about it."

"I appreciate the warning."

"Shhh!" Joyce hisses from the desk. Dani and Sam smile at each other. He opens his laptop again.

Dani looks down at her own computer. She thinks about Sam starting over here, becoming a caretaker, a beloved teacher. She wonders if she would be a good teacher and decides she would. She understands teenagers; she's never forgotten what it's like to be one, to be full of adult desires and still under the thumb of your parents, at the physical and emotional mercy of their whims, shaped by things over which you have no control. She tries to envision herself standing in front of a class and wonders if it is possible to speak with authority without sounding like a prick. Sam, it seems clear to her, is not a prick.

"What are you working on?" he whispers.

"I'm trying to finish a novel."

He raises his eyebrows. "How long have you been writing it?"

People usually ask what the novel is about, so his question takes her by surprise. There is a lot, actually, that is surprising about this afternoon. This feeling she is feeling as she looks at Sam is a surprise. "Eight years," she says.

"That's a long time to think about one story."

"Yes," Dani says, studying him. "It is."

She spends the afternoon writing the missing scene of her book. She has gone over the events of that day so many times in her mind that once she actually starts writing, the words come quickly. As she writes, she realizes that one of the many reasons she has put off writing this scene for so long is that she'd always assumed it would be cathartic to voice the truth, to give the events of that weekend when Colin died structure and syntax and a vocabulary of meaning, and she had not been ready for catharsis. She didn't think she deserved it—the possibility of healing. But now she realizes she'd been wrong to think this process held the possibility of catharsis—she feels no better as she writes the final words than she did when she started this book all those years ago.

Still, it's done, and this is something. She sends the pages to the library's printer and listens as the machine churns to life.

16

⌒⌒⌒⌒⌒

Kate

Kate can't believe she agreed to this. Is it Avalon that makes her do things she wouldn't normally do? Is it being with Vanessa and Dani? She hopes she isn't doing it to seem cool. This possibility turns something inside of her and makes the whole night feel off from the start.

She walks down the beach to the spot where she and Gabe planned to meet—far enough from Dani's father's house that Dani and Vanessa won't be able to watch from the deck unless they dig out the binoculars, which Kate wouldn't put past them. Gracie bounds ahead of her. Technically, dogs aren't allowed on the beach, but Kate figures it's okay now that the sun is setting. Tomorrow night, on the Fourth of July, there will be more people on the beach at this hour, but tonight, Sunday, it is nearly empty.

Gracie is licking Gabe's face when Kate catches up with her and has already made a mess of the striped towels he had laid out. A paper shopping bag is on its side.

"Gracie!" Kate says. Gracie knocks Gabe's sunglasses off his face with her tongue. "*Gracie!*"

Gabe laughs and grabs his glasses before Gracie can crush them. "Hi," he says, standing. He leans toward Kate and kisses her cheek. By the time they look down, Gracie has licked an entire plate clean. Who knew what it had held—Gracie would eat anything, right down to the plasticware.

"Oh no," Kate says. She grabs Gracie's collar and tries unsuccessfully to get her to sit. "I'm so sorry. She's normally pretty well behaved, but she has this thing with food. It turns her into a wild woman." Kate can't believe she is back here, introducing another man to her dog. She remembers when Peter met Gracie for the first time. The three of them had gone for a walk and Gracie had basically scrabbled down the entire length of the sidewalk in a crouch, releasing a stream of unpick-upable diarrhea, a deeply apologetic look on her face. Kate had been so embarrassed that she was actually rendered speechless. But Peter, it turned out, was unflappable, making a small joke about securing some chicken-liver-flavored Pepto-Bismol and then kindly ignoring the situation.

"Are you a wild woman?" Gabe asks Gracie, ruffling the fur on her head. Her thick tail whips at the air. "Are you a crazy, wild woman?" In the midst of this petting, Gracie suddenly freezes, nose quivering, and then takes off, sand flying, toward a flock of tiny gray birds that skitter like windup toys along the edge of the water. "She's awesome," Gabe says. "And don't worry, there's more food in the bag."

Kate steps out of her flip-flops and sits cross-legged on the towels, glad she wore her cute white jeans and not a dress. She rests her hands on her knees but they look strangely pale and limp, so she moves them. Gabe opens a bottle of wine. He fills a plastic cup for Kate and she pretends to take a sip before setting it on the sand.

"What a night," Gabe says, leaning back on his palms. The wet swath of sand left by the receding tide glows beneath the setting sun. There's a slight breeze off the ocean that stirs Kate's hair, lifting it from her neck. Down the beach, a middle-aged couple sits side by side in chairs, reading books. A few walkers dot the coastline. Gracie races around, kicking up sand and barking into the breeze, wearing what can only be described as a shit-eating grin.

"She's happy," Kate says, laughing. Gabe laughs too. He passes her a small container of olives, and she relaxes a little. Anyone who could watch Gracie's display of joy and not laugh is someone Kate does not want to know.

"I'm happy too," Gabe says. "Thanks for joining me."

She turns to face him, maneuvering an olive in her fingertips, scraping the meat from the pit with her front teeth. It is salty and oily and she already knows she will end up eating the entire container, weird dried basil leaf and all. "So what's your deal?" she asks.

"My deal?"

"Why aren't you at some house party right now, tapping a keg with your buddies? Or buying shots for college girls at the Princeton?" These questions come out more aggressively than she'd intended, but she is suddenly feeling very nothing-to-lose about this whole situation.

"Because I'm with you," Gabe responds. He does not seem fazed by her dovetailed questions or her tone. He's smiling at her with an easy set to his shoulders and a cheerful look in his blue eyes. After a beat of time, he adds, "Also, I'm not really into crowds."

This answer satisfies her. She wonders if she has caught him before anyone he loves has died, before he has made any life-changing mistakes. She breathes in this possibility, his brightness, his kindness and optimism.

"Would you prefer water?" he asks. Kate follows his gaze down to her untouched cup of wine. She looks back at him.

"Yes," she says. "I would."

Vanessa and Dani were the ones who had summer flings. Back then, Kate desperately wanted to join their ranks, but those sorts of romances had never materialized for her. The boys who liked her were serious and almost uniformly short; they spent their summers on anthropology digs or at science camps, not in Avalon. She never had her friends' aptitude for feigning indifference. They were aloof and unpredictable, and guys flocked to them—continue to flock to them. Kate was always trying too hard. It would never strike her as anything less than supremely unfair that men faulted women for trying.

The last time she was on the beach in Avalon after the sun had set was at that party eight years earlier. The night had felt magical to Kate. The sky was velvety black, pricked by countless stars. The air was warm and sweet, the sand cool. She was with her best friends and her brother in the place she loved most in the world. They were on the cusp of everything changing. Soon, they would head back to college for their senior year—well,

Kate and Dani and Vanessa would, at least; they would begin to think seriously about their futures. That summer—that night, even—seemed like the last time Kate was allowed to think only of the present. Even before she knew that summer was the end of something, she sensed it. She was exhilarated and she wound up drunk. And then Dani told that story about Kate hiding in the dryer when the cops came to break up the party, and Colin had looked right at her and laughed. *Live a little*, Dani had sniped, lighting up a joint that she knew Kate would refuse to smoke. Vanessa had wandered away with Jeremy, not even attempting to defend her. If Kate had been a little less drunk, if that night had felt a little less magical, a little less monumental, if Colin wasn't always telling her to loosen up . . .

These are all excuses. She did what she did and no one told her to do it. She did it.

Gracie is still leaping and racing, barking at nothing, running into the water and then out again. *What would it be like to gallop through the world with such openhearted joy?* Sometimes Kate finds herself living vicariously through her dog.

And so when Gabe leans in to kiss her, she does not pull away. He puts one hand behind her head and the other on her shoulder and they kiss for a long time. Kate feels herself drawn toward him, into him. She is not thinking of anything but that moment, the feel of Gabe's lips against hers, the pressure of his fingers entwined with her hair.

The cold water makes her eyes snap open. Gracie is shaking her fur, a long head-to-toe shimmy, splattering Kate's white jeans with dark, wet sand. "Gracie!" Kate shrieks, leaping to her feet. Maybe it is that the perfect kiss has been ruined, or maybe it is being on the beach in Avalon after the sun has set, or maybe it is simply that she has eaten too many olives, or maybe it is—and it surely *is*—the fact that she is pregnant, but all of a sudden she feels certain she is going to be sick. She turns and heaves but all that comes out is a pitiful retching sound. She clamps her hand over mouth, but doesn't turn back to face Gabe. She's never been more humiliated in her entire life.

"Kate!" she hears him say. "Are you okay?"

She stumbles a few feet away, holding her stomach. She misses her orderly apartment in Philadelphia. She misses the life she had a month ago, a full, busy life that in all but its darkest moments kept her safe from the sharp ache of her memories, the truth about what she did to her brother.

"I'm sorry," she says, turning back to face Gabe. He is standing in the middle of the beach towels with his head cocked to the side, his brow furrowed and his body tense, like a dog that has been asked to stay. "I'm so sorry. I really do like you. But I'm pregnant." She turns and begins to run down the beach toward the house. Gracie leaps ahead of her, barking so loudly that Kate can't hear if Gabe calls her name.

By the time she climbs the steps to the upper deck, she is out of breath and crying so hard that her eyes already feel swollen. Vanessa and Dani are lounging on chaises and spring to their feet when they see her.

"What happened?" Vanessa asks. She guides Kate to a chaise and sits down beside her. Dani drops to her other side.

"He kissed me," Kate says. Her breathing is ragged, her words punctuated by a hiccup.

"Quelle horreur!" Dani breathes, smiling.

"It's not funny, Dani!" Kate says. "I'm pregnant!"

Dani looks at her, her expression softening. "I'm sorry," she says. She wraps her arm around Kate. "I'm sorry," she says again.

Gracie stretches out at Kate's feet and sighs. She smells of the sea. Kate can feel Vanessa and Dani exchanging a glance behind her head. "I should never have gone out with him," she says, hardly realizing she is saying the words out loud. Her mind is turning.

"We thought it would help you stop thinking about Peter," Vanessa says. "That's the point of this whole trip, isn't it?"

Kate looks out at the ocean. Colin had always loved swimming at night. Why was that? What was it about the dark water that had appealed to him? Had they always been so different? From the moment they were born? She takes a deep breath.

"There are other reasons why I wanted to come here," she says.

Vanessa and Dani are silent, but Kate can feel how her words make their bodies tense.

She lays her right hand on her belly. She imagines her guilt as a poisonous cloud, stunting the baby's growth. Colin is everywhere here, just as she had known he would be. She had known all along.

"I set that fire," she says. "At the party on the beach the weekend Colin died."

There is leaden silence, and then Vanessa says, "What are you talking about?"

"I was so drunk and I thought, why not? I wanted to be reckless for once. It seemed like my last chance." Kate's eyes are pegged on Gracie. "I wanted to do something stupid and wild and not think about the consequences. At least, I think that's what I was thinking. I was so drunk."

"Colin set the lifeguard stand on fire," Vanessa says. Her voice is strained. Kate looks at her.

"No, he didn't. I did." She tells them how she had sat with Colin's friend Tony on the lifeguard stand. Maybe he had egged her on, maybe she was

trying to impress him. She was drunk and it had
been so hard not to admit to Tony that she had a
crush on him. She didn't remember much more
than holding a lighter up to some cardboard.
How had she burned an entire lifeguard stand? It
seems an impossible feat. But she had. Colin ran
up, saw the lighter in Kate's hand and tried to kick
sand on the fire. But he was too late; the lifeguard
stand was burning, crackling, sending smoke into
the night sky. Kate was mesmerized. After long
minutes spent watching Colin throw sand on the
fire, Kate had finally snapped out of it and joined
him. They heard sirens in the distance; someone
in one of the beachfront homes must have seen the
smoke and called 911. Tony ran off into the dunes,
yelling for them to do the same.

"Get out of here, Kate!" Colin said. She didn't
see her friends anywhere. They both started running, but when Kate finally slowed down, all the
way out on Dune Drive, Colin wasn't beside her.

The next morning, when she woke in her bed,
she was confused. The events of the night were
hazy. For a moment, seeing Colin arrive at the
bungalow with his citation in hand, she thought
he had actually done it and was furious with him
before she remembered. *She* set the fire. It was a
stupid prank and it would change everything.

"Colin didn't want me to get in trouble," Kate
tells Vanessa and Dani. They're sitting completely

still on either side of her; Dani's hand is no longer on Kate's shoulder. "He said I had so much to lose, and he had nothing. So I let him take the blame. I was so selfish and I just let him. I didn't even put up a fight." Her face is wet with tears. "He must have thought I didn't have any faith in him. He must have thought I believed him when he said he didn't have a future. I was his sister and I didn't even stand up for him."

Vanessa is crying now too, one hand covering her mouth. She looks stunned. Kate feels a rush of shame.

"You've been keeping this secret all this time?" Dani asks. Her skin is sallow below her tan, but her brown eyes are dry. "Why?"

"Because," she breathes, "I know what letting Colin take the blame did to him. He was getting better, he was smoking less, he seemed happier. He was going to get his life on track, and I let him do something that set him back again. I pushed him. And then he took those drugs and he swam out into the bay and he died." She begins to sob. "I hate myself for doing that to him."

"Kate, it wasn't your fault," Dani says.

"It was," Kate says. "Don't you understand? It was *my fault*." This is the truth. She spent her whole childhood trying not to make a big mistake that would change the direction of her life, and then in one drunken summer night she'd done it anyway. Except it wasn't her life she had destroyed—it was her brother's. Her twin brother, who was the opposite of her in so many ways, and whom she had loved in such an over-whelming, deeply complicated way that at times it feels like the great love of her life. There are stories about twins who feel each other's pain across continents, who know the exact moment the other breaks a bone. Kate and Colin hadn't had that. But there was *something* between them, an invisible thread that Kate sometimes thinks had also tied her to the world and kept her from feeling adrift. And then she broke it.

She was the one who called her parents and told them Colin had died. She would never forget the sound of her mother's grief, the way it crashed through the phone, causing Kate to shiver in a way she would not be able to quell for weeks. Later, when the police told her parents about the fire on the beach, Kate could see that her parents did not consider the incident an important piece of the puzzle of Colin's death—it was low on Colin's rap sheet, a harmless prank. To her great, enduring shame, Kate never told them the truth. She would now though. She would go home and tell them, and Peter too.

"Maybe I'm being punished," she says. Her throat feels stripped raw. "Peter leaving, the baby—"

"The baby isn't punishment," Vanessa says.

"*None* of it is punishment," Dani says. "Don't say that."

"I'm sick of not saying it. I *need* to say it. I think about Colin every day. What I did to him. What I could have done differently. I feel like everything changed that summer and I can't find my way back."

"I think about that too," Dani says. Kate realizes Dani's hands are trembling.

"I do too," Vanessa says.

Still, her friends look shocked. They are horrified by what Kate has told them, and she wonders if they will ever understand, let alone forgive her.

It gets worse the next morning. Dani smiles weakly when Kate sits on the high stool beside her at the kitchen counter. The circles under Dani's eyes have deepened and her hair has the sheen of grease.

"Are you sick?" Kate asks. She doesn't feel so well herself. She can't believe Dani and Vanessa now know her secret. Also, there is a person growing inside of her, sapping away her energy. She can't quite wrap her mind around this. The night before, they'd each gone to bed early. Kate had thought there was no chance she would be able to sleep, she was still wound too tightly, but she'd dropped into unconsciousness like a stone into water.

"No," Dani says, but her voice is gravelly. "Just tired," she adds, clearing her throat.

"Oh," Kate says. She's having trouble reading Dani's mood. The air between them feels dense, and she has the urge to cut through the silence by repeating her admission from the night before: *I set the fire and I let Colin take the blame and he died the next day.* If she says this to someone every day for the rest of her life, will she feel better? She imagines herself telling strangers as she walks the city streets with Gracie, telling her clients, telling her parents—what will her parents say? She realizes she is more worried about what her friends are feeling; her parents, she knows, will never stop being her parents. But will Dani and Vanessa be her friends now that they know the truth? They loved Colin too. This is part of the reason she has always loved them: because they loved Colin.

Kate lifts a heaping spoonful of cereal to her lips. "Vanessa's still sleeping?" she asks, chewing.

Dani nods and then slides off the stool. She walks across the room and out onto the deck without another word. Kate watches her, stunned. Vanessa is the one who deals in silence, not Dani. She realizes that she had certain expectations about how her friends would process the news that she was responsible for her brother's death. She knew they would be shocked and then angry. She knew Vanessa would take a significant length of time to warm to her again—she tended to become cool when she felt betrayed. And she'd expected Dani, who had always been so close with Colin, to be vocal with her fury. Dani lashed out when she was hurt; she didn't retreat. This quiet, cut only by the metallic scrape of the screen door opening and shutting as Dani walks out onto the deck, frightens Kate. She slides off the stool and follows Dani outside.

At first, the deck looks empty. Then she sees that Dani is standing at the corner near the street. It's a strange place to stand. Her arms are crossed and her brow is furrowed.

"I understand why you're angry with me," Kate begins, but Dani's eyes widen and she lifts her finger to her lips. She mouths something. Kate hurries over.

"Jeremy Caldwell is downstairs," Dani whispers.

"Here?" Kate begins to say, but Dani shushes her. *With Vanessa?* Kate mouths.

Dani nods, pointing directly below her to indicate that they are on the lower deck. Kate and Dani look at each other, lips pressed shut, and listen.

"—didn't want to wait until tonight," Jeremy is saying.

"You were always so impatient," Vanessa responds. Even though Kate is surprised that Jeremy has suddenly appeared, she takes a moment to jot a note in her *This Is How to Flirt* mental folder.

"And you weren't? You would shut off the coffeepot halfway through brewing a cup just so you could start drinking it, and then you would turn the pot back on to brew the rest."

"I still do that," Vanessa says, laughing.

"Patience is overrated."

"Jeremy—" Vanessa says and then her voice falls off.

Kate can hear them moving and wishes she could see them better. She can only catch glimpses of them through the wooden deck slats. How far apart are they? Are they sitting? Are they touching? She wants to run downstairs and stand between them, stretch her arms out wide so they can't get near each other. She doesn't think she can sit back and listen as Vanessa makes this mistake.

"I had to see you," Jeremy is saying. "I know how that sounds. I hate when clichés really do express how you feel. It makes this seem so ordinary, like it's happened a thousand times before to a thousand other people."

"It has," Vanessa says. Kate is heartened by this; Vanessa hates being ordinary.

And then Jeremy says, "Tell me you haven't thought about what would have happened to us if Colin hadn't died."

Kate feels that spinning sensation building within her, drawing the oxygen from her lungs. Dani looks at her.

"Of course I have," Vanessa says.

"I know you felt terrible. You tried to make things better by breaking up with me, but that was so many years ago. Please tell me that all this time has at least brought you some clarity. We didn't do that to him. He was already messed up, anyone could see that. You didn't do anything wrong."

"I did," Vanessa responds. Her voice is so clear that it is as if she is standing beside Kate and Dani, looking directly into their eyes and saying the words. When she replays this conversation in her head later, Kate will remember that in this moment it seemed the entire island went unnaturally quiet: the breeze died and the dune grass stilled, the ocean seemed to retreat, no birds flew overhead. "Colin loved me and I broke his heart."

Kate breathes in sharply. Dani reaches out and grabs her elbow. They stand there together, hearing everything.

17

Vanessa

"People don't die of broken hearts," Jeremy is saying. He is, finally, angry. He had been upset when Vanessa broke up with him in the days after Colin died eight years earlier, but he had not seemed angry. This anger has built over the intervening years. The restraint he'd demonstrated at Breslin Bar, that simmering heat, has changed. Something has provoked him and he can't mask his feelings for her.

Vanessa realizes how strange, how serious, it feels to be with Jeremy in broad daylight, without even a cocktail as subterfuge. This should make their meeting feel less underhanded, but somehow it does the opposite. The shaded lower deck, nestled against the foliage of the dunes, hidden from the blunt beauty of the beach and the glare of the sun, feels built for clandestine conversations, but Vanessa wishes she had walked Jeremy out to the beach, farther from the house. His sudden arrival—hours earlier than their planned meeting—had thrown her off; she had not had time to prepare herself.

"Anyway," Jeremy says, "I'm really not here to talk about Colin."

It doesn't matter if you talk about him; Colin is always with us.

"You loved me, didn't you?" he asks.

"Yes," Vanessa says. "You know I did."

"We were great together."

"We were."

There are two Adirondack chairs on the deck, but they are standing and Vanessa knows this is because they want to be closer to each other than the chairs will allow. There seem to be two conversations happening at the same time—the one that is taking place out in the open, and the one that is taking place within the chemistry between them. Jeremy's eyes are dark and glittering in the shade, and she is shocked by the strength of her urge to pull him toward her. Her desire is a slippery thing; just when she thinks she has it under control, she feels its whispered breath in her ear, asking her if she remembers how it feels to press her hands against his smooth, tan back, to kiss the soft lobe of his ear. She blinks and realizes he is looking at her expectantly.

"I asked if you were happy," Jeremy says quietly. "I really need to know."

She feels steady in his gaze; she feels, she realizes, like herself. *This must have been how Drew felt when Lenora looked at him.* She does not want to empathize with Drew, but she understands the temptation now—the temptation of the emotions of another life, another age, emotions they'd agreed to trade in for something else, something they thought might last.

She does not know the answer to Jeremy's question. He looks at her, interpreting her silence, and all the while the pull between their bodies is working its magic, its pure and beautiful science. He reaches out and traces her jawline with his thumb, and it feels exactly the way she remembers it felt when she was twenty-one years old. Her pulse quickens. She closes her eyes and inhales deeply, taking in the hot summer scent of his skin.

There is something building inside of her so suddenly that it takes her a moment to realize that it is a feeling of control. She feels powerful, dizzy, and clearheaded all at once. The feeling takes her breath away.

I am not going to do this.

She opens her eyes. She puts her hands on Jeremy's chest and pushes, gently but firmly.

"I'm sorry," she says. Even as she hears herself echoing the words her husband used when he pulled away from Lenora, she knows she means them; she doesn't want to hurt Jeremy again. She has been so careless with others' hearts. "I'm married. I'm a mother."

"Vanessa," Jeremy says, gazing at her. "You're more than that."

Of course I am. And: *I am not.*

"It's not too late for us," Jeremy says. "I know you think it is, but it's not. We can pick up where we left off."

That, Vanessa thinks, *is the last place I want to be.* She thinks of how devastated she felt after Colin died, losing first him and then Dani, how her friendship with Kate wilted in the heat of everything else.

"Jeremy, there's something you don't know about that weekend—something I've never told anyone. I wasn't with you the entire night that Colin died. That's what we told the police, but it wasn't true."

Jeremy is full of tells; his eyes flicker over her as she speaks. She had forgotten this about him. It's disorienting to consider all of the things she has forgotten about that summer; it had felt indelible, but some pieces are lost forever.

"I went back to the bay where we saw Colin swimming earlier in the night and he was still there," she says. "I swam out to him and told him that I was in love with you. I yelled at him for starting that fire—which, it turns out, he didn't even do." For a moment, Vanessa loses her train of thought. Kate's confession still shocks her. It clicks everything she thought she understood about that weekend a notch out of place, like changing the code of a safe. "I told Colin that I loved you," Vanessa continues, her heart hammering in her ears, "and then I swam back—"

Above, there is a stampede of feet. Vanessa's stomach twists. Kate races down the stairs from the upper deck. Dani is close behind her.

"What are you saying?" Kate is yelling. She looks as if she's been slapped—pink circles burn on her cheeks. "What are you *saying*? You left him out there to die?"

Vanessa's mind races. All these years, she has kept this information from Kate and for a moment she begins devising ways to backtrack. Then she takes a breath, sees the fierce set of Kate's face, and understands there is nothing to think about, it's too late. Kate has already heard everything.

"Oh, Kate," she says. She holds out one of her hands though she has no idea why; she doesn't expect her friend to take it. "Colin and I dated that spring before he died. We didn't tell you because we knew you'd be upset. I should never have dated him. Or kept it from you. I—"

"You left him out there?" Kate asks again, interrupting her. "You were swimming with him and then you left him?" Her fingers are clenched in fists at her sides. Vanessa has seen her like this only once before.

"Maybe you should sit down," Dani says, putting her hand on Kate's shoulder.

Kate spins toward Dani. "Did you know?"

Dani glances at Vanessa. "No. I thought there was something between them, but I didn't know for sure. I didn't know she was with him that night."

"I cared about him," Vanessa says. She's still trying to paint a whole picture for Kate; she's clinging desperately to the hope that context will keep Kate from hating her. "I really did. I had a crush on him for years. We started seeing each other that spring. He would visit me in New York—"

"You left him out there!" Kate says again. All she wants to hear about is the night in the bay.

Vanessa begins to cry and once she starts she does not know how she will ever stop. "I met Jeremy and I fell in love with him. I let myself get swept away."

All three women look at Jeremy. He is standing at Vanessa's side, his face stiff with a mix of discomfort and sympathy.

"You can't help who you love," he says quietly, looking at Vanessa.

Dani narrows her eyes. "Yes, you can."

Vanessa isn't sure whom she believes.

"So you decided to break this news to my brother once he had swallowed a bunch of pills and was swimming in the bay in the middle of the night? The night after he'd spent the night in a holding cell?" Kate's voice is weirdly high, but somehow, she has not shed a single tear.

"I didn't know about the pills, Kate. Please believe me. I thought he had smoked some pot. I had no idea how far gone he was. I think about that night every single day. In my head, I stay with him until we both get out of the water and walk home together. I refuse to leave until he gets out. I stand on the dock and wait for him. Why didn't I do that? Why didn't it even occur to me that something bad could happen? All I had to do was one simple thing and he would be alive." She's gesturing around her and when she stops speaking, her hands fall to her sides.

Kate's lips are pressed so tightly together they have paled. Vanessa's legs feel boneless. Jeremy is at her elbow, steadying her. She turns to him.

"I'm so sorry, Jeremy. I should have explained everything to you. You didn't deserve to be treated the way I treated you. I just—I couldn't be with you after Colin died. I was in too much pain, and I felt like our relationship could never be the same again. I couldn't see you and not think of what I did to Colin." She swallows. "And now I'm married. I have a family."

Jeremy's shoulders sag. "Okay," he says. He gazes at her for a moment and then wraps his arms around her, pressing his cheek against the top of her head. "Okay," he says again. He holds her tightly, and Vanessa takes a deep breath in his arms. All of these men she has loved, she has really loved them all. "Good-bye, Vanessa," Jeremy says softly, looking down at her one last time before releasing her. He steps off the deck and disappears around the corner of the house. Vanessa hears his car door shut, the engine turning, tires crunching against the sand-blown road. He is gone, and Vanessa knows she might not ever see him again.

It's just the three of them now, a wary, wavering triangle.

Kate takes a long, ragged breath. Her eyes are still puffy from her crying jag the night before; the blue in them is vibrant. "What was the last thing Colin said to you?" she asks.

Vanessa does not have to consider this for even an instant; their final conversation has replayed in her mind thousands of times. " 'Go,' " she says.

Kate thinks about this for a moment and then says, "I feel as if I never really knew either of you." Her mouth twists to the side and she bites into her lip, holding in a sob. "You or Colin. I don't understand how you could have kept this from me."

"You knew us better than anyone," Vanessa says, but she would feel the same way in Kate's shoes—embarrassed and enraged that she had been left in the dark. She had done this to her friend, a woman who never betrayed her in all the years they had known each other. "I was afraid you would be mad at me for being with him. I thought if I could keep being with Colin a secret, I could be with him and keep our friendship the same too. What should I have done?"

"You should have dated someone else," Dani says. It's the first time she has addressed Vanessa. She sounds like a dampened version of herself, as if she's speaking through one of the cup-and-string contraptions they used to hang between the decks.

This is what Dani had done, Vanessa knows. She had loved Colin too and she had buried her feelings. "Is that what you would have wanted?" Vanessa asks Kate.

Kate sniffs. She's no longer really listening. "You left Colin out there in the bay," she says, staring at the dunes. "You just left him there."

Looking at Kate's unfocused blue eyes, Vanessa sees Colin that night in the bay, the numb look on his face as he sank below the cold, black water. Yes, she'd left him out there. "Kate," she says. "I am so sorry." She's ready to plead for forgiveness, to lay her head in Kate's lap.

Kate doesn't even look at her. "I need to lie down," she says. She turns and walks back up the stairs.

Dani looks as if she is about to walk away too. "I owe you a huge apology, Dani," Vanessa says, reaching out to stop her from leaving. "That fight we had—those things I said—I was feeling so awful. I wanted to blame someone else, and I lashed out at you." Even before there was an official cause of death, Vanessa thought that drugs had made Colin lose consciousness in the water. When the police showed up on their doorstep, she'd realized immediately what she hadn't understood when she was swimming with him—Colin had been more than just a little stoned, he'd been *really* high. He'd been with Dani most of the afternoon and when Vanessa pieced this together, she screamed at Dani, sure they'd been doing drugs. She yelled at Dani, unfairly, when she knew Colin had never needed any help finding drugs, when she was the one who'd actually been out there in the bay with him—*she* was the one who could have saved him.

"Jeremy is the reason you came here this weekend, isn't he?" Dani asks. It's as though she hasn't heard a word Vanessa has said. "You came here to see him."

"Dani," Vanessa says. She doesn't know how to answer. "There are so many reasons I came."

Dani shakes her head. She is so disgusted she looks physically ill. She turns and climbs the stairs without another word.

Alone, Vanessa sinks down into an Adirondack chair. She wipes her face. In the silence, the hard chair neither comfortable nor uncomfortable beneath her, she tries to slow her breathing. Her thoughts twist and expand.

She and Kate and Dani used to do gymnastics down here in their bathing suits after a day on the beach. They would try to pace their cartwheels perfectly down the length of the deck—if their hands hit the far edge of the deck halfway through the final cartwheel, they could spring off it and land on the small patch of grass that separated the deck from the hydrangea bed. Vanessa remembers spinning through the air, hoping her hands would land in the right place, that surprising swell of momentum over the edge of the deck, the squishy thud when her feet landed in the grass. They could do this for hours—the spinning, the landing, the laughing. Eventually Dr. Lowenstein would call them upstairs to shuck corn or to sprinkle salt on thick slices of tomato or to set the table. They'd eat out on the deck, lighting citronella candles to deter the bugs, and sometimes Dr. Lowenstein would surprise them with a key lime pie from the produce market on Ocean or bowls of strawberries set on mounds of Cool Whip—a strange and delightful confection that Vanessa's own mother would never have kept in the house and that Vanessa was sure her childhood would not have been complete without.

Vanessa had bought Cool Whip on a whim after spotting it at the market near their New York apartment a few weeks earlier. She and Drew and Lucy had sat out on the balcony and dunked strawberries right into the tub again and again until they'd worked their way through half of it. Lucy, perched on a chair in her little yellow dress, had smacked her lips after each bite, hopped up on happiness and sugar. Drew had propped open the door to the condo, and the Desmond Dekker song playing on the stereo had poured outside. Because they were in front of Lucy, Vanessa had let Drew spin her around the small balcony, making her dizzy, transporting her through time.

At least Drew had told her what happened with Lenora. Vanessa had never had the courage to tell Kate what she did to Colin. Kate had to overhear the news. Her friendship with Kate was a kind of covenant too, and Vanessa had broken it. Though these betrayals are not linked, she asks herself if forgiveness might be one act providing the momentum for another, the possibility, but not the promise, of a soft landing at the end.

18

Dani

Dani hopes a walk on the beach will soothe her pounding head. She wears her dark sunglasses and Susanna's ridiculous pink hat and a long black T-shirt over her bikini and jogs barefoot over the hot sand until her feet sink into the wet sand at the water's edge. She has a book in her hand, not because she thinks she'll actually read it, but because just carrying it might make her feel better. She has never felt so raw in her entire life; she feels as if all of the nerve endings in her body are exposed, crackling at the slightest hint of contact. Her mind is rife with metaphors, searching for a way to give words to what is happening to her. One drink would be enough to calm her. Just one tiny pill would be plenty. When she tries to summon the hope she felt when she was talking with Sam yesterday, she cannot. It's the Fourth of July and the library is closed. She walks until she is shin-deep in the ocean and then turns and keeps walking along the coast, the cold water slapping at her skin.

Even from the water, she can hear laughter hanging in the air. Some of the older beach-goers have stuck small American flags into the sand beside their raised beach chairs. A group of guys are drinking cans of Bud Light and shielding their Wawa hoagies from the huge seagulls that hover above and peer down with aggressive glints in their beady eyes. She knows how those seagulls feel. Her mouth is so dry. *Water, water everywhere, nor any drop to drink.*

She'd always known there was a spark between Colin and Vanessa, a different version of the one that existed between Colin and herself, the one she smothered into platonic submission. Those sparks were only natural. No matter how long or how well you knew a boy, no matter if he was the brother of your best friend, if you were a heterosexual teenage girl, you were going to feel a spark with a rebellious, good-looking boy. The question was only what you did with that spark. Did you fan it, letting it grow and gather heat? Or did you extinguish it, knowing just how it all would end if you did not?

Now that Dani understands the timing of Vanessa's relationship with Colin, she is furious. She knows how Vanessa operated back then, making a boy the center of her universe right up until the moment someone else caught her eye. Dani is a little ashamed to realize this trait is something she used to admire in Vanessa, before she realized Vanessa had set her hooks into the heart of someone who actually mattered to her.

She sits in the shade under the pier for a long time trying to read her book, but her mind won't allow her to slip away.

It's clear now that this weekend is a disaster. This doesn't feel like much of a shock. Maybe these years of wandering the country, losing herself in anything and everything, have been building to this—the final disintegration of a friendship that had been wavering on the point of collapse all that time. Kate had set that fire and let Colin take the blame. Vanessa had broken Colin's heart and left him alone in the bay, in a drugged-out stupor, in the middle of the night. Dani is surprised and confused by these revelations—all these years, she'd thought she was alone in her guilt. It's hard for her to process this news, to reframe the story she has told herself about that weekend. Their confessions don't make her feel any better about what she did—if anything, on top of everything else, she now feels to blame for the guilt that has weighed on her friends all these years. Their confessions are small compared to the truth she has been carrying.

From the moment she enters the house hours later, Dani senses that something is wrong. Her feet are still wet from rinsing them in the outside shower and she nearly slips when she pulls open the sliding door to the living room. She steps inside and stops short.

Kate is standing in the middle of the room as if she's been waiting. Gracie sits beside her, her tail wagging slowly; she looks as confused as Dani feels by the energy in the room. Then Dani sees. Kate is holding her manuscript, the one Dani printed out at the library yesterday. Dani tries to remain calm as her mind races.

"You gave him the drugs," Kate says.

"It's fiction, Kate," she says, knotting her hands together. "It's a novel."

"It is not! These people have different names but they are *us*."

Vanessa appears at the top of the stairs. "What are you talking about?" she asks, looking back and forth between them.

"Dani gave Colin the drugs he took the night he died," Kate says without taking her eyes off Dani. "It's in her book."

Vanessa looks at Dani. "So I was right?" she asks, her eyes wide.

Dani's head hurts so badly that she feels herself wincing. She remembers the afternoon she and Colin spent drinking at the Princeton as if it were yesterday. It was when they'd biked back to the bungalow that Dani showed him the pills. A guy she'd met in one of her creative writing classes at Brown had sent them to her a week earlier; apparently she gave off the vibe that alprazolam was the way to her heart. She and Colin each took one, swallowing them right on the steps of the bungalow. Dani looked at the bag and then at Colin. "Why don't you take them home?" she'd told him, handing him the bag. There were at least ten pills left. "You and your buddies in Philly will get more use out of them than I will here with Kate and Vanessa." Colin had shoved the bag into his pocket, and Dani didn't think about it again—not even when she woke up on the bungalow's couch much later and realized the television was still on but Colin was no longer beside her. She thought he must have gone out to meet friends. It was only the next morning when the police showed up on the doorstep and held out Colin's soggy citation that she remembered giving him those pills. Handing over that bag had felt like such a small, uncomplicated act; as it turned out, it was the defining moment of her life, the moment when everything changed.

She never told anyone about those pills. Somehow, Vanessa was the only one who had guessed the truth. Even the therapist she'd seen briefly when she got back to Brown had never put the pieces together, handing Dani her first prescription as though she were giving her blessing.

"You were right," Dani tells Vanessa. She crosses her arms and presses her fingers hard into the hollow spaces between her ribs. The pain centers her a little, but not much.

Kate's face twists.

"Kate—" Dani begins, but Kate shakes her head sharply and Dani falls silent.

Kate turns to face Vanessa. "You knew?" The words hang in the air for a moment.

"No," Vanessa says. "But I thought, maybe. It's what we fought about after Colin died. She denied it and made me feel horrible." She looks at Dani, her face tight with anger. "All these years, I've felt guilty for accusing you of something so terrible. You've been acting pissed off at me for eight years, and the whole time I was right. You made me feel awful, as if I didn't deserve your friendship."

"I was in shock," Dani says. Her eyes are so dry they sting. "And I was afraid. I gave him those drugs—"

"How could you?" Kate asks. Her voice trembles with grief. "You were supposed to look out for him. You were supposed to be his friend!"

"I didn't know he was going to take them all. I didn't know he was going to go swimming in the middle of the night," Dani says. Her excuses are halfhearted. She doesn't believe in her innocence any more than they do. "I thought he was mad at himself for setting that fire. I thought I understood him. I thought I could help cheer him up."

"With a truckload of pills?" Vanessa asks. "That was your remedy?"

It was idiotic. Dani knows this. She'd thought she was so much older than her twenty-one years; she'd thought they were all invincible. The word "sorry" is like a penny dropped into a fountain; it's far too small to represent her wish. "I will regret that day for the rest of my life," she says, and "I'm so sorry," because she needs to say the words—needs her friends to hear them—even if they are inadequate. "I wish I could go back and do that whole weekend over." When neither Kate nor Vanessa will meet her gaze, she closes her eyes.

"Kate, you have to know that Dani loved Colin," Vanessa says, and Dani opens her eyes to look at her. "But she would never act on it. She's a better friend than I am. She's loyal. You and Colin were her family."

You were my family too, Dani thinks, but the look in Vanessa's eyes tells her she's too angry to hear these words. She is not absolving Dani; she is trying to make Kate feel better.

Is Vanessa right? Was she in love with Colin? She felt differently about him than she has about any other guy before or since. Was that love? How do you know what love is? Is it the way she feels for her father, the emotion she is careful to keep in check in case it pushes him away? Is it the way she still occasionally longs for her mother, a woman who clearly does not long for her, whose daily silence is daily rejection? The solid, unchangeable feeling she has for Kate and Vanessa? She wishes there were a test—a love breathalyzer. She wishes she could explain that she writes about her friends so that she can remember what it is to know someone in the huge, encompassing way she once knew them—and what it is to be known and loved in return. She has been punishing herself with this story, but maybe she has also been saving herself with it. She has been holding her friends and this place in her heart all this time, even when she has been far away and alone.

None of this matters. Kate will never forgive her. Dani gave Colin the drugs that made him lose consciousness and drown when he was twenty-one years old. Dani won't ever forgive herself either.

She hates herself for feeling a wave of self-pity, but there it is, crushing her. She looks at Kate, wishing she would say something, but Kate has sunk down into the couch and is cradling her head in her hands. Vanessa still stands at the top of stairs. Dani can tell she wants to comfort Kate, but there is tension between all of them, the room hums with it. No one is trying to comfort Dani. Of course they're not. If their friendship was fractured before, now Dani has delivered the final blow. A clean break.

Kate has felt guilty about that fire for years, and yet she still managed to create a life for herself—she has a job, a best friend, and, soon, a baby. Vanessa, too, who has clearly never forgiven herself for leaving Colin alone in the bay, has a family, a life. Soon they'll both be mothers, adults, and Dani will still be Dani—fucked up and fancy-free. She's losing her father to a woman named Suz. She doesn't have a home, or a job, or friends. She doesn't even have her health, which she has pushed to its limit.

Those pills. Her heart hits a bump and then picks up speed.

She walks over to the couch and puts her hand on Kate's shoulder. She's embarrassed by how frail it looks there, before Kate shakes it away.

Dani turns. She stops next to Vanessa for a moment at the top of the stairs. Vanessa looks pale, as though she is holding her breath until Dani passes. Dani heads down the stairs.

In her room, she pauses for a moment. It's still light outside, but there are a few pops of firecrackers, practice rounds for the evening's celebrations. The sound sends a jolt through Dani. She hears Gracie's nails scrabbling against the hardwood upstairs. All over the island, people are celebrating. She can't remember the last time she felt truly lighthearted; it's the ghost of a feeling now, flitting through her thoughts, slipping through her grasp, the memory of a dream not even from yesterday, but from years ago.

She crosses the room and digs through her duffel bag until she finds what she is looking for. The pills are weightless in her hand. *This* feeling, the weight of pills in her hand, she remembers.

19

Kate

Gracie has wedged herself under the coffee table. She looks up at Kate with a furrowed brow. She hates loud noises. Thunderstorms make her curl into a tight ball. In Philly, a motorcycle once backfired beside them and Gracie had been so frightened that she'd reared back out of her collar and taken off in a blind, hunted sprint. Kate had chased her down the sidewalk, watching her dart around strangers and barrel toward the busy intersection ahead. At the last moment, a man in a suit had reached out and grabbed Gracie by the scruff of her neck, making her yelp.

Why hadn't any of them reached out a hand to stop Colin?

"Do you want to be alone?" Vanessa asks.

Kate shrugs but the answer to this question has

always been the same and Vanessa knows it. She sinks into the couch beside Kate.

"I'm so sorry," she says. "I need you to know that I love you and I never meant to hurt you. Colin and I . . ." Vanessa trails off and sighs. "I should have told you. And I was an idiot for not realizing he could get hurt out in the bay that night."

Kate rests her head on the couch cushion and stares at the ceiling. Dani gave Colin the drugs he took the night he died; Vanessa went swimming with Colin that night and left him there. She is enraged, devastated, heartbroken. A part of her doesn't even want to try to stop these feelings from building; she wants to take the lid off and let the foamy, furious heat of her emotions spill out over everything. But another part of her is already feeling it dissipate. In the end, what is it worth, being so angry about the mistakes they've all made? A day that goes by without letting the people she loves know that she loves them feels like a waste to her, a gross and dangerous game. She does not understand how her friends do not already know this about her, how they could have kept these secrets from her for so many years.

"What happened to us?" she asks, turning her head toward Vanessa. "We used to be there for each other."

Vanessa's face softens. "It's not too late," she says. Kate shivers. There is a prickling sensation traveling up her spine. She straightens, glancing over her shoulder at the staircase. "Do you think Dani is okay?" she asks.

"No," Vanessa says. Then she looks more closely at Kate's face and seems to understand what she is asking. She leaps to her feet at the same moment Kate does and in an instant they are rushing down the stairs, Gracie scrambling to catch up behind them.

Downstairs, the doors of all three bedrooms are ajar, but the bathroom door is shut. Kate flings it open.

Dani is standing by the sink. She spins around. Her face is pale and taut. "Holy fuck," she says. "You scared me."

"What are you doing?" Kate demands. Dani's hands are balled into fists at her sides and before Kate even realizes what she is doing, she grabs them, wrenching Dani toward her. Dani spreads her fingers wide. Her hands are empty; her fingers tremble. Dani squeezes them back into fists and Kate releases her.

"Dani," Vanessa says, her voice strangled. "You have to tell us. What did you do? Did you take something?"

"No," Dani says. She gestures toward the toilet. Green pills are floating on the surface of the water. While they watch, Dani flushes the toilet and they are gone.

Kate turns and throws her arms around Dani. "I'm not going to let you go," she says.

Dani is silent for a moment. "Okay," she says then. Kate squeezes her until she releases a half laugh, half sigh, a sound of surrender and relief.

"I lost my job," Dani tells them. They're sitting under the umbrella on the upper deck. Even in the shade, it's a scorching hot afternoon, but Dani has a beach towel wrapped around her shoulders. "Well, to be explicit, I was fired. It's the one thing I seem to be getting better and better at."

"What do you mean?" Vanessa asks.

"I've been fired twelve times since I graduated from college."

"Oh, Dani," Kate says. All these years she's been worried about Dani, but she's never said anything. Why hasn't she said anything?

"Don't pity me," Dani says, not sounding at all like herself. It's clear that she is embarrassed—Dani, whom Kate had always thought was somehow incapable of embarrassment or self-consciousness, who always seemed so secure in who she was and where she was going. Twelve jobs in seven years. The thought alone sends a panicked tremor through Kate.

"I can't help it," Kate admits. "I feel terrible for you. I always thought you were on some amazing adventure."

"Well, I was, in a way. It depends on your definition of amazing. Unbelievable? Yes. It's hard to believe I've been fucking up for seven years straight. I've been asleep."

"I don't believe that," Vanessa says. "You've been living the way you want to live. You've been chasing your dream. What more is there than that?"

Kate watches as Dani and Vanessa lock eyes. For a moment, Dani looks almost wistful. Then she shakes her head. "That's whitewashing. I've been hiding. I haven't done the work it takes to claim I've been chasing my dream."

"We're only twenty-nine," Kate says. "Everyone says your thirties are when you come into your own." She'll be a cheerleader for the people she loves until the day she dies.

"It's okay," Dani continues. "I mean, it's not, but it is. I've tapped out my bank account so I was going to move home, but I'm pretty sure Mrs. Suz Lowenstein will not be psyched about me crashing in her love nest."

"You can stay with me," Kate says.

Dani looks at her. Something flickers across her face; it's gone before Kate can interpret it. "I think I'm going to stay down here for a while," she says. "It turns out cities aren't so great for me right now."

"But you'll be all alone," Kate says. She's worried about this plan. The fact that Dani does not trust herself with those pills in her luggage—the fact that she had those pills in the first place—shows Kate that things are much worse than she had ever guessed. She decides that when she gets back to Philadelphia, she will invite Dr. Lowenstein to coffee and tell him that she is worried about his daughter. Dani might be mad at her for this, but she would rather lose Dani's friendship than lose Dani. Dani might never know why her father will suddenly begin calling her more, checking in with her at odd hours, why he wants to spend his weekends with her in Avalon even after Labor Day has come and gone. She might just think it's because her father loves her, and this, of course, will be a version of the truth.

"I'm okay with being alone," Dani says, but there is the slightest tremble in her voice when she says this, so slight that most would not even notice it. Kate and Vanessa exchange a glance. The glance does not go unnoticed by Dani. "If it doesn't work out, I'll come to Philly," she promises. "We can be roommates again."

They had shared a room in the bungalow that summer before their senior year of college, Dani on the top bunk, yelling, "Dear God, please shut up!" when Kate wouldn't stop talking and shaking the bed frame with her laughter when they heard Vanessa and Jeremy Caldwell making out so loudly their noises could be heard over the drone of the enormous box fan. Even Kate didn't really care whose towel was whose and they sat on beach chairs on the pile of rocks in front of the house when they were too lazy to go to the beach, and they fought about whose turn it was to clean the toilet. Someone was always passed out on the scratchy plaid sofa, and sometimes that person was Colin. His hair would be matted in the morning and one side of his face would be red and raw as if he'd been in a fight, or contracted a rash. "The sofungus is spreading," Dani would say, and Colin's laugh would crack open the bungalow and the sun would pour in.

They're all silent for a moment, remembering.

"Let me ask you something," Vanessa says, turning to Dani. "Do you think you wanted us to find your manuscript?"

Dani looks surprised. "No."

"But you want to get it published, right?" Kate asks. "So you knew we were going to read it someday."

"Someday."

"I don't want to be in your book," Vanessa says. Kate can tell she has been thinking about this for a while. "Not that you would bother to ask my permission."

"Oh, don't worry, V," Dani says. "There is no book. I'm done with that. I'm going to start something new. I don't think it was a book, anyway, it was . . . a way to punish myself, reliving that summer and what I did over and over again."

Kate envisions her twin brother's death as a lever pulled, sending them each hurtling down a different track. "The book is beautiful," she says. "I didn't read the whole thing and I hated what I did read, but it's beautiful."

Dani laughs. "*Ankthadavaka ouyadavaka*. It will be my book-in-a-drawer. Every writer needs one."

"You're ready for a new chapter," Vanessa says. She is clearly relieved.

"To turn the page," Kate says, straightening.

"To close the book." This is Vanessa again.

"Yukity yuk yuk," Dani says. "You two are hilarious."

Later, Kate walks inside with Gracie on her heels. She is careful to shut the screen door behind them. The house is cool. Downstairs, she sits on the bed in the room she thinks of as her own. She hears Gracie lapping the water in the toilet down the hall.

"Gracie!" she yells. Gracie trots into the bedroom looking not in the least sheepish, not even when she knocks into the bowl of fresh water on the floor and sends the water in it sloshing over the side. "Take a load off," Kate says. Gracie flops down, her big tongue hanging out the side of her mouth, and looks up at Kate expectantly.

"Okay," Kate says. "Here we go." She takes a deep breath and dials Peter's number. She has no idea where he is right now, a fact she is surprised to find only slightly bothersome.

He picks up after one ring. "Hi, Kate," he says.

"Hey," she says.

"How are you?"

At the sound of his voice, Kate feels a fluttering sensation in her stomach. She does not know if it's the baby or something else. It could be any number of things—love or regret or fear or hope.

"I'm okay," she says. "I'm in Avalon with Vanessa and Dani."

"Oh, Kate—" Peter begins, but Kate interrupts him.

"No, really, I'm okay," she says again. Peter knows that Avalon is where Colin died, and that her panic attacks began soon after that summer, but he does not know the details that make the story complete—as it turns out, she'd hardly known them herself.

"Good," Peter says. "I'm glad you're okay." He hesitates. "I miss you. I know I shouldn't say that. It's not constructive."

As she listens to him, Kate thinks that if he had not broken up with her, she would have been happy with him for the rest of her life. But she is going to be happy without him, too, because she will insist on it, because, despite everything, she is a happy person. Kate realizes this knowledge has been buried in her this whole time, a seed awaiting sun.

"I miss you too," she says. "That's normal, right? You don't just flip that off like a light switch. I don't know. Vanessa thinks there's some sort of half-life equation to breakups; it takes half the length of the relationship to fully get over someone. But if you ask me, it's pretty clear Vanessa's own situation proves that equation doesn't work. She still isn't totally over someone she dated for like a month eight years ago."

"But she's married," Peter says.

"Apparently, marriage doesn't make preexisting problems go away. Shocking, I know."

Peter laughs. "What are you guys doing tonight? For the Fourth?"

"I don't know."

"Really?" Peter sounds startled. "No plans?"

Is this momentous? Kate wonders. Maybe it is. "Nope," she says. She can feel something shifting between them. "So," she says. "I-have-to-tell-you-something-I'm-pregnant-eight-weeks-pregnant-and-I'm-keeping-it." She says this in one long rush.

"What? Kate. *What?* You're pregnant?" He does this repeating thing when he's thrown off guard.

"You're pregnant?" he asks again, this time louder. Listening to him ask all these questions, even the same ones over and over, Kate can't help it, she's smiling.

"I'm pregnant."

"You're *pregnant*."

"Yes."

"Wow. Okay. I—I'm speechless, honestly. I'm. Well. Wow. How are you feeling?"

Kate knows he is searching for the right thing to say, that saying the right thing is important to him. "Oh, I'm fine. A little tired. A little, you know, *pregnant*. But I want you to understand that I don't think this changes anything. I mean, it changes some things, of course, but it doesn't need to change everything. You can be as involved as you want to be. I'm sure you want some time to think about that." She means everything she says and yet, at the same time, it feels as if she is reading dialogue intended for a live studio audience.

"Right. But, well," Peter says, "I'd like to see you when you get back so we can talk about this in person."

"Oh, of course. I'm sorry I delivered the news over the phone. I finally worked up the nerve to tell you and I wanted to do it before I lost it again."

"I understand," Peter says. "Wow. A baby." And then, after a pause, he says, "I really meant it when I said I missed you."

Kate hesitates, gauging her reaction to his words. It feels as if so much has changed since she sat on the couch and listened to him break up with her. She thinks of that kiss with Gabe on the beach, the deep swimming-pool blue of his eyes. The secrets her friends have revealed to her, the confession she made about the fire. Things would be different between the three of them now. Better. They can't change what happened; they can only move forward. Peter is the one who prompted these changes, he is the one who encouraged her to talk about what happened to Colin, to take that risk. She wants to tell Peter that she took his advice, that she faced the truth about the past and that he was right, it did help her. She wants to tell him about the fire. But there's time. It suddenly doesn't seem important to say everything right now. There is time. They'd be in each other's lives forever now, one way or another.

"We'll talk about everything when I get back to the city," she says. "Face-to-face."

After Kate hangs up, she slides down to the floor and sits close to Gracie. Her forever person is out there somewhere, and he might be Peter. But who knows, really? There is so much you cannot plan. Still, she can't help it: she has a sudden vision of herself lying on the couch, a newborn baby asleep on her chest and Gracie stretched out nearby. She thinks of weekends spent pushing a stroller, sand castles, a growing hand in hers, a striped shirt for the first day of kindergarten at PFS. He might, she thinks, be a boy; a grandson for her parents. Then again, maybe she's a girl. Kate lays her hand on her belly and feels the potential of roots forming, of blossoms wild and bright.

20

Vanessa

The sun is finally slipping behind the house, losing its hold above and throwing the deck into shadow. The drudging, tender-skinned shuffling sound of beach exodus rises up to where Vanessa and Dani sit on the deck overlooking it all. Vanessa remembers that they slept on these same chaises one summer night in high school; they'd fallen asleep a little spooked by the enormous, scarred sky, and awakened, covered in bug bites and still exhausted, peeling blankets away from their sweating bodies when the sun cracked the surface of the ocean at six in the morning.

"I think she's actually going to forgive me," Dani says.

"I think you're right."

"She'll forgive you too," Dani adds. "I didn't want to say 'she's going to forgive *us*' because I don't want you to think I'm lumping what you did in with what I did. They're not the same. I know that."

"Oh, I don't know," Vanessa says. "We all made some hugely dumb mistakes. And I'm sure we'll regret them forever, forgiveness or not. One of mine was picking that fight with you after Colin died."

"But you were right. I gave him the drugs."

Vanessa had said more than this during their argument. She'd accused Dani of enabling Colin, and this wasn't true. More often than not, the drugs were flowing in the opposite direction; in the last few years of Colin's life it seemed to Vanessa that every time she saw Colin with Dani, he was slipping something into her hand or pulling her away from them. Colin, who had a family that loved him—even *liked* him, which was surely more than he deserved at times—was the one who influenced Dani, with her poisoned understanding of love, her mother who barely acknowledged her existence, her father who treated her like a friend instead of a daughter, her nose always in a book, her hair around her face obscuring that strange look of transportation—of *relief*—on her face as she read. Dani had looked out for Colin for years; she'd taken away his keys and called him cabs; in high school she had frequently disappeared just before class only to arrive a few minutes late with Colin in tow—she'd run out to the park down the

street, pulled Colin back into school by the sleeve
of his coat.

"You were his friend," Vanessa says. "You
made a mistake."

Dani shrugs but Vanessa can see that she is
grateful.

Kate opens the sliding door and steps onto the
deck. "Well," she says. "I told Peter that I'm pregnant."

"What did he say?" Vanessa can perfectly imagine buttoned-up Peter, his mouth dropping at this
news.

"I think he wants us to get back together."

"Because you're pregnant?"

"No, something was different about this conversation. Even before I mentioned the baby." She
bites her lip, trying not to smile. Vanessa grins at
her and sees that Dani is doing the same. Kate sits
on the end of Vanessa's chaise and hugs her knees
to her chest. "Anyway. What were you guys talking about?"

"Drew," Dani says, looking sidelong at Vanessa.

"No, we weren't."

"And Jeremy."

"We were not!"

"Well," Dani says. "We are now."

"I'll start," Kate says, raising her hand. "I think
you loved Jeremy, but if you'd been *in* love with
him, you wouldn't have let him go. I don't think

people can walk away from true love. I don't think that's possible."

As Kate says this, Vanessa remembers how she'd spent a lot of that summer eight years earlier thinking about her life in New York City, feeling eager to get back to it. She'd loved that summer with Kate and Dani, but when you know you're on the cusp of something—the rest of your life—it's hard to be in the moment, you're always looking ahead. Jeremy lived in Philadelphia and Vanessa lived in New York. Their relationship was exciting, and hiding it from Colin had added to its drama, but had she ever expected to keep dating him when she returned to New York? She'd forgotten this part of the story.

"Maybe you're right," Vanessa says. Something had dawned on her as she'd stood in front of Jeremy, and now she is prodding her memory, feeling for it. "I think maybe I missed *me* more than I missed Jeremy."

"You've always been a bit of a narcissist," Dani says.

"Shut up," Vanessa says, but she's smiling, shaking her head.

"What do you mean?" Kate asks her.

"When I quit my job at the gallery to stay home with Lucy, I think I lost track of myself."

"I thought you loved being home with Lucy," Kate says.

"I do," Vanessa says. "I really do. I had no idea I'd feel so . . . maternal." She thinks of brushing Lucy's curls into pigtails, the weight of Lucy in her lap when they read together. Then she thinks of the way art connects her to the world, and to herself. "But I loved working in the gallery too. I wish I could be in both places at once."

"Well, you can't," Dani says.

Vanessa laughs. "Thanks for the tip." She'd really missed Dani.

"Lucy will be in preschool soon," Kate says. "Maybe you could go back to the gallery then."

"Maybe. But Drew wants to have another baby."

"Is that what you want?" Dani asks.

"Someday, sure," Vanessa says. "But now? I don't know. I feel like I'm just on the verge of finding myself again."

"Maybe he wants you to have a baby because he's afraid of losing you," Kate says.

She'd never thought of it this way.

"I think the key," Dani says, "is to decide what you want to do and run with that, whatever it is."

"Yes," Kate says. "Make a decision and commit yourself. What else can you do?"

"Commit myself," Vanessa repeats.

"Into an asylum," Dani says.

"To your *life*," Kate says. "Whatever you want that to be."

* * *

Vanessa walks out to where the ocean meets the shore. The wet sand is dazzling, golden and glowing below the setting sun. The sea foam is tinged with pink. She takes a deep breath. It's one of her favorite smells, the smell of the beach at sunset, rivaled only by the milky warmth of her daughter's neck. Her call interrupts Drew and Lucy in the middle of their dinner.

"What are you having?" she asks, pressing the cell phone to her ear so she can hear her husband over the tumble of the ocean.

"Macaroni and cheese," he says.

"Of course." Drew and Vanessa are equally inclined to cook out of boxes.

He tells her that soon they'll head up to the building's rooftop deck to watch the fireworks. In the background, Vanessa can hear Lucy attempting to repeat the word "fireworks." Lucy has no idea what this word means; she's excited because her father is excited, and the sound of her little voice, which sounds even smaller over the phone, makes Vanessa's heart contract. She can picture them sitting side by side at the round white Saarinen table in the kitchen. Drew has surely put too much pasta in Lucy's bowl—he still has no sense of the portions for a two-year-old—and he'll finish her dinner after his own. Tomorrow, he'll run an extra mile on the High Line before work. Vanessa wishes she were at the table with them, both of them. She's ready, she realizes, to go home.

"Guess who we saw at the playground this morning," Drew says.

Vanessa braces herself, thinking of little Emma's beautiful mother. She can only imagine how this woman must have smiled at her husband, seeing him at the playground twice in once weekend. Vanessa shakes her head abruptly at the thought. This can't go on.

"Who?" she asks.

"Teri and Nick and little Luke."

Vanessa breathes. "They were at the playground with their three-week-old?"

"I know," Drew says. "Rookies."

They both laugh. On their weekend trips to the playground together, Drew and Vanessa find it hard not to snicker when a couple shows up with a mewling, sticky-eyed newborn. They exchange a look that they have perfected by now, a look that silently recalls the conversation they have had countless times on their walks home from these encounters: *Do they think that baby is going to leap out of their arms for a turn on the slide? They should take advantage of their baby being a baby! Do adult things! Go to a museum! Have dinner with friends! Get drunk on martinis and rock the car seat with your foot when the baby gets fussy! Save yourself—for now. Soon enough, you'll be living at the playground.* But the truth is, they'd done the same thing when they were new parents. You feel that mewling, sticky-eyed newborn curl up against your heart and all of a sudden you find yourself doing all kinds of things you never would have thought you would do.

"How are they?" Vanessa asks. She's been thinking about Teri, wondering how she—and her gallery—is fairing in these early weeks.

"Zombies in love," Drew says. It's another old joke—their nickname for the sleep-deprived, infatuated parents of newborns. If they ever form a band, they've decided, this is what they will call it: Zombies in Love. Drew had made this joke a week after they brought Lucy home from the hospital, and Vanessa remembers how the sound of her own laughter—throaty and strong—had been a relief, as welcome as the first bite of sashimi that she'd had in nearly a year.

"Teri said that Francine Martin signed with her gallery," Drew says. "I'm sure you already know that."

Weeks before the news became public knowledge, Teri told Vanessa that she had convinced the painter Francine Martin to switch representation from Nocelli to her own gallery. Martin was small potatoes for Nocelli but a coup for Teri's

fledgling gallery, and Teri's career. The whole
thing caused a bit of a scandal. This stuff was better than celebrity gossip to Vanessa. She lapped
it up. She hadn't told Drew because they had not
been speaking much by then. She'd put it on her
Things I Would Tell Drew If I Didn't Want to Kill Him
list.

Since Drew and Vanessa first met at Francine
Martin's opening at Nocelli, Vanessa always
hoped that he would buy her one of Martin's
pieces as an anniversary present, but this never
happened. Drew never really liked Martin's
paintings, and marriage meant they both had to
like the artwork that hung on their walls.

"Anyway," Drew says, "the opening for her first
show with Teri is in a few weeks and Teri invited
us. I thought we could go. I know how much you
like her work." He pauses. Vanessa waits and he
continues. "And then I thought, why don't we
make a day of it? Ask your mom if she'll come up
and take care of Lucy—you know how happy that
would make both of them. We could gallery-hop,
go to the party, have a late dinner. . . ."

Vanessa is quiet, listening, already envisioning
this day, seeing herself chatting with Teri about
art and babies, babies and art. Drew misses her.
She has been distant for months and now he has
spent three full days without her and he misses
her. The truth is that she misses him too; it's not,

she realizes finally, that she can't walk away, it's that she doesn't want to. And even though she can feel how much Drew misses her, she knows the thrill of the chase as well as anyone, she knows what it's like to want something because it seems out of reach. She wonders how long she and Drew can play this game, the seesaw of their relationship ever tilting, never still. Maybe forever. She finds that the possibility of this excites her. Then again, right now she is on top.

"Vanessa?" Drew asks. "Are you there?"

She spots a pink shell and picks it up for Lucy.

"Yes," she says, turning back toward the house. In her mind, she's already packing. "I'm here."

21

Dani

Dani wishes she could concentrate on these last hours with Kate and Vanessa—it's nighttime now and they will leave Avalon in the morning—but she is questioning whether she can really do this, live a sober life in Avalon. She is angry with herself for flushing those pills, still picturing the last one swirl out of sight. Just knowing they were there, if she needed them, helped. Now that they're gone, she feels a clench of panic. Then again, she's not a quitter. She said she would do this, so she would. She would try.

She's going to scrap her book and start something new. There's a risk to this. She could spend her entire life writing books she won't publish. Some old dogs just can't learn new tricks. But she remembers now that Kate once told her this is a lie: even the oldest dog can learn a new trick, you just need to know what motivates them. *Never underestimate an old dog,* Kate had said.

"The fireworks are going to start soon," Vanessa says. All three of them laugh. Maybe it's the lazy, bored way she said those words, or maybe it's the fact that they've had their fill of fireworks before the actual show even begins—either way, they laugh together. They're lying on the chaises on the upper deck. Above them, the sky is midnight blue and darkening. Below, the shadowed dunes whisper.

"I don't like fireworks," Dani says.

"Of course you don't," Vanessa says.

"What's not to like?" Kate asks. "They're pretty."

"Art for the people," Vanessa offers.

"That's a stretch," Dani says.

"I'm starving," Kate says, propping herself up on an elbow. "What's for dinner?"

"Pizza?" Dani suggests. She turns to Vanessa. "I'll order if you pay."

Vanessa rolls her eyes. "You're irresistible."

Dani calls Circle Pizza from her cell phone. They lie in companionable silence for a while, listening to the Grateful Dead and the occasional pop of distant fireworks. Eventually, Kate swings her feet to rest on the floor. She stands, groaning. "I'm going to take a shower," she says. "I'll be out by the time the pizza gets here." Kate has always had a sixth sense for the timing of food delivery. In high school when Dani and her father would order an early Sunday dinner of Thai food, the doorman would announce Kate's arrival minutes before their food arrived.

Vanessa follows Kate downstairs to change out of her bathing suit, leaving Dani alone on the deck. A light breeze is coming off the ocean and a few stars are now visible above. She wonders how many times she has sat on this deck, under this configuration of stars. The Grateful Dead is still spilling out onto the deck from the inside stereo.

She's a summer love for spring, fall, and winter.

It's her father's favorite song. Dani picks up her cell phone and when her call goes straight to voice mail, she pictures her father sitting across from Susanna at a table in a restaurant. Suz will be at the table from now on. *It is what it is*, she thinks, listening to the sound of her father's recorded voice.

"Hey, Dad," she says. "It's me, Dani, your favorite daughter. I just wanted you to know we found the beach tags. Also, as it happens, I left my congratulations next to the coffeepot as well. I'm sorry I forgot to tell you. Like father, like daughter, I guess. Anyway, call me." She imagines her father listening to this message at some point and smiling, the strange and funny language of love that will warm the conversation they'll have whenever they finally get hold of each other.

Dani is still alone on the upstairs deck when the doorbell rings. She hurries inside and down the stairs, grabbing the cash that Vanessa left on the entryway table. She gives the pizza delivery guy a generous tip; with all of the Fourth of July barbecues taking place on the island tonight, he's probably not making much money. The screen door slams behind her as she turns, pizza box in hands. Kate, of course, is standing there, looking freshly scrubbed. Her water-darkened hair gives her freckled skin an ethereal quality.

"Oh, hello there, gooey goodness," Kate says to the pizza box.

Dani feels a burst of joy spin and flash inside of her just as, outside, there is the machine-gun crack of fireworks. Kate's jaw tenses. She turns toward the staircase and cocks her head as though listening for something. When Kate looks at Dani again, her eyes are wide.

"Where's Gracie?" she asks.

A bristly heat wraps around Dani's neck. "I don't—" she begins, but Kate is already racing up the stairs.

Dani is halfway up the steps when she hears footsteps behind her. She looks back, but it's just Vanessa. In the living room, Kate is staring at the screen door to the deck. It's open. Dani drops the pizza box onto the kitchen counter and rakes her fingers through her hair, her pulse loud in her ears. She'd left the door open in her hurry to get downstairs when the pizza arrived. She had done this.

"Gracie!" Kate yells. The house is silent. She runs out to the deck and Dani and Vanessa follow. "Gracie!" The breeze has picked up, and Gracie's name is lost in it.

"Gracie!" Dani yells.

"Gracie!" Vanessa yells.

Don't do this, Gracie, Dani thinks, gritting her teeth. *Please.*

Kate is hurrying down the outside staircase now. She's standing in the middle of the street when Dani and Vanessa catch up with her. All three of them are barefoot.

"Fireworks spook her," Kate says. She points at Vanessa. "She might be hiding somewhere in the house. Check under the beds. Check everywhere."

Vanessa jogs back toward the house.

"I'm going this way," Kate says to Dani, pointing toward First Avenue just as a car flies by, surely going faster than the twenty-five-mile-an-hour speed limit. Another car flies by in the opposite direction. *People drive too damn fast on this island.* Dani remembers seeing a dead cat by the side of the road when they'd pulled off the bridge. "You take the beach," Kate says and then she's off, running down the block.

Dani turns and hurries along the winding path through the dunes to the beach, feeling the pavement quickly give way to sand under her bare feet. To the north, fireworks explode in the sky, one burst of color after another, raining sparks down on the ocean. The pier glows with each burst above, disappearing between sets into the inky night. Dani turns to look south. It's darker this way, so this is the direction she runs, yelling for Gracie.

As she nears the water, something cuts into her foot. She stumbles, foot throbbing, and keeps running, five, maybe ten blocks of beach. The Wildwood Ferris wheel is in the distance, its lights spinning through the air, tracing the same circle over and over.

"Gracie!" she yells. "Gracie!"

The look on Kate's face, the panic and the fear, is replaying in Dani's mind as she runs. *This isn't worth it*, she thinks. *It's not worth loving something that can so easily be lost.* Still, she doesn't stop running. She hasn't run this fast, or this far, in years. She left that door open. She can't believe she left that door open. Her mind is racing ahead of her feet, building the story of what will happen if she doesn't find Gracie.

And then she sees her.

Gracie is snout-deep in a Tupperware container

in the middle of a picnic dinner that has turned into a scene of multigenerational bedlam. An older couple is racing around, trying to catch a flurry of white napkins that are flying in the wind; a younger man is unsuccessfully attempting to yank Gracie away by the collar; a red-haired kid with sunburned arms and a face full of snot and sand is wailing while a woman frantically waves a lollipop in front of his face.

"Gracie!" Dani calls. Gracie's ear flicks in recognition as she wolfs down a few final bites.

The man looks at her. "Is this your dog?" he asks angrily.

"She knocked our son over!" the woman says. "She ate our potato salad!"

"I'm so sorry," Dani says, but she can't help it, she's laughing and she can't seem to stop. She's never been so happy to see a dog in her whole life. The relief that is coursing through her is like a drug, like that elusive, soaring high of her first hit of Ecstasy with Colin all those years ago. She didn't think she'd ever feel that way again.

"Come on," she says, grasping Gracie's collar. The potato salad is ancient history now and Gracie comes easily, tail wagging. Tears sting Dani's eyes, surprising her.

She hobbles back toward the house with Gracie's collar gripped tightly in her fist. Her lungs feel hot and raw, her feet cut and bruised. "You're

a bad, bad dog," she mutters, still smiling, and
Gracie wags her tail. "Goddamn fleabag." She
ruffles Gracie's head.

The fireworks show is over now. Pun intended,
Dani thinks. There is darkness everywhere except for the moon on the ocean and the glow of
houses beyond the dunes. They're nearly back to
the Thirty-Eighth Street beach when Dani sees
Kate running through the dry sand toward them.
Vanessa lags behind her. When Kate reaches
them, she drops to her knees and throws her
arms around Gracie, who licks the side of her face
and then belches loudly.

Kate snorts a laugh, wiping at her tears. She
looks up at Dani. "Thank you."

"I was the one who left the door open," Dani
says.

"It could have been anyone."

Dani isn't sure if this is true. It seems to her that
Kate or Vanessa would not have let this happen,
that they operate on a more thoughtful level than
Dani, even on the days when Dani is really trying. Maybe Kate can read these thoughts, because
she pulls Dani down to sit beside her in the sand
and puts her arm around her. Vanessa joins them,
huffing and puffing as she lowers herself down to
Dani's other side. They sit in a row—Gracie, Kate,
Dani, then Vanessa—looking out at the ocean.

"Someone once told me," Kate says, "that you

have to give yourself permission to be happy. You have to decide you deserve it."

Vanessa groans. "You sound like my mother. Please don't tell me you're drawing energy from crystals."

"I've always loved your mother," Dani says. "She bakes a mean pot brownie."

Vanessa asks Kate who gave her these words of wisdom.

"I can't remember," Kate says. The slow way she says this makes Dani think she is not telling the truth. Was it Colin? It doesn't sound at all like Colin, but that was the thing about Colin—there was always something unknowable about him, even then.

"Anyway," Kate says, turning to Dani, "my point is that you deserve it. Happiness."

Tomorrow evening, hours after Kate and Vanessa have left, Dani might eye the sunset and crave a drink. But not, she realizes, tonight. Tonight she is with Kate and Vanessa and they know the truth about what she did to Colin and they're sitting here with her anyway. Her body is still aching and warm and she can imagine her bones finally thawing, and for now, this feeling of warmth is enough.

O. K. Dani traces these letters on her thigh, like she used to do back in Friends Meeting at PFS. Even in the dark, Kate and Vanessa know what she is doing and smile. It's a strange feeling, being aware that she is changing even as it's happening. She thinks of the bathroom door where her father used to mark her growth from summer to summer with a Sharpie pen, the funny feeling she got when she saw the space between the lines, the shock when there was no longer any space and she realized she was grown.

"Maybe," Vanessa says, "none of us did this to Colin."

Dani holds her breath.

"Or maybe we all did," Kate says.

Dani looks at Kate. Her words are a small current of air in a room without a window, an impossible thing, a gift.

"I can't believe we have to leave tomorrow," Vanessa says.

"I know," Kate says.

Dani can feel the hum of their excitement—Kate has a job and a city she loves to return to, a baby to plan for, and Vanessa has her own little family, imperfectly in love with one another.

"But you'll be back, right?" Dani asks.

"Sure," Vanessa says. "Next summer."

"Next summer?" Dani asks. "What about *this* summer? The whole point of the Fourth of July is to whet your appetite for the rest of the season."

"*That's* the whole point of the Fourth of July?" Vanessa asks. "Are you sure?"

"Speaking of appetite," Kate says, standing and wiping the sand from her knees, "should we go eat that pizza?"

Dani knows Kate has had that pizza on her mind for a while now, probably ever since she saw Gracie was okay. A Kate is a Kate is a Kate. Vanessa rises too and pulls Dani to her feet. For just a beat of time, none of them move, and Dani catches a glimpse of a new novel unfolding—a cast of quirky characters in a beach town in the off-season, a teacher who looks like Hemingway, a lost dog, and maybe even, if Dani can stomach it, a happy ending. Gracie barks and races forward and they all begin to run, not wanting to lose her again.

Acknowledgments

Thank you to my husband, Phil Preuss, whose love, support, and continued willingness to endure the pressure of being my first reader mean the world to me. Phil, you are a brave man, and I love you. Finley and Avelyn, you fill me to the brim with joy and gratitude.

Thank you to my parents, Carol Mager and James Donohue, for their love, and for bringing me to Avalon, New Jersey, when I was still in the womb and every summer since. Part of me is always with you in Avalon.

Thank you to Jeanette Perez, an exceptional editor, whose insight enriches my work time and time again, and a warm, spirited, and much-cherished friend. I am indebted also to a wonderful team at William Morrow, including, but not limited to Liate Stehlik, Jennifer Hart, Kaitlyn Kennedy, Tamara Arellano, and Carolyn Bodkin.

I am beyond grateful for the guidance of my kind and whip-smart agent, Elisabeth Weed, whose enthusiasm for this book from its earliest pages brought tears to my eyes. Thank you also to Jon Cassir at CAA for representing my books in the world of film and television.

Thank you to Carol Mager, Meg Kasdan, Sarah Blanton, and Francesca Grossman, whose thoughtful feedback on the first draft of this book made it stronger, and whose encouragement made me stronger.

Thank you to Jay Donohue, Brianna Andersen, Ellen Mager, Mimi Mager, Jackie Mager, Barbara Preuss, Charles Preuss, and the many other friends and Donohue, Mager, and Preuss family members who have been so lovingly supportive and excited for me. My appreciation knows no bounds.

Finally, thank you to the generous readers, book bloggers, and booksellers who have reached out to me, encouraging me and flooding me with awe at the kindness of strangers. Then again, perhaps no book lover is truly a stranger. Thank you, then, new friends. I'm so glad we've found one another.

A Conversation with
Meg Donohue

When did you start writing?

I can't remember a time when I didn't love to write. My parents are both lawyers and it seemed like there was a yellow legal pad on every surface in our house when I was growing up; I must have filled fifty of them with my stories. During those early years, which I refer to as my "Damsels-in-Distress Period," I was really wrestling with the roles that beautiful orphan princesses and horses play in our society. I remember taking a writing class in third grade with a teacher I loved named Mrs. Watters, so I was certainly hooked on writing by then. I still remember the poem I wrote for her class: When a secret is told / its heart turns cold / and it's banished from the world of untellables. / It lives alone / in a tower's cone, / broken and unsellable. Thank you. Thank you very much. (Even then I was obviously a little obsessed with secrets.)

Do you remember the first book you fell in love with and why it affected you so strongly?

I'm sure I fell in love with many books before reading Emily Brontë's *Wuthering Heights*, but it's the one that immediately comes to mind. I loved how it was dark and atmospheric and romantic and the characters were all so deliciously tormented. So much angst! I lapped it up, copying long passages into my journal. I remember feeling completely transported to those windswept moors and damp, shadowy manors—maybe that's when I first fell in love with the idea of novels with mood-inspiring settings. I wonder what I would think of *Wuthering Heights* now? I should reread it.

Who are some of your writing influences? Do you have influences outside of the literary world?

I find I'm influenced more by specific books than writers. Siri Hustvedt's *The Blindfold* really captivated me when I read it in college and for years afterward—it's a book I return to time and time again. More recently, I've loved and been influenced by Jennifer Close's *Girls in White Dresses* and J. Courtney Sullivan's *Maine* (see my Summer Reads list on page 345 for more on these novels). Outside of books, I love music and movies and art, but books are easily my main influence. If I fall in love with a book, I'm writing the whole time I'm reading it, jotting down notes and dog-earing pages so I can go back and study how the writer moved the plot along or made me feel a certain way. Nothing makes me long to write quite like reading something I love.

What's the best writing advice you ever received?

Write every day. It's common advice and I'm not sure where I first heard it or read it, but the more I embrace it, the better I write. And I don't embrace it nearly as much as I should because I have young children and am also a world-class procrastinator, but I do write at least four days a week. When you're disciplined enough to write most days, magical things start happening. Your thoughts are never far from your story, you're immersed in the world you're building, and suddenly ideas and connections and dialogue appear in your mind like gifts. The more you write, the more open and receptive you are to inspiration.

Where do you write? Do you have any writing rituals? Or perhaps vices that help you get through writing a novel?

Unlike Kate, I am not a creature of habit. Sometimes I write at a café; sometimes I write at a desk in my bedroom. Sometimes I drink coffee; sometimes I drink tea. Sometimes I listen to music; sometimes I don't. I'm all over the map depending on my mood and how much childcare I have on any given day. One of my many vices is checking social media (mostly Twitter) too frequently throughout the day, but there is such a warm community of writers posting all sorts of helpful and supportive writing- and industry-related news that I only feel horribly guilty doing so about half the time.

If All the Summer Girls *were to be made into a movie, which three actresses would you pick to play Dani, Kate, and Vanessa?*

This is actually really hard for me! I see Kate, Vanessa, and Dani so clearly as real women that it's difficult to think of actresses who could fill their flip-flops. I suppose Anna Kendrick could embody Kate's girl-next-door combination of intelligence, self-consciousness, and warmth, and she's fair and brunette to boot. As for Vanessa—perhaps Jessica Szohr? She's gorgeous and could pull off that Chelsea gallerist mix of downtown style and uptown sophistication. And I feel like Kirsten Dunst could capture Dani's troubled, sardonic, adventurous edge and unlikely blondeness.

The ups and downs of female friendships have been at the heart of your novels. What is it about this relationship that you find inspiring to write about?

Friendships have a fascinating ebb and flow; they're never static. There's something about childhood friends in particular—the friendships that have withstood decades of change—that are especially endearing to me and ripe with storytelling possibility. Being with an old friend might be the closest we get to traveling through time—when else are you so acutely reminded of the person you used to be than when you are with someone who has known you through all of your various self-reinventions? I'm also interested in writing stories that explore the lives of more than one woman, and writing about women who are tied by the bonds of friendship allows me to create a tapestry effect in which multiple families and conflicts and settings are woven together.

The settings of your novels tend to be a big part of the plot and the characters' lives. How do you decide where to set a book and how does place inform what you write?

With both of my novels, the decision of setting has been tied to the earliest seeds of the story. For *How to Eat a Cupcake*, I think my first imaginings of the novel included a cupcake shop in San Francisco's Mission District, a neighborhood that is so diverse and complex and teeming with energy that its ambiance and potential conflicts practically write themselves. For *All the Summer Girls*, I was eager to write about summertime, and for me, as for the novel's protagonists, summer is Avalon, New Jersey. So, again, the setting was right there in my thoughts from the beginning. Once I started thinking about that setting, and putting in the hard time of writing, that magical thing I mentioned earlier started happening: it seemed like the setting offered up all sorts of metaphors and themes. For example, before I sent Dani walking through San Francisco, it never occurred to me that both Avalon and San Francisco are set on seven-mile-long landmasses surrounded by bay and ocean. That connection only occurred to me—to Dani, really—when I sent her wandering through the city.

How much of what you write comes from your own experiences? Are any of your characters based on real people?

Sometimes a character might initially come to me with a collection of traits that I've culled from various people I've met, or from myself, but once I'm fifty pages into writing a novel, if that character hasn't completely taken on a life and identity of her own that is far removed from anyone I know, then I'm doing something wrong. I pepper my work with a few of my own experiences, and I almost always use settings with which I have deep familiarity. But once I set those fictional characters loose in those nonfictional environments, they experience things in a way that is all their own. So even the parts of my novels that might contain some echo of my personal history become little more than jumping-off points. One of the great joys I get from writing fiction is that it feels so wonderfully free to me—the possibilities are endless. It wouldn't be nearly as fun or rewarding for me if I were only recounting my own experiences, or inserting people I actually know into the story.

If you were not a writer, what would your dream job be?

This is hard because being a novelist is truly my dream job. I guess I've always been a little envious of singers, but I envy their talent more than their job. How amazing would it be to just open your mouth and sing in your own beautiful, unique voice, or to record a song so that when someone listens to it for just a couple of minutes, she is instantly sent back to the time in her life when she first heard the song, or she's moved to dance or cry or sing along? That is a beautiful talent. Sadly, I'm a terrible singer. I did karaoke recently and at one point when I was singing on stage I realized that not a single person in the audience, made up primarily of close, supportive friends, would meet my eye. I heard the sound of that dream shattering. Okay, it might have been glass breaking. Either way, I think I'll stick with writing.

The Coldest Winter
I Ever Spent

What sparks inspiration? It's a question I'm asked with some frequency, and one that can be tricky to answer. It is often difficult to retrace the steps I've taken to develop a story, to identify the moment, the spark, that sent me off and running down a particular narrative path. Other times, the root of a story remains so vivid to me that I could practically stub my toe on it. *All the Summer Girls* has a distinct root like that, and it serves as a wonderful reminder that the most unlikely occurrences can be a source of inspiration, opening doors to places that I did not expect to go. So what surprising thing sparked this novel that is, in a way, an ode to the East Coast summer? In a word: fog.

As a Philadelphian accustomed to East Coast seasons—and one with particular fondness for summertime, the muggier the better—I was shocked by San Francisco's weather when I first arrived in the city on an August afternoon five years ago. Damp gray fog moved quickly over our new home and snaked its way under my clothes, making me shiver. My husband and I had spent the days leading up to our arrival in San

Francisco driving the length of the country in short-sleeved shirts, our skin golden from a stay at my parents' beach house in Avalon, New Jersey. We hurried into our new home and dug through stacks of moving boxes until we located our heaviest down-filled parkas. And then we turned on the heat. The heat! In August! Only our dog seemed pleased with this turn of events, his fur coat finally coming in handy.

Before that day, I'd always figured Mark Twain was using artistic license when he so famously said "The coldest winter I ever spent was a summer in San Francisco." Turns out, I was wrong. (On two counts, actually: apparently the quote, though commonly attributed to Twain, is of unknown origin.) Five summers later, I still haven't come to terms with that August chill. I don't think I ever will. Don't get me wrong—I am in love with San Francisco. But like any passionate love affair, there are times when I loathe this city nearly as much as I love it, and those times are frequently in the summer, when I'm wearing a wool sweater and thick slippers, and dreaming of the beach in Avalon.

Which is exactly what I found myself doing—shivering through another San Francisco summer and pining for Avalon—when the seeds of *All the Summer Girls* first planted themselves. As a novelist, you spend a lot of time thinking about your book; you immerse yourself in the story you're telling, and sometimes it's hard to shake the story from your thoughts even during your nonwriting time. So I figured that if I were going to spend the next year deeply immersed in a place and a time, where better than Avalon, New Jersey, in summertime?

Like the protagonists in this book, I grew up spending time each summer in Avalon. For more than a decade of my youth, my parents rented a tall, crumbly Victorian home a few blocks from the beach. It had the sort of nooks and crannies that enchant a child, and an excruciatingly hot attic room where my cousins and I slept in rows on the floor. The house used to be red so we called it the Red House . . . until the year we showed up and found it had been painted blue. After that, we called it—wait for it—the Blue House. There was a big—or so it seemed at the time—kitchen with a peeling linoleum floor on which lobsters were raced (in a cruel turn, the winner would be dropped into the pot first). Out front, there was a wide wooden swing hanging from chains on the wraparound porch. In the back, there was a small yard where, above my head, an ever-changing rainbow of beach towels hung from the clothesline, and my bare feet were bruised by pebbles and pine needles (this was before landscapers and irrigation systems descended on those sandy-soiled New Jersey beach towns and turned them lush with greenery). My grandfather would create boats out of sand for us to play in at the beach, and after dinner he would walk us down Dune Drive to Dippy Don's for bubblegum ice cream. My father was the oldest of eight siblings and nearly every summer another cousin—who only a year earlier had seemed like a baby—reached an age when he could be inducted into the fold by way of mischief. The elderly neighbors once called the police because they thought we were being robbed—turned out they just spotted two of my cousins shimmying down the side of the house using bedsheets they had tied together to form a long rope. At night, my cousins and I would stay up late in the sweltering, sloped attic, plotting these schemes— stunts that often involved unscrewing every lightbulb in the house a half turn or hiding all the toilet paper in the cobwebbed crawl space under the porch or hanging an uncle's underwear on the front screen door and spraying it with the Fart Spray we'd bought in the ever-marvelous kids' aisle at Hoy's Five and Dime— while two stories below our parents and aunts and uncles would stay up late drinking beer and laughing so loudly it seemed to make the old house shake.

Later, Avalon became a place where I also spent time with friends. I rented a house there with my best friends from childhood the summer after we graduated from high school, and—just as it was for Kate, Vanessa, and Dani—that was a magical time for me, both in the actual moment and in retrospect. We were so free and it seemed so much lay before us and we just had a whole lot of fun. I'm relieved that, unlike the friends in this book, no tragedies befell us; that summer holds nothing but happy memories for me.

So when it's August in San Francisco and I'm pulling on my winter coat, in my mind I'm in Avalon— reading on the beach, soaking up the sun, or riding a bike under a star-filled sky. Ironically, it seems the cool San Francisco summer sends me straight back to the warmest summers of my life. I'm very grateful to have spent this past year in Avalon, even if only on the page. So, thank you, San Francisco fog, for the spark of inspiration. You've reminded me that there is great comfort—warmth, even—to be found in memory, and that we are never far from our favorite places, or our childhood, when we hold them in our heart. Summer, after all, when boiled down to the emotions it so often invokes—happiness and hope—is a state of mind.

Meg Donohue's Favorite Summer Reads

My favorite novels are ones that I call "smart page-turners"—they're fast-paced, frequently funny, and laced with astute observations. For me, the only thing better than a smart page-turner is a smart page-turner that takes place during my favorite season: summer. Here's a list of six summer novels I've recently loved and am sure to reread, probably on beaches, in the years to come.

Girls in White Dresses by Jennifer Close

I fell in love with this group of women as they poignantly and hilariously fumbled their way through questionable relationships and career choices during those hazy postcollege years when nothing seems to go the way you thought it would. The dialogue sparkles, the friendships are touching and real without veering anywhere near sappy, there's a hysterical chapter entitled "Summer Sausage" that allows me to feel perfectly justified including this book in a Summer Reads roundup, and the novel ends with what might just be my favorite final line of any book, ever. I'm certain Lena Dunham and fans of her show *Girls* would adore this novel as much as I do.

A Big Storm Knocked It Over by Laurie Colwin

Reminiscent of Nora Ephron, Colwin writes with warmth and wit about marriage, motherhood, work, and food. This novel isn't set exclusively in summer, but the protagonist—a New York book designer—and her husband frequently visit his family's country home during weekend escapes from the city, and the idea of that special home-away-from-home always invokes the idea of summer for me. A delightful exploration of how even an essentially happy life is full of novel-worthy twists, this book manages to be both realistic and refreshingly hopeful.

The Adults by Alison Espach

When this novel opens, it's summertime in a muggy, green-lawned Connecticut suburb and Espach's memorable teenage protagonist is about to experience all kinds of heartbreak without ever losing her bright, funny voice. (When asked what the theme of her father's fiftieth birthday party should be, she replies, "Man, aging dramatically!") If you're a fan of intelligent coming-of-age fiction and fresh writing, and you're okay with laughing out loud on the beach while you read, this is the book for you.

The American Heiress by Daisy Goodwin

Starting in one oceanside setting (Newport, Rhode Island) and ending in quite another (Dorset, England), this juicy historical novel details an American heiress's adventures in love and title hunting. The upstairs-downstairs plot draws easy comparisons to *Downton Abbey,* but as I followed heiress Cora Cash's exploits I found myself equally reminded of another winsomely headstrong, quintessentially American heroine: Scarlett O'Hara. A highly entertaining romance with fascinating period details and evocative writing.

Maine by J. Courtney Sullivan

This layered novel reveals the rich inner lives of the Kelleher family matriarch, her daughter, her daughter-in-law, and her granddaughter, all of whom have complex relationships with one another and the family's summer home on the coast of Maine. The story is somehow both character-driven and briskly paced, moving between decades-old flashbacks and the present as one heart-wrenching secret after another is revealed over the course of a summer.

Beautiful Ruins by Jess Walter

Beautiful Ruins has everything you could possibly desire in a summer read—gorgeous settings (the Italian coast with a splash of Old Hollywood); a large cast of intriguing characters (including a cameo by real-life actor Richard Burton); great writing; and a fun, decades-spanning plot in which numerous story lines—including several moving love stories—are masterfully juggled. This book is like a buffet that offers up all of my favorite foods in one sitting. I devoured it, enjoying every last page.

Have You Read?
More by Meg Donohue

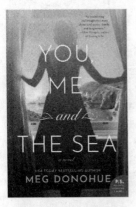

YOU, ME, AND THE SEA

As a child, Merrow Shawe believes she is born of the sea: strong, joyous, and wild. Her beloved home is Horseshoe Cliff, a small farm on the coast of Northern California where she spends her days exploring fog-cloaked bluffs, swimming in the cove, and basking in the light of golden sunsets as her father entertains her with fantastical stories. It is an enchanting childhood, but it is not without hardship—the mystery of Merrow's mother's death haunts her, as does the increasingly senseless cruelty of her older brother, Bear.

Then, like sea glass carried from a distant land,

Amir arrives in Merrow's life. He's been tossed about from India to New York City and now to Horseshoe Cliff, to stay with her family. Merrow is immediately drawn to his spirit, his passion, and his resilience in the face of Bear's viciousness. Together they embrace their love of the sea, and their growing love for each other.

But the ocean holds secrets in its darkest depths. When tragedy strikes, Merrow is forced to question whether Amir is really the person she believed him to be. In order to escape the danger she finds herself in and find her own path forward, she must let go of the only home she's ever known, and the only boy she's ever loved . . .

"An enchanting and imaginative story about soulmates, family, and forgiveness. With its sparkling allure of Northern California's rugged coast and aura of mystery and romance, I was swept away by this evocative modern take on *Wuthering Heights*."

—Elise Hooper, author of *Learning to See* and *The Other Alcott*

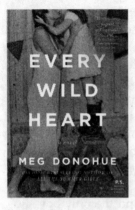

EVERY WILD HEART

Passionate and funny, radio personality Gail Gideon
is a true original. Nine years ago when Gail's husband
announced that he wanted a divorce, her ensuing on-
air rant propelled her local radio show into the na-
tional spotlight. Now, *The Gail Gideon Show* is beloved
by millions of single women who tune in for her advice on the power of self-reinvention. But fame comes
at a price, and escalating threats from a troubled fan
make Gail worry for the safety of her daughter, Nic.

Fourteen-year-old Nic has always felt that she
pales in comparison to her vibrant, outgoing mother.
Plagued by a fear of social situations, she is most comfortable at the stable where she spends her afternoons.
But when a riding accident lands Nic in the hospital,
she awakens from her coma changed. Suddenly, she
has no fear at all and her disconcerting behavior lands
her in one risky situation after another. And no one,

least of all her mother, can guess what she will do next . . .

"*Every Wild Heart* should be on every reader's list of new books to savor. It's a heartfelt, funny, poignant and suspenseful story of a good woman trying her best, making mistakes, picking up the pieces and moving on—a celebration of what it means to be a working mother."

—Susan Wiggs, #1 *New York Times* bestselling author of *Family Tree*

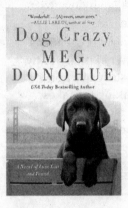

DOG CRAZY

As a pet bereavement counselor, Maggie Brennan uses a combination of empathy, insight, and humor to help patients cope with the anguish of losing their beloved four-legged friends. Though she has a gift for guiding others through difficult situations, Maggie has major troubles of her own that threaten the success of her counseling practice and her volunteer work with a dog rescue organization.

Everything changes when a distraught woman shows up at Maggie's office and claims that her dog has been stolen. Searching the streets of San Francisco for the missing pooch, Maggie finds herself entangled in a mystery that forces her to finally face her biggest fear—and to open her heart to new love.

"Even if my daughter hadn't recently rescued a dog, our first, I would have fallen in love with Meg Donohue's *Dog Crazy*. On these pages you will find love, healing, forgiveness and pure unbridled joy of the human and canine kind."

—Adriana Trigiani, *New York Times* bestselling author of *The Shoemaker's Wife*

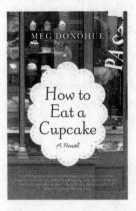

HOW TO EAT A CUPCAKE

Free-spirited Annie Quintana and sophisticated Julia
St. Clair come from two different worlds. Yet, as the
daughter of the St. Clairs' housekeeper, Annie grew
up in Julia's San Francisco mansion and they forged a
bond that only two little girls oblivious to class differ-
ences could—until a life-altering betrayal destroyed
their friendship.

A decade later, Annie bakes to fill the void left in
her heart by her mother's death, and a painful secret
jeopardizes Julia's engagement to the man she loves.
A chance reunion prompts the unlikely duo to open
a cupcakery, but when a mysterious saboteur opens
up old wounds, they must finally face the truth about
their past or risk losing everything.

"A sparkling, witty story about an unlikely, yet redemptive, friendship. Donohue's voice is lovely, intelligent, and alluring. Grab one of these for your best friend and read it together—preferably with a plate of Meyer lemon cupcakes nearby."

—Katie Crouch, bestselling author of *Girls in Trucks* and *Men and Dogs*